infinity

Also by Sherrilyn Kenyon

The Dark-Hunters, Volume 1
The Dark-Hunters, Volume 2

CHRONICLES *of* NICK

infinity

SHERRILYN KENYON

St. Martin's Griffin ❧ *New York*

INFINITY. Copyright © 2010 by Sherrilyn Kenyon. All rights reserved. Printed in the United States of America. For information, address St. Martin's Press, 175 Fifth Avenue, New York, N.Y. 10010.

www.stmartins.com

ISBN 978-0-312-59907-2

First Edition: June 2010

10 9 8 7 6 5 4 3 2 1

To the fans who've been with the Dark-Hunters from the beginning—thank you for the support, the laughs, and for being so eager to read each new installment. For Monique, whose energy is boundless and who has done so much to bring this series, as well as the Dark-Hunters and the manga, to life. For my friends, who keep me sane, and especially Kim, who read every bit of it hot off the presses and ran the book through our teen cold readers to get their stamp of approval.

To my ever wonderful husband for making lots of dinners (okay, that should probably be lots of reservations LOL) while I worked diligently on this. And most of all to my sons, who inspire me every day; especially Madaug, who helped me come up with the opening line—I am a socially awkward mandork—and who graciously allowed me to use his name as one of the characters. And to Ian, who wanted to stab a zombie with a pencil. I love all of you and am grateful every day that you're a part of my life.

And last, but not least, Casey Woods, who won the contest to be a character in the book. We'll be seeing a lot more of you in book two :)

ACKNOWLEDGMENTS

While I am and have always been a huge zombie fan, I want to acknowledge two special people whose brains I picked while writing the book.

To my zombie savant and horror movie cohort, Evyl Ed, who also agreed to play Bubba in several Bubbisodes. Thanks for the invaluable insight and keen comments.

And to my favorite exorcist, Mama Lisa, who fights the good fight every day and who understands demonology in a way few people do.

Thank you both.

infinity

PROLOGUE

Free will.

Some have called it the greatest gift bestowed on humanity. It is our ability to control what happens to us and exactly how it happens. We are the masters of our fate and no one can foist their will on us unless we allow it.

Others say free will is a crap myth. We have a pre-ordained destiny and no matter what we do or how hard we fight it, life will happen to us exactly as it's meant to happen. We are only pawns to a higher power that our meager human brains can't even begin to understand or comprehend.

My best bud, Acheron, once explained it to me

 1

like this. Destiny is a freight train rolling along on a set course that only the conductor knows. When we get to the railroad crossing in our car, we can choose to stop and wait for the train to pass us by, or try to pull out in front of it and beat that bad boy across.

That choice is our free will.

If we choose to rush ahead, the car we're in might stall on the tracks. We can then choose to try and start the car or wait for the train to plow into us. Or we can get out to run, and fight the destiny of the train slamming into us and killing us where we stand. If we choose to run, our foot could get caught in the tracks or we could slip and fall.

We could even say to ourselves, "there's no way I'm dumb enough to fight the train" and hang back to safely wait. Then the next thing we know, a truck rams us from behind, throwing us straight into the train's path.

If it is our destiny to be hit by the train, we will be hit by the train. The only thing we can change is how the train turns us into hamburger.

I, personally, don't believe in this crap. I say *I* control my destiny and my life.

No, nothing controls me.

Ever.

I am what I have become because of the interference and secrets of one creature. Had things been done differently, my life would have been a whole other enchilada. I would not be where I am today and I would have had a life worth living instead of the nightmare my life has become.

But no, by keeping his deepest secrets, my best friend betrayed me and turned me into the darkness I have come to embrace. Our fates and destinies were mashed together by a freak event that happened when I was a kid, and I curse the day I ever called Acheron Parthenopaeus my friend.

I am Nick Gautier.

And this is my life and how things should have been. . . .

CHAPTER 1

I am a socially awkward mandork."

"Nicholas Ambrosius Gautier! You watch your language!"

Nick sighed at his mother's sharp tone as he stood in their tiny kitchen looking down at the bright orange Hawaiian shirt. The color and style were bad enough. The fact it was covered in l-a-r-g-e pink, gray, and white trout (or were they salmon?) was even worse. "Mom, I can't wear this to school. It's . . ."—he paused to think real hard of a word that wouldn't get him grounded for life—"hideous. If anyone sees me in this, I'll be an outcast relegated to the loser corner of the cafeteria."

As always, she scoffed at his protest. "Oh, shush. There's nothing wrong with that shirt. Wanda told me at the Goodwill store that it came in from one of those big mansions down in the Garden District. That shirt belonged to the son of a fine upstanding man and since that's what I'm raising you to be . . ."

Nick ground his teeth. "I'd rather be a delinquent no one picks on."

She let out a deep sound of aggravation as she paused while flipping bacon. "No one's going to pick on you, Nicky. The school has a strict no-bullying policy."

Yeah, right. That wasn't worth the "contract" paper it was written on. Especially since the bullies were illiterate idiots who couldn't read it anyway.

Jeez. Why wouldn't she listen to him? It wasn't like he wasn't the one going into the lion's den every day and having to traverse the brutality of high school land mines. Honestly, he was sick of it and there was nothing he could do.

He was a massive loser dork and no one at school

ever let him forget that. Not the teachers, the principal, and especially not the other students.

Why can't I flash forward and bypass this whole high school nightmare?

Because his mom wouldn't let him. Only hoodlums dropped out of school and she didn't work as hard as she did to raise up another piece of worthless scum—it was a harped-on litany permanently carved into his brain. It ranked right up there with:

"Be a good boy, Nicky. Graduate. Go to college. Get a good job. Marry a good girl. Have lots of grandbabies and never miss a holy day of obligation at church." His mom had already road-mapped his entire future with no diversions or pit stops allowed.

But at the end of the day, he loved his mom and appreciated everything she did for him. Except for this whole "Do what I say, Nicky. I'm not listening to you because I know better" thing she said all the time.

He wasn't stupid and he wasn't a troublemaker. She had no idea what he went through at school, and every time he tried to explain it, she refused to listen. It was so frustrating.

Gah, can't I catch swine flu or something? Just for the next four years until he was able to graduate and move on to a life that didn't include constant humiliation? After all, the swine flu had killed millions of people in 1918 and several more during outbreaks in the seventies and eighties. Was it too much to ask that another mutant strain of it incapacitate him for a few years?

Maybe a good bout of parvo . . .

You're not a dog, Nick.

True, no dog would be caught dead wearing this shirt. Whizzing on it would be another matter. . . .

Sighing in useless angst, he looked down at the crap shirt he wanted desperately to burn. Okay, fine. He'd do what he always did whenever his mom made him look like a flaming moron.

He'd own it.

I don't want to own this. *I look epically stupid.*

Man up, Nick. You can take it. You've taken a lot worse.

Yeah, all right. Fine. Let them laugh. He couldn't stop that anyway. If it wasn't the shirt, they'd humiliate him over something else. His shoes. His haircut.

8

And if all else failed, they'd insult his name. Nick the dick, or dickless Nicholas. Didn't matter what he said or did, those who mocked would mock anything. Some people were just wired wrong and they couldn't live unless they were making other people suffer.

His Aunt Menyara always said no one could make him feel inferior unless he allowed them to.

Problem was, he allowed it a lot more than he wanted to.

His mom set a chipped blue plate on the side of the rusted-out stove. "Sit down, baby, and eat something. I was reading in a magazine that someone left at the club that kids score much higher on tests and do a lot better in school whenever they have breakfast." She smiled and held the package of bacon up for him to see. "And look. It's not expired this time."

He laughed at something that really wasn't funny. One of the guys who came into his mom's club was a local grocer who would give them meat sometimes when it expired since all the guy did was throw it out anyway.

"As long as we eat it quick, it won't make us sick."

Another litany he hated.

Picking up the crispy bacon, he glanced around the tiny condo they called home. It was one of four that had been carved out of an old run-down house. Made up of three small rooms—the kitchen/living room, his mom's bedroom, and the bathroom—it wasn't much, but it was theirs and his mom was proud of it, so he tried to be proud too.

Most days.

He winced as he looked at his corner where his mom had strung up dark blue blankets to make a room for him on his last birthday. His clothes were kept in an old laundry basket on the floor, set next to his mattress that was covered with *Star Wars* sheets he'd had since he was nine—another present his mom had picked up at a yard sale.

"One day, Mom, I'm going to buy us a really nice house." With really nice stuff in it.

She smiled, but her eyes said she didn't believe a word he spoke. "I know you will, baby. Now eat up and get to school. I don't want you dropping out like me." She paused as a hurt look flitted across her face. "You can see exactly what that gets you."

Guilt cut through him. He was the reason his mom had dropped out of school. As soon as her parents had learned she was pregnant, they'd offered her one choice.

Give up the baby or give up her nice home in Kenner, her education, and her family.

For reasons he still didn't understand, she'd chosen him.

It was something Nick never let himself forget. But one day he was going to get all that back for her. She deserved it, and for her, he'd wear this god-awful shirt.

Even if it got him killed. . . .

And he'd smile through the pain of it until Stone and his crew kicked his teeth in.

Trying not to think about the butt-whipping to come, Nick ate his bacon in silence. Maybe Stone wouldn't be in school today. He could get malaria or the plague, or rabies or something.

Yeah, may the smarmy freak get a pox on his privates.

That thought actually made him smile as he shoved the grainy powdered eggs into his mouth and swallowed them. He forced himself not to shiver at the taste. But it was all they could afford.

He glanced at the clock on the wall and jerked. "Gotta go. I'm going to be late."

She grabbed him for a bear hug.

Nick grimaced. "Stop sexually harassing me, Mom. I gotta go before I get another tardy."

She popped him on the butt cheek before she released him. "Sexually harassing you. Boy, you have no idea." She ruffled his hair as he bent over to pick up his backpack.

Nick put both arms through the straps and hit the door running. He launched himself from the dilapidated porch and sprinted down the street, past broken-down cars and garbage cans to where the streetcar stopped.

"Please don't be gone. . . ."

Otherwise he'd be doomed to another "Nick? What are we going to do with you, you white-trash dirt?" lecture from Mr. Peters. The old man hated his guts, and the fact that Nick was a scholarship kid at his snotty overprivileged school seriously ticked Peters off. He'd like nothing better than to kick him out so that Nick wouldn't "corrupt" the kids from the good families.

Nick's lip curled as he tried not to think about the way those decent people looked at him like he was nothing. More than half their dads were regulars at the club where his mom worked, yet they were called decent while he and his mom were considered trash.

The hypocrisy of that didn't sit well with him. But it was what it was. He couldn't change anyone's mind but his own.

Nick put his head down and ran as he saw the streetcar stopped at his station.

Oh man. . . .

Nick picked up speed and he broke out into a dead run. He hit the platform and leapt for the streetcar.

He'd caught it just in time.

Panting and sweating from the humid autumn New Orleans air, he shrugged his backpack off as he greeted the driver. "Morning, Mr. Clemmons."

The elderly African-American man smiled at him. He was one of Nick's favorite drivers. "Morning, Mr. Gautier." He always mispronounced Nick's last name. He said it "Go-chay" instead of the correct "Go-shay." The difference being "Go-chay" traditionally had an "h" in it after the "t" and, as Nick's mom so often said, they were too poor for any more letters. Not to mention, one of his mom's relatives, Fernando Upton Gautier, had founded the small town in Mississippi that shared his name and both were pronounced "Go-shay." "Your mom made you late again?"

"You know it." Nick dug his money out of his pocket and quickly paid before taking a seat. Winded and sweating, he leaned back and let out a deep breath, grateful he'd made it in time.

Unfortunately, he was still sweating when he reached school. The beauty of living in a city where even in October it could hit ninety by eight A.M. Man, he was getting tired of this late heat wave they'd been suffering.

Suck it up, Nick. You're not late today. It's all good.

Yeah, let the mocking commence.

He smoothed his hair down, wiped the sweat off his brow, and draped his backpack over his left shoulder.

Holding his head high in spite of the snickers and comments about his shirt and sweaty condition, he walked across the yard and through the doors like he owned them. It was the best he could do.

"Ew! Gross! He's dripping wet. Is he too poor to own a towel? Don't poor people ever bathe?"

"Looks like he went fishing in the Pontchartrain and came up with that hideous shirt instead of a real fish."

"That's 'cause he couldn't miss it. I'll bet it even glows in the dark."

"I bet there's a naked hobo somewhere wanting to know who stole his clothes while he was sleeping on a bench. Gah, how long has he owned those shoes, anyway? I think my dad wore a pair like that in the eighties."

Nick turned a deaf ear to them and focused on the fact that they really were stupid. None of them would be here if their parents weren't loaded. *He* was the scholarship kid. They probably couldn't have even spelled their names right on the exam he'd aced to get in.

That was what mattered most. He'd much rather have brains than money.

Though right now, a rocket launcher might be nice too. He just couldn't say that out loud without the faculty calling the cops on his having "inappropriate" thoughts.

His bravado lasted until he reached his locker, where Stone and crew were loitering.

Great, just great. Couldn't they pick someone else to stalk?

Stone Blakemoor was the kind of creep who gave jocks a bad name. They weren't all like that and he knew it. Nick had several friends who were on the football team—starters, no less, not seat warmers like Stone.

Still, when you thought of an arrogant jock-rock, Stone was aptly named. It was definitely a self-fulfilling moniker his parents had labeled him with. Guess his mom had known while he was in the womb that she was going to birth a flaming moron.

Stone snorted as Nick stopped beside his group to open his locker. "Hey, Gautier? I saw your mom naked last night—shaking her butt in my dad's face so that he'd put a dollar in her G-string. He got a good feel of her too. Said she's got a nice set of—"

Before he could think better of it, Nick swiped him upside the head with his backpack as hard as he could.

And then it was on like Donkey Kong.

"Fight!" someone shouted while Nick wrapped Stone in a headlock and pounded him.

A crowd gathered round, chanting, "Fight, fight, fight."

Somehow Stone escaped his hold and hit him so hard in the sternum it took the breath from him. Dang, he was a lot stronger than he looked. He hit like a jackhammer.

Furious, Nick started for him, only to find one of the teachers suddenly between them.

Ms. Pantall.

The sight of her petite form calmed him instantly. He wasn't about to hit an innocent person, especially not a woman. She narrowed her eyes at him and pointed down the hall. "To the office, Gautier. Now!"

Cursing under his breath, Nick picked his backpack up from the tiled beige floor and glared at Stone, who at least had a busted lip.

So much for not getting into trouble.

But what was he supposed to do? Let the weasel scum insult his mom?

Disgusted, he entered the office and sat in the corner chair outside the principal's door. Why wasn't there an undo button for life?

"Excuse me?"

Nick looked up at the softest, sweetest voice he'd ever heard. His stomach hit the ground.

Dressed all in pink, she was gorgeous, with silky brown hair and green eyes that practically glowed.

Oh. My. God.

Nick wanted to speak but all he could do was try not to drool on her.

She held her hand out to him. "I'm Nekoda

Kennedy, but most people call me Kody. I'm new to the school and kind of nervous. They told me to wait here, then there was a fight and they haven't come back and . . . I'm sorry, I babble when I'm nervous."

"Nick. Nick Gautier." He cringed as he realized how stupid he sounded and how behind he was on her conversation.

She laughed like an angel. A beautiful, perfect . . .

I am so in love with you. . . .

Get a grip, Nick. Get a grip. . . .

"So, have you been going here long?" Kody asked.

Work, tongue. Work. He finally choked an answer out. "Three years."

"You like it?"

Nick's gaze went to Stone and the others heading into the office. "Not today, I don't."

She opened her mouth to speak, but Stone and crew surrounded her.

"Hey, baby." Stone flashed her a cheesy grin. "You new meat?"

Kody grimaced and sidestepped them. "Get away from me, you animals. You smell." She raked a repugnant stare over Stone's body and curled her lip. "Aren't you a little old for your mom to be picking out your clothes for you? Really? Shopping at the Children's Place at your age? I'm sure there's some third-grader dying to know who bought the last navy I-sore shirt."

Nick bit back a laugh. Yeah, he really, really liked her.

She went to stand by Nick and put her back against the wall so that she could keep an eye on Stone. "Sorry we got interrupted."

Stone made a sound like he was about to vomit. "Why are you talking to the King Loser Dork? You want to talk about ugly? Look at what he's wearing."

Nick cringed as Kody examined the sleeve of his shirt.

"I like a man who takes fashion chances. It's the mark of someone who lives by his own code. A rebel." She cast a biting glare at Stone. "A real lone wolf is a lot sexier than a pack animal who follows orders and can't have an opinion unless someone else gives it to him."

"Oooo," Stone's friends said in unison as she got the better of him.

"Shut up!" Stone shoved at them. "No one asked you for your opinions."

"Nekoda?" the secretary called. "We need to finish with your schedule."

Kody gave Nick a last smile. "I'm in ninth grade."

"Me too."

Her smile widened. "Hope we have some classes together. Nice meeting you, Nick." She made sure to step on Stone's foot as she walked past him.

Stone yelped and mumbled an insult for her under his breath. Then he and his three friends sat down in the chairs that were opposite Nick's.

Ms. Pantall walked past them to go talk to Mr. Peters.

They're going to cream me over this. . . .

As soon as she was gone, Stone tossed a wadded-up piece of paper at him. "Where did you get that shirt, Gautier? Goodwill or did you find it in a Dumpster? Nah, I bet you rolled a hobo for it. I know you people couldn't afford even something that tacky."

Nick refused to rise to the bait this time. Besides, he could handle insults directed at him. It was the ones against his mom that elevated him to fighting mad.

And this was why most private schools had uniforms. But Stone didn't want to wear one and since his father all but owned the school. . . .

Nick got to be mocked for the clothes his mom thought were respectable. *Why don't you ever listen to me, Mom? Just once . . .*

"What? No smart comeback?"

Nick flipped him off. . . . At the same exact moment Peters came out and saw him.

Lady Luck is definitely on vacation today.

"Gautier," Peters growled. "Get in here. Now!"

With a heavy sigh, Nick got up and went inside the office he knew as well as his own home. Peters stayed outside, no doubt talking to Stone while he was forced to wait. He took the chair to the right and sat there, staring at the pictures of Peters's wife and kids. They had a nice house with a yard, and in one photo his daughters played with a white puppy.

Nick stared at them. What would it be like to live that way? He'd always wanted a dog, but since they could barely afford to feed themselves, a pooch was out of the question. Not to mention their landlord would die if they had one in their rented condo even though there wasn't much more damage a dog could do to the run-down shack.

After a few minutes, Peters came in and went to his desk. Without a word, he picked up the phone.

Nick panicked. "What are you doing?"

"I'm calling your mother."

Terror ripped through him. "Please, Mr. Peters, don't do that. She had to work a double shift last night and tonight too. She's only going to get about four hours of sleep today and I don't want to worry her about nothing." Not to mention she'd beat his butt royally for this.

He dialed the number anyway.

Nick ground his teeth as anger and fear whipped through his entire being.

"*Miss* Gautier?" Could there be any more loathing in his tone? And did he always have to stress the fact that his mom had never married? That always embarrassed her to death. "I wanted to let you know that Nick is being suspended from school for the rest of the week."

His stomach hit the floor. His mom was going to kill him when he got home. Why couldn't Peters just shoot him and put him out of his misery?

Peters glared mercilessly at him. "No, he was fighting again, and I'm sick of his thinking he can come in here and attack decent people anytime he feels like it for no apparent reason. He has to learn to control his temper. Honestly, I'm tempted to call the police. In my opinion, he should be sent to public school where they can handle troubled kids like him. I've said it before and I'll say it again. He doesn't belong here."

Nick died a little with every word. *Kids like him . . .*

He zoned out so that he wouldn't have to hear the rest of Peters's tirade about how worthless he was. He already knew the truth in his heart. The last thing he needed was someone else voicing it.

After a few minutes, Peters hung up the phone.

Nick gave him a sullen stare. "I didn't start it."

Peters curled his lip. "That's not what the others said. Who am I supposed to believe, Gautier? A hoodlum like you or four honor students?"

He was supposed to believe the one telling the truth, which happened to be the hoodlum. "He insulted my mother."

"That's no excuse for violence."

That went down his spine like a shredder. The sanctimonious pig—Nick couldn't let that go unanswered. "Really? Well, you know, Mr. Peters, I saw your mom naked last night and for an old broad, she has really nice—"

"How dare you!" he shouted, coming to his feet to grab Nick up by his shirt. "You foul-mouthed little—"

"I thought you said insulting your mom was no excuse for violence."

Peters trembled as rage mottled his skin. His grip tightened and a vein throbbed in his temple. "My mother isn't a Bourbon Street stripper. She's a good, God-fearing woman." He shoved Nick away from him. "Get your things and get out."

God-fearing, huh? Strange how Nick and his mom went to mass every Sunday and at least twice during the week and the only time he ever saw Peters or his mom there was on holidays.

Yeah . . .

Hypocrite to the core. He despised people like Peters.

Nick scooped his backpack up from the floor and left. There was a security guard waiting outside the office to escort him to his locker.

Just like a criminal.

Might as well get used to it. Some things ran in the blood. *At least he's not handcuffing me.*

Yet.

Hanging his head low, he tried not to look at anyone as the other students sniggered and whispered about him.

"That's what happens when you come from trash."

"I hope they don't let him back in."

"Serves him right."

Nick ground his teeth in anger as he neared his locker and reached for the combination lock.

Brynna Addams was pulling her books out, two doors down. Tall with dark brown hair, she was very pretty and one of the few people who hung with Stone and crew that Nick could stand.

She paused to look at them with a frown that only deepened when she saw the guard with him. "What's up, Nick?"

"Got suspended." He paused before he swallowed his pride. Again. "Could I ask a favor?"

She didn't hesitate. "Sure."

"Could you get my assignments so that I don't fall behind?"

"Absolutely. You want me to e-mail them to you?"

And I stupidly thought I couldn't feel any worse. "Don't have a computer at home."

Her cheeks darkened. "Sorry. Um, where do you need me to take them?"

Nick was grateful she was decent—unlike the rest of the jerks she ran with. "I'll come by your house after school and get it."

She wrote down her address while he pulled all of his books out. "I'll be home about four."

SHERRILYN KENYON

"Thanks, Brynna. I really appreciate it." He tucked the paper in his back pocket, then allowed the security guard to escort him off campus.

Heartsick over having to face his mother, he made his way back home to their side of the ghetto and dreaded every step that took him closer to his door.

Inside their crappy house, his mother was waiting on him with a stern frown on her face. Dressed in a threadbare pink robe, she looked about as tired and ticked off as he'd ever seen her.

He dropped his backpack to the floor. "You should be asleep, Mom."

Her eyes cut him to the quick and made him feel even lower than Peters had. "How can I sleep when my boy's been thrown out of school for fighting? You of all people know how hard it is for me to keep you there. How much money it takes. What I have to do to pay for your books and lunches. Why would you be so stupid as to throw this chance away? What were you thinking?"

Nick didn't say anything because the truth would kill her and he didn't want her to feel as bad as he did when there was nothing she could do about it.

28

I'm the man of the family. It was his job to protect her. It was all he knew.

Take care of your mom, boy, or you'll answer to me. You lip off to her and I'll cut out your tongue. You make her cry and I'll kill you myself. His father was pretty worthless, but the one thing about him was that he made good on his threats. All of them. And since he'd already killed twelve people, Nick figured he wouldn't think twice about killing him either. Especially since his father had no great love of him.

So he kept his anger locked in and refused to say anything to hurt her feelings.

Unfortunately, his mother gave him no reprieve. "Don't you get sullen on me, boy. I'm sick of that look on your face. Tell me why you attacked that kid. Now."

Nick clenched his teeth tight.

"Answer me, Nick, or so help me, I'll spank you, even at your age."

He had to stop himself from rolling his eyes at her ludicrous threat. Even at fourteen, he was more than a head taller than his tiny mother and he had a good forty pounds on her. "He made fun of me."

SHERRILYN KENYON

"And for that you'd jeopardize your entire future? What were you thinking? He laughed at you. So what? Believe me, that's not the worst thing that will ever happen to you. You have to grow up, Nicky, and stop acting like a baby. Just because someone mocks you is no reason to fight. Now is it?"

No. He swallowed attacks against him all the time. What he wouldn't suffer were attacks against his mom. And he shouldn't have to. "I'm sorry."

She held her hand up. "Don't even go there. You're not sorry. I can see it in your eyes. I am so disappointed in you. I thought I'd taught you better, but apparently you're determined to grow up into a no-account criminal just like your daddy, in spite of everything I do to keep you straight. Now go to your room until I calm down. You can stay there for the rest of the day."

"I'm supposed to work this afternoon. Ms. Liza needs me to help move her stock around in the storeroom."

She growled. "Fine. You can go, but then it's straight home. You hear me? I don't want you wasting time with any of those hoodlums you call friends."

"Yes, ma'am." Nick headed to his "room" and pulled the blankets closed. Sick and tired of it all, he sat down on the old, lumpy mattress and leaned his head back against the wall where he saw the pieces of the ceiling that were discolored and peeling up.

And then he heard it. . . .

The sound of his mother's tears coming through the wall of her bedroom. God, how he hated that sound.

"I'm sorry, Mom," he whispered, wishing he'd strangled Stone where the creep stood.

One day . . . one day he was going to get out of this hellhole. Even if he had to kill someone to do it.

It was nine o'clock when Nick left Liza's store. He'd already picked up his assignments from Brynna at her huge mansion of a house on his way into work. Then he'd put in five hours so that he could save money for his "college fund." 'Course at the rate it was accumulating, he'd be fifty before he could go. But something was better than nothing.

Liza locked the door to her shop while he stood behind her to shield her from anyone who might be watching them. "Good night, Nicky. Thanks for all your help."

"Night, Liza." He waited until she was safely in her car and on her way home before he headed down Royal Street toward the Square. The closest streetcar stop was over behind Jackson Brewery. But as he neared the Square, he wanted to see his mom and apologize for getting suspended.

She told you to go straight home. . . .

Yeah, but he'd made her cry and he hated whenever he did that. Besides, the condo was really lonely when he was there alone at night. They didn't have TV or anything else to do.

And he'd already read *Hammer's Slammers* until he could quote it.

Maybe if he apologized, she'd let him hang out at the club for the night.

So instead of turning right, he made a left and headed for her club on Bourbon Street. The faint sounds of jazz and zydeco music coming out of stores and restaurants soothed him. Closing his eyes as he walked, he inhaled the sweet smell of cinnamon and gumbo as he passed the Cafe Pontalba. His stomach rumbled. Since he hadn't been at school, his lunch had consisted of more powdered eggs and bacon, and he had yet to eat dinner . . . which would be those nasty eggs again.

Not wanting to think about that, he walked down the narrow alley to the back door of the club and knocked.

John Chartier, one of the huge burly bouncers who watched out for the dancers, opened it with a fierce frown—until he saw Nick. A wide smile spread over his face. "Hey, buddy. You here to see your mom?"

"Yeah. Is she on stage yet?"

"Nah, she's still got a few minutes." He stood back so that Nick could walk down the dark back hallway to the green room.

He paused at the door to the room where the dancers dressed and rested between performances, and knocked.

Tiffany answered. Absolutely stunning, she was

tall and blond . . . and barely dressed in a G-string and lacy top.

Even though he'd been raised around women dressed like that and was used to it, his face flamed bright red as he kept his gaze on the floor. It was like seeing his sister naked.

Tiffany laughed, cupping his chin in her hand. "Cherise? It's your Nicky." She squeezed his chin affectionately. "You're so sweet the way you won't look at us. I knew it was you when you knocked. No one else is so nice. All I can say is your mama is raising you right."

Nick mumbled a thank-you as he stepped past her and made his way to his mom's dressing station. He kept his gaze down until he was sure his mom was covered by her pink bathrobe.

But when he caught her furious glare in the chipped mirror where she was putting on her makeup, his stomach hit the floor. There was no forgiveness in that face tonight.

"I thought I told you to go straight home."

"I wanted to say I was sorry again."

She put down her mascara wand. "No, you didn't. You wanted to try and make me tell you that you didn't have to stay on restriction. I won't have it, Nicholas Ambrosius Gautier. And your paltry apology doesn't change the fact that you knew better. You have to learn to think before you act. That temper of yours is going to get you into serious trouble one day. Just like it did your father. Now go home and contemplate what you did and how wrong it was."

"But Mom—"

"Don't 'but Mom' me. Go!"

"Cherise!" her handler shouted, letting her know it was time to go on stage.

She stood up. "I mean it, Nick. Go home."

Nick turned around and left the club, feeling even worse than he had when he'd left Liza's. Why wouldn't his mom believe in him?

Why couldn't she see that he wasn't trying to play her?

Whatever . . . He was tired of trying to convince the world, and especially his mom, that he wasn't worthless.

On the street, he headed down Bourbon toward Canal, where he could pick up a closer streetcar. He hated when his mom treated him like a criminal. He was *not* his father. He would *never* be like that man.

Fine, I'll never protect your honor again. Let them insult and mock you. See if I care. Why should he bother when doing the right thing made her so mad at him?

Angry, hurt, and disgusted, he heard someone call his name.

Pausing, he saw Tyree, Alan, and Mike across the street, hanging outside a tourist bead and mask store. They waved him over.

Nick crossed the street to tap his fist against theirs. "What's up?"

Tyree leaned his head back in silent salute to him. "Hanging. What you doing?"

"Heading home."

Tyree slapped at the collar of Nick's orange shirt. "Boy, what you got on? That shit's hideous."

Nick slapped his hand away. "Clothes. What's that crap you got on and what truck did it fall off of?"

Tyree snorted and preened. "These my Romeo threads. They make all the ladies call me tasty."

Nick scoffed. "Tasty-crazy. Them ain't no Romeo duds. Those fashions by Geek Street."

They all laughed.

Mike sobered. "Look, we got a thing tonight and we could use a fourth. You want in? It should be worth a couple hundred dollars to you."

Nick's eyes widened at the sum. That was a lot of money. Tyree, Mike, and Alan were hustlers. Though his mom would have a stroke if she ever found out, he'd been known to help them a time or two when they'd scammed locals and tourists. "Pool, poker, or craps?"

Alan and Tyree exchanged an amused look. "This is more a job of watchdog. At least for you. We got the big boss from Storyville who's paying us to shake down some deadbeats. It'll only take a couple of minutes."

Nick screwed his face up. "I don't know about that."

Tyree tsked. "C'mon, Nick. We don't have much

time before we have to be there and we really need someone to watch the street. Five minutes and you'll make more money than working a month for that old lady."

Nick looked back toward his mom's club. Normally, he'd have told them to forget it, but right now . . .

If everyone's going to call me a worthless delinquent, I might as well be one.

'Cause living right sure wasn't paying off for him. "You sure it's five minutes?"

Tyree nodded. "Absolutely. In and out and we're done."

Then he could be home and his mom wouldn't be the wiser. For once, he enjoyed the thought of sticking it to her, even though she would never know about it. "All right. I'm in."

"Good man."

Nick looked at Alan, who was nineteen. "Can you guys give me a ride home after?"

"For you, boy? Anything."

Nodding, Nick followed them over to a seedy part

of North Rampart. Tyree put him on the street, blocking an alley.

"You stay right here and watch for the Five-O. Let
us know if you see anyone."

Nick inclined his head to him.

They vanished into the shadows while he stood
there, waiting. After a few minutes, an old couple walked
past him on the sidewalk. By their dress and manners,
he could tell they were tourists just taking a late stroll
off the beaten path.

"Hi there," the woman said to him, smiling.

"Hi." Nick returned the expression. But his smile
died an instant later when Alan leapt out of the shadows to grab the woman while Tyree knocked the man
into a wall.

Nick was stunned. "What are you doing?"

"Shut up!" Alan snarled, pulling out a gun. "All
right, grandpa. Give us your money or the old ho gets
it right between her eyes."

Nick felt the color drain from his face. This couldn't
be happening. They were mugging two tourists?

And I'm helping. . . .

For a full minute he couldn't breathe as he watched the woman cry and the man beg them not to hurt her.

Before he even realized what he was doing, he grabbed Alan's hand that held the gun and knocked it away. "Run!" he shouted at the couple.

They did.

Tyree started after them, but Nick tackled him to the ground.

Alan caught him by the collar of his shirt and jerked him back. "Man, what are you doing?"

Nick shoved him. "I can't let you mug someone. That wasn't the deal."

"You stupid . . ." Alan hit him in the face with the gun.

Pain exploded in Nick's skull as he tasted blood.

"You're going to pay for that, Gautier."

The three of them descended on him so fast and furious that he couldn't even see to fight back. One minute he was standing and the next he was on the ground with his arms wrapped around his head to protect it from the gun Alan was beating him with. They stomped and beat on him until he lost all feeling in his legs and one arm.

Alan stepped back and angled the gun on him. "Say your prayers, Gautier. You're about to become a statistic."

CHAPTER 2

✹

Nick wanted to lash out so badly he could taste it. *I won't die like this. Not beaten in a gutter by people who're supposed to be my friends. Guys I've known and played with my whole life. I won't.*

Yet here he lay.

Helpless. Weak.

Defeated.

Not only were his taste buds drenched with blood, he felt like he was suffocating on it. His mind ached to fight until they were begging him for mercy—it wanted him to get up and make them eat their teeth, but his body refused to cooperate. Nothing was listening to him. Heck, he couldn't even keep them from hitting him.

Unable to do anything at all, he glared his hatred at Alan and hoped that the look alone would haunt the rat for the rest of eternity.

Alan laughed as he squeezed the trigger.

Holding his breath, Nick waited for the sound that would end his life.

Out of the darkness, a blur rushed in at the same instant Alan fired the gun. One moment, Tyree, Alan, and Mike were laughing at his pain while they insulted him. In the next, they were flying through the air and hitting the ground near him hard enough to break bones.

Nick froze as he tried to figure out where he'd been shot, but his body hurt so much that he couldn't tell. *Maybe it missed me. . . .*

Lying on the street, he caught a flash of blond hair and black clothes as someone attacked his ex-friends.

Alan cried out and the gun landed on the ground beside him.

The blond man tsked. "Shame you're too young to

kill. But in two years, I catch you doing this crap again, you won't live long enough to rethink it." With one hand, he threw Alan into the street like a rag doll.

In a swirl of black and a flash of silver, the man turned to face Nick. He didn't know why, but the guy reminded him more of a rich stockbroker than someone able to take down street-hardened gangbangers. And he wasn't all that old either. Maybe his late twenties.

Maybe.

Nick could barely draw his breath as the man came forward with the walk of a vicious predator. He was dressed all in black. An expensive leather coat draped around a body that was lethal. But it was the flash of silver on a pair of black boots that caught his attention.

One of them had a knife protruding from the toe. A knife that retracted as he came closer. The man knelt down, his brow furrowed into a deep frown. "They made a mess of you, kid. Can you stand?"

Nick slapped at his hand as the man reached out

to touch him. He didn't need help from anyone. Especially not a stranger.

He tried to push himself to his feet, then everything went black.

Kyrian Hunter barely caught the skinny kid dressed in a foully orange Hawaiian shirt before he hit the street. That hideous thing had saved his life. So bright it practically glowed, it'd called out to him as he'd been walking by and had alerted him to the fight.

From what he'd seen, the kid was a tough little scrapper. He'd give him that. And the boy could take a vicious beating without begging for mercy. There weren't many adults who could have gone through what he had without crying.

That alone made him respect the kid.

He glared at the other punks, who were running down the street as fast as they could. The ancient warrior and predator inside him wanted to hunt them down and kill them for what they'd done.

SHERRILYN KENYON

But the man in him knew this one, the one who'd put his life on the line to save the elderly couple, wouldn't live if he did. The cowards could unfortunately wait for another butt-whipping.

He tilted the kid's face so that he could see his features. The short brown hair was saturated with blood, and a huge cut would most likely leave a scar right above his left eyebrow. His nose was broken and by the looks of it, his jaw might be too. If not broken, they'd pounded it real good. Blood poured from his shoulder where he'd been shot.

Poor kid.

Picking him up, Kyrian carried him to his car so that he could get him to the hospital before he bled out and died.

Kyrian paced the waiting room, where several dozen other people sat in various states of agitation and illness. It'd been almost two hours since he'd handed the teenager over to the staff and still no word about the kid he'd found.

Was he even still alive?

Checking his watch, he growled. He really didn't have the time to stay here, waiting. . . .

He had important duties to attend to and, with luck, more lives to save before dawn.

"What are you doing here, General?"

He froze at the deep, thickly accented voice. Since Acheron was an eleven-thousand-year-old omnipotent immortal, he was the last person Kyrian had expected to find in a hospital. Not like the man could ever break a bone or get sick.

He turned around slowly to find Acheron just inside the doorway. At six foot eight with dark green hair and dressed in black Goth gear complete with a spiked leather motorcycle jacket, he was an impressive sight that made everyone who saw him swallow in fear. But it wasn't just his height that gave people pause. It was the lethal aura of I'll-kick-your-butt-so-hard-your-ancestors'-ears-will-ring. Anyone who came near him could feel the unearthly power that bled from the pores of this particular . . .

Being.

"What are *you* doing here?" Kyrian asked.

His eyes completely shielded by a pair of opaque Predator sunglasses even though it was almost midnight, Acheron cut loose with a lopsided grin that antagonized him. "I asked *you* first."

If it'd been anyone other than Acheron making that smart-aleck comment, Kyrian would give him a higher dose of attitude. But attitude didn't work on Acheron. It just pissed him off, which was never a good thing. "I found a kid getting a major ass-whipping on the street. I don't know who he is but I don't want to leave him here without an adult to watch over him. He was pretty badly mangled in the fight and not old enough to be left alone."

Acheron tilted his head as if he was listening to voices only he could hear. Kyrian hated whenever he did that. It creeped him out to think what all whispered to the ancient being. Most of all, it creeped him out to think what all the man knew about him that Kyrian had never told him. . . .

"Name's Gautier. Nick Gautier. He's a fourteen-year-old student at St. Richard's High School on

Chartres who lives in the Lower Ninth on Claiborne Ave."

Kyrian was impressed. "You know him?"

There was no hint of emotion from Acheron. "Never seen him before."

"Yet you know his name?"

That cocky grin returned to irritate Kyrian. "I know lots of things, General." Acheron held his hand up and a piece of paper appeared out of nowhere between his fingers. He held it out to him. "His mother's an exotic dancer named Cherise Gautier. You can reach her here. But be warned. She has a sharp tongue where her son's concerned and if she thinks you've hurt him or caused him to be hurt . . . she's going for blood."

Kyrian took the paper from his hand. "I'd ask you about those Jedi mind tricks of yours, but I know you won't answer."

Acheron tucked his hands into the pockets of his scuffed jacket that had two chains wrapped around the shoulder of it. "No comment, but I will say this." He paused before he spoke again. "Nick isn't Jason.

It's a different time and place, General. Don't let the past ruin your future."

"Meaning what, oh great Yoda?"

Acheron didn't elaborate. "You take care of the kid. I'll take care of your patrol tonight. I could use the target practice."

"Thanks for understanding." After all, Acheron was his boss and could have easily reamed him for not doing his duties.

Acheron inclined his head before he made his way out of the room and through the double doors that led to the parking lot. And with him went that powerful charge in the air.

Yeah, Acheron was one scary SOB. But Kyrian wasn't exactly comforting himself. Acheron had trained him and he'd been a master pupil, especially when it came to killing things that shouldn't be living in the first place.

Glancing at the number in his hand, he pulled his phone out and called Nick's mother.

* * *

Nick groaned as he blinked open his . . .

Eye.

Uh, gah, what happened? His head was throbbing and one eye had something over it that prevented him from opening it. *Please don't tell me I've put out an eye.* His mom would flip sideways. It was her biggest fear.

Don't play with that fill-in-the-blank, Nick. You could lose an eye. It was her favorite rant no matter what object he touched, and she'd kill him if he was now a cyclops.

God, I'll never get a girlfriend now. Women don't date freaks.

"Careful, kid."

Nick paused as he realized he was in a hospital room. He tried to sit up, but someone stopped him. His panic increased as he recognized the blond man from the fight. "Where am I?"

"Hospital."

"Really? No kidding? And here I thought I was at McDonald's." Nick glared at the stupid answer. "I can't be here. We can't afford it."

The man ignored his rampant sarcasm, keeping his

features completely impassive. "Don't worry about the price. It's on me."

Yeah, right. "We don't take charity." Nick winced as pain tore through his skull and he realized his arm was in a sling. *Don't you dare break a bone, Nicky. I can't afford no doctor bill like that. Whatever you do, don't get hurt.*

Nick felt ill over everything that'd happened. "My mom's going to kill me."

"I doubt it."

If the stranger only knew . . . "Yeah, well, I don't. I happen to have known the woman since the day I was born and she's going to beat me until I bleed." He looked up at the stranger who'd saved his life.

He was huge. Probably around six-four with short blond hair, he was dressed all in black. High-end black. Nice pants, Ferragamo boots and, unless Nick missed his guess, the button-down shirt was silk with leather cuffs and collar—not that fake stuff they sold at the Dollar Store where he and his mother bought clothes. As for his coat, the leather was so soft, it didn't even make that crackling leather sound.

This guy was definitely loaded.

"Why can't I move my arm?" Nick was starting to panic.

"You were shot."

"Where?"

"Your shoulder."

Before Nick could say another word, he heard his mother's distressed cry. From the side where his vision was blocked, she appeared and wrapped her arms around him.

"Oh my God, baby. Are you all right?" She bawled as she saw the bandage on his head and over his eye. "What did they do to you? Why weren't you at home like I told you? Dammit, Nicky, why don't you ever listen to me? Just once in your life!"

"It wasn't his fault."

His mother released him instantly. She turned toward the stranger, who was still in the far corner of the room. "Who are you and why are you here?"

He held his hand out to her. "Kyrian Hunter. I'm the one who called you."

She shook his hand. There was a stark contrast

between her tan secondhand frayed wool coat, cheap white vinyl boots, and the red sequined polyester skirt Nick knew belonged to one of her dancing outfits. His tiny mom was a beautiful woman, but the heavy, overdone stage makeup made her look a lot older than her twenty-eight years and he hated when she teased her blond hair out for shows. It made her look cheap and his mom was anything but. "Thank you for that, Mr. Hunter. Where did you find him again?"

Nick panicked. If Kyrian told her where he was when he'd been shot, she'd shoot him again just for good measure.

"He was in the Quarter, trying to protect an old couple from being mugged. They got away and the scum who'd held them up was beating on him when I saw them and stopped it."

Tears glistened in her eyes. "You saved my baby?"

Kyrian nodded.

She sobbed even harder.

Nick felt like total crap. It was a good thing his dad wasn't here. He'd cut his throat for upsetting her like this. "Don't cry, Mom. I'm so sorry I got shot. I should have done what you said and gone home. . . . I'm just so sorry."

She wiped at her cheeks where her makeup was now streaked by the tears. "You didn't do nothing wrong, baby. You're a hero. A wonderful hero and I couldn't be prouder of you."

Nick winced at the lie. He wasn't a hero. *I'm a hoodlum . . . just like my scum-sucking father.*

He met Kyrian's gaze and something in his eyes made him think that Kyrian might actually know the truth. If he did, he didn't bust him for it, which only made Nick feel all the worse.

His mother drew a ragged breath. "The doctor told me you'd have to stay here for a few days, maybe a week or more. I don't know how we're going to afford—"

"Don't worry about it. I'm taking care of the bill."

She narrowed her eyes at Kyrian. "I can't let you do that."

"It's all right. Least I can do for him. There aren't many kids his age who'd take a bullet to keep a stranger safe."

Still, she looked doubtful.

Kyrian offered her a kind, tight-lipped smile. "I have the money, Mrs. Gautier." Wow, unlike Peters, he didn't sneer her name. He actually said it like he respected her. "And no one to spend it on. Trust me. You're not taking a dime from me or my family that'll be missed."

She bit her lip. "That's mighty kind of you. Especially after everything you've already done getting him here and all." She took Nick's uninjured hand into hers and squeezed it. "I can't thank you enough for saving my baby, Mr. Hunter. Nicky's all I got in this world. I'd die if anything ever happened to him."

Something dark flitted through Kyrian's eyes that reminded Nick of a ghost tormenting him. Some past pain that his mother's words conjured up.

Kyrian pulled out his wallet and opened it. "This is my number." He gave his mother a small business card. "If you need anything at all, don't hesitate to call me. Any time, day or night. I don't sleep much so don't worry about disturbing me."

She tried to give it back, but Kyrian wouldn't allow it.

"Look," he said firmly. "I know you don't know me or trust me at all. I don't blame you. But there are people in the world who can give without asking for anything back. I'm one of them."

She shook her head. "And I know how much stuff like this costs. I can't take that kind of money from you or anyone else. Ever."

Kyrian's dark brown gaze went to Nick. "Then let him work it off."

Nick sputtered indignantly. "Excuse me?"

They ignored him.

"Don't be ridiculous," his mom said. "It'd take him forever to earn this kind of money back."

Uh, yeah . . . Last thing Nick wanted was to be indentured over a doctor bill.

Kyrian returned his wallet to his pocket. "Then what do you want to do? Have the hospital turn him out into the street before he's fully healed? Wounds like that, he could get gangrene and lose a limb or die."

Hopeless despair glistened in her blue eyes and the sight kicked Nick straight in the gut.

"Mrs. Gautier . . ." A tic worked in Kyrian's jaw. "I know you can't tell it by looking at me, but I've had a hard life. I've lost everyone who was ever important to me and I know what it's like to be kicked hard when you're down. You've got a great kid there. He deserves a chance. Let him work for me, part time, after school for a year, and we'll call it even."

She glanced at Nick, who wasn't so sold on this idea. "Doing what?"

"Washing my car. Running errands."

His mom scowled. "What kind of errands?"

"Yeah," Nick interjected, "I ain't no babysitter or dog walker."

Kyrian rolled his eyes. "I don't have kids or a dog." He returned his gaze to Nick's mom. "He'd pick up groceries. Some dry cleaning. He can work with my groundskeeper trimming hedges or help my housekeeper clean the outside windows. Nothing dangerous or illegal."

That didn't sound too bad, but Nick already had a

job that he liked most days. "What about Ms. Liza, Mom? Who'll help her in her store?"

Kyrian frowned at him. "Liza Dunnigan?"

"You know her?" Nick asked in surprise.

Another tight-lipped grin broke over his face. "Yeah. We go way back. And I think she'd understand if you worked for me for a while."

His mom's hand tightened on his. "I don't know . . . what do you think, Nicky?"

Nick looked at the sling on his arm. There really was no way they could afford this bill. If Kyrian would pay and his mom wouldn't have to suffer . . .

"As long as he's not a pervert and Liza doesn't mind, I can work for him, I guess."

Kyrian laughed. "I'm not a pervert."

"You better not be 'cause I'll quit if you are."

Kyrian shook his head. "So it's settled?"

Indecision played in his mom's gaze before she nodded. "Thank you."

"No problem. Now if you two don't mind, I have an appointment I need to keep."

Nick frowned.

"This late?" his mom asked suspiciously.

Kyrian nodded. "I do a lot of international business that requires me to work late at night. Like I said, I don't sleep much." And with that, he was gone.

Now that they were alone, his mom gave him her full attention. "What do you really think?"

"I think I'm really glad I'm not dead and you're not killing me over getting shot and being in the hospital, running up bills we can't afford."

Her lips trembled. "Baby, how could I be mad at you for something like this? I just wish I made enough money that you didn't have to work too. If you'd been at home—"

"Don't, Mom, please." The guilt of it was killing him.

She lifted his hand to her lips and kissed his bruised knuckles. "All right, sweetie. You just rest. Don't you worry or think about nothing except getting better." She pulled one of her black hair bands from her pocket and slicked her hair back into a sedate ponytail.

Nick smiled, knowing she did that for him so he

wouldn't be embarrassed by her over-teased hair. Then she went to the sink to wash off her makeup and pull off the fake glitter eyelashes. She was so much prettier without all that goop on her face that he didn't understand why they made her wear it.

Once she looked like his mom again, she slid into the bed beside him and held him close.

Normally, he'd be pushing her away 'cause it felt like she was stifling him. But tonight, while he ached and hurt, he was glad to have her hold him close.

It'd always been just the two of them in this world. Team Fabulous. That's what she'd called them as far back as he could remember. Together they could make it through anything.

She brushed his hair back from his temple and gave him a light kiss there. "You are my little man, Nickyboo. And I'm so grateful I have you. You're the only thing I've ever done right in my entire life and if anything ever happened to you, they'd have to dig two graves 'cause I couldn't live a single day without my baby beside me."

Her words almost succeeded in making his eyes

tear up, but he was too tough for that. Nothing could make *him* cry. Nothing. "I love you, Mom."

"I love you too, baby. Now go to sleep. You need to get better so I can beat your butt for getting hurt."

Smiling at her empty threat, Nick closed his eyes, but he couldn't sleep. His mind kept replaying the look on Alan's face as he'd pulled the trigger. The creep had tried to kill him. . . .

And if it was the last thing he did, he was going to get even. As his dad would say, *Our blood don't run. Sometimes we want to. Sometimes we ought to. But we don't ever run from anyone or anything.*

Next time he met up with Alan's "crew" they were going to feel the full wrath of Nick Gautier. . . .

CHAPTER 3

><

Nick learned a new lesson in misery as he lay in bed, alone, in the hospital for days on end, bored out of his mind. His mom stayed with him as much as she could, as did Menyara, but they couldn't be here constantly. Kyrian would stop in and visit at night and some of the dancers from his mom's club in the daytime. Still, he spent most of the time by himself.

Scariest part?

School was starting to look good. He shivered in revulsion of that awful thought.

"Hi . . . um, Nick, wasn't it?"

He opened his eye to find Nekoda of all people

standing in the doorway. With her hair pulled back into a thick ponytail and dressed in a volunteer's uniform, she came deeper into the room.

Heat stung his cheeks as she looked at his ragged state of ick. Nick cleared his throat. "Yeah, it's me, but I like to think I looked better when we met. 'Cause right now, I'm pretty much hogging all the ugly."

She laughed. "No offense, but yeah, you did look a bit better. But I have to say you really rock the crazy headgear you have going right now. Not an easy thing to do to make *that* look good." She winked at him.

He could only imagine how foul he appeared. His head was still wrapped up, his exposed eye bruised and swollen. One shoulder was in a sling to keep it still and the other arm attached to monitors and an IV. He had a faded-out hospital gown that was freckled with the oh-so-manly-looking flower things all over it. Gah, at this point, he'd rather be back in his orange Hawaiian shirt.

All he needed to look like a bigger goober was to drool on himself. Which he might do if she kept talking to him.

She stopped next to his bed and glanced over all the monitors that beeped and hummed. "So what happened to you?"

"I got shot."

Her brows arched high. "In the eye? Is that why it's covered?"

"No. I got hit there with a board, a fist, a foot, and probably a few other things. There's a bunch of stitches above my eye. Doc says the bandage for that can come off tomorrow. I'm sure I'll look even better then." His voice was thick with sarcasm. "I was clipped in the shoulder."

"Oh," she said, calming down as she scowled at his sling. "Did it hurt?"

He wanted to say no, duh, but his common sense caught his tongue before he insulted her. Even though it still hurt, he straightened up into his tough posture. "Nah. I took it like a man."

She shook her head at him and didn't comment on his bravado. "So why did you get shot? One of your witticisms go awry?"

Nick wasn't sure how to answer that. He didn't

want to take credit for something he hadn't really done—like saving people he'd helped put in harm's way. So he settled on a lesser truth. "Wrong place. Real wrong time."

"Did you see who shot you?"

"No," he lied. He hadn't even told the police who it was even though they'd bugged him several times. Rule one on the street: Narcs don't live long. Besides, he intended to settle this score on his own and the last thing he wanted was for Alan and group to be protected by prison walls when he went for them.

This was going to be between "friends."

"Like they say in the movies and shows, it all happened so fast. . . ."

She fretted over him. "Well, I'm sorry you got shot. It explains why I haven't seen you in school."

His ears perked up at that. She'd been looking for him? *Man, for that news, I'd take a bullet any day.* It was all he could do not to give her a goofy grin.

She leaned closer. "But I'm happy you lived and that you're okay."

"Yeah, me too. It would have really cramped my

future plans had I died. . . ." He flashed what he hoped was a charming smile at her then changed the topic. "So you work here?"

"Volunteer. Twice a week," she corrected. "I'm told things like this look good on a college application."

Wow, she was worried about that already? It made him feel like a slacker. "We're only in ninth grade."

She shrugged. "Yeah, but every year from now until graduation matters and everything we do affects if and where we get in. So I'm trying to make a difference."

"Gah, you sound like my mom."

"Sorry." She wrinkled her nose up in the most adorable way. He didn't know why, but it made his stomach tighten and heat flood his cheeks—if he kept that up, he'd be able to rent himself out as a light-house at night.

"So can I get you something to drink?" she asked. "Some ice? I have magazines and books on my cart if you want something to read."

"I'd kill for Nintendo."

She laughed. "No Nintendo on the cart. Sorry."

"You got any manga?"

"Manga?" She scowled. "What's that?"

Crap. It was too much to hope she'd share some of his more unusual interests. "Japanese comic books. I'm addicted to them."

"No, sorry again. I do have some Batman and Spider-Man if you're interested?"

"That'd be great." They were a lot shorter than the manga, but at least it'd eat up a couple of minutes while he read through them. "You got any science fiction or fantasy?"

"We have a couple of Dune books."

"Now that I could definitely go for."

She smiled. "I'll be right back."

Nick watched as she walked out of the room with a shake to her hips that ought to be illegal and in some states probably was. She really was beautiful. He didn't know what it was about her hair, but it really made him want to touch it. It just looked so soft and smooth. It probably smelled good too.

Just like her skin.

What are you thinking? She's so far out of your league. . . .

Girls like her didn't date loser dorks who mugged tourists. She was the kind who went on to date jocks and marry lawyers and surgeons and stuff.

He could just imagine the type of childhood she'd had with maids and tutors and birthday parties with presents wrapped in something other than hand-decorated grocery sacks. Her parents would probably flip out and die if they knew she was even talking to filth like him.

"Here you go." She returned and handed him a stack of books and comic books.

Nick smiled. "Bless you."

"Any time." She stepped back from the bed. "Well, I better get going. I still have to make my rounds and visit other patients. I promised Mrs. O'Malley that I'd play rummy with her today."

Wow, that was real sweet of her. "Okay. Thanks so much for stopping in and for the books."

She inclined her head to him. "Take care."

"You too."

Then she was gone. Nick sighed as depression set in. He hated that he was stuck here, but most of all he hated that he'd never be worthy of a girlfriend like Nekoda. He could bluster and pretend all he wanted to. It wouldn't change anything. She'd still go home to her nice house and he'd have to crawl back to the gutter where he'd been born.

Trying not to dwell on things he couldn't change, he opened a book and started reading.

Nick sighed and shifted, then jerked awake as he felt like he was falling out of bed. He blinked open his eye to find himself still in the hospital, alone.

Gah, this sucked. Wishing he'd slept longer than two hours, he reached for his tray to get another book and froze. There was a small box that hadn't been there before.

He frowned, reaching for it, then opened it up. Inside was a pink Nintendo and a small note.

Sorry for the color. Pink's my thing. But I hope this'll keep you from going crazy so that you won't have to kill anyone. I figure I can do without it for a few days if it'll spare your sanity.

Get better soon,
Kody.

He stared at the note as a wave of emotion over- whelmed him. It was the nicest thing anyone had ever done for him. The box was filled with games for it, from classics to strategy to shooters.

What an incredibly nice thing for her to do. It really touched him.

Picking it up, he held the system in his hand. For some reason, it made him feel weirdly close to her. Systems were personal. They were an extension of yourself. From the color to the stickers . . . It all came from within and it was something that you kept close to you. Something you guarded and pro- tected.

And she'd loaned him hers.

Not many people would do that. Especially not someone as hot as Kody. The girl was crazy.

Maybe she likes you.

That thought made his blood race like fire through his veins. Could it be possible?

She's dangerous to you. Avoid her.

He scowled at the deep, scary voice in his head. It sounded almost demonic. WTH?

"I am going crazy from boredom." Only a lunatic would want to avoid a girl as nice and pretty as Kody.

D id he take it?"

Nekoda tensed as she felt the air around her stirring. The power was palpable and it was one she was intimately familiar with.

Sraosha. Her guide and mentor.

Nekoda locked the door of the storeroom to keep anyone else in the hospital from innocently coming in and seeing Sraosha's form. Tall and graceful, he was so beautiful that it was hard to look straight at him. His powers were so great that they manifested as an ever-moving aura that illuminated his skin with a bright yellow glow. His long blond hair flowed around his shoulders as he narrowed his gaze on her . . . a gaze that had no eyes. Only a smoky black cavity that was as frightening as it was peculiar.

"I left it for him," she whispered. Nick had no idea that her Nintendo allowed her to keep an eye on him so long as he was around it.

Sraosha nodded. "What do you think of this one?"

He was younger than the other Malachais she'd fought. More innocent. Sweet even.

Don't let him seduce you.

That was the last thing she could afford to have happen.

"He seems . . ." She had to choose her word carefully. "Different."

"Do you think he's the one?"

"I don't know." Since the dawn of time, they'd hunted for the right Malachai. The one who could turn against the dark forces that had sired it and fight with them against the Source so that she could free her brothers.

But to date, they had lost every Malachai they'd tried to save. The darkness within each one was more than they could resist. And who could blame them?

All of their bloodline was born to cause pain. Born to wield the darkest powers imaginable. Just as Nekoda had been born to the light.

Nick was still a kid who had no idea who and what he was. But she knew exactly the kind of violence he'd been bred for.

And he terrified her.

"Menyara swears we can save him."

Sraosha scoffed. "She's too close to this one. She's blind to what he really is."

Perhaps that was true, but Nekoda had no such attachment to him. "Have no fear. I'm not blind to him. His glamour doesn't charm me."

"Make sure you don't fall victim to it. Remember, that's only one of many powers he'll possess. Powers that will work on all mortals and immortals alike. As you've seen, evil is already beginning to tempt him and that will only worsen as he matures."

Nekoda swallowed as she saw in her mind the events that led up to his being shot. "He pulled back before hurting them."

"*This* time. But that single act of drifting toward

violence against another has unleashed his Cimmerian Magus. The dark powers are uniting now to train him. Can't you feel it?"

Yes. It permeated everything here and it sent a feral chill down her spine. There were ten lessons that had to be taught to every Malachai. Every one of them would make him stronger.

More corrupt.

It would shape him into a tool of evil that would come for her and her people and wreak absolute misery on everyone who came into contact with him.

The first lesson was necromancy. But not just communication with the dead. Reanimation and control.

No matter how hard Nekoda tried, she couldn't see Nick becoming like the others. Surely he wouldn't embrace such a cold power.

You made the mistake of that thought before.

She winced as she remembered his father and how wrong she'd been then. Had she struck when she'd been told to, she would have saved countless lives.

It's the light inside of you that wants to believe in the goodness of other people. Even the Malachais. She'd shown the elder Malachai mercy and he'd spat in her face and embraced his own brand of evil.

No matter what, she wouldn't be so stupid again.

"Have no fear, Sraosha. I've learned from my mistake. This time, I won't fail. If we can't turn him, I *will* kill him."

"You better remember that. Because this one is even stronger than his father and now he's being embraced and trained by the Dark-Hunters. If we don't turn him, he will be the one who finally destroys us all."

And she would be the one to blame for the death of humanity.

CHAPTER 4

W elcome home, Nicky!"
Nick opened his eyes to find himself
in their crappy living room with Aunt
Menyara standing in front of him, holding an actual
store-bought chocolate cake with the same happy
words written on it that she'd just uttered. He was
stunned by the small crowd around her who shouted
her words at him.

Wow . . .

Petite like his mother, Menyara had smooth choc-
olate-brown skin that glowed in the flickering can-
dlelight. Her sisterlocks were held back from her
beautiful face by a wide yellow scarf she'd tied around

her head that trailed down her back, just past her hair. The yellow was mirrored in her peasant blouse that was tucked into a bright orange skirt that fell all the way to her ankles.

Skinny silver bangles lined both of her arms and they jingled as she angled the cake for him to see her beautiful handwriting. "It's your favorite, *cher*. We're so glad you're home."

Nick blushed as his gaze went from her to the rest of the dancers who worked with his mom who'd come over for his party. Even John and Greg, two of the bouncers from the club, were here.

They were clapping and smiling at him, making him extremely uncomfortable with the attention as they congratulated him on being a hero.

Funny, he felt more like a fraud.

Menyara put the cake down on the counter for him. "C'mon, *cher*, and blow out the candles before they ruin your beautiful cake."

He always loved the lilt of Menyara's Creole accent whenever she spoke. A voodoo priestess and midwife, Aunt Mennie, as he called her, was also his godmother and his mother's best friend.

She'd been the one who'd brought him into this world and who'd taken his mom in after her parents had tossed her out. When he'd been too young to go to the club with his mom, Mennie had been the one who kept him. For that alone, he'd do anything in the world for her.

"Thanks, everyone," he muttered as he went to the cake and blew out the candles.

His mom stood behind him with her hand on his uninjured shoulder. "We're all so proud of you, baby."

"That's right." Greg, a huge bear of a man with long brown hair and pockmarked skin, stepped forward to hand him a box. "We took up a collection for you at the club. Hope you like it."

Their kindness touched him. It felt more like a birthday than a return home from the hospital.

Ripping the box open, he found a Street Fighter video game and a T-shirt that said: NICK GAUTIER. SUPERHERO OF THE DAY.

Nick didn't have the heart to tell them that he didn't have a gaming system here. Any more than he could tell them that he hadn't been a hero. He'd only been trying to make something right that he'd let go terribly wrong.

"Thanks, everyone. I really appreciate it."

Tiffany stepped around Greg and pulled an envelope out of the box. "You forgot this."

Nick handed the box to his mom before he took the envelope, but since his left arm was still in a sling, he couldn't open it.

"Here, child." Menyara took it and opened it for him.

He gaped as he saw five twenty-dollar bills in her hand. "What's that for?"

Tiffany smiled. "Your college fund. We know it's not much, but it'll cover most of the days of work you missed while you were in the hospital."

He looked at his mom, who was smiling in gratitude. But he didn't feel grateful. He felt weird about it, especially knowing how hard all of them worked for it. "I can't take this."

John snorted. "Take it. Don't make me have to whup your butt and put you back in the hospital, snot-wad. Just be grateful for it and don't ever spend it on drugs or cheap women 'cause I know what I'd have done with it at your age and we're all raising you to be better than that."

Nick didn't know what to say. "Thanks, guys. I really appreciate it."

Then someone turned up the music to play Aerosmith's "Walk This Way" and the party started even though it was hard to move in their small condo. Then again, the dancers were used to being up on the thin catwalk in the club so they did what they did best and made his face so red with their dance moves that he was sure it glowed neon.

Nick took the money to his jar they kept under the kitchen sink and dropped the twenties inside while his mom and Menyara cut the cake and handed out slices to everyone.

"You okay, child?"

He nodded as Menyara handed him his cake and a plastic fork. "Just tired."

There was something in her gaze that made him wonder if she could read his mind. It was eerie.

"Your mom told me that you'll be working for a man named Kyrian Hunter. Is that so?"

"Yeah. I gotta pay him back for the hospital bills."

"Then I want you to watch yourself, Nicholas. This man, he's . . ."

When she didn't finish the sentence, he finished for her. "Evil?"

She laughed and brushed her hand through his hair. "No, not evil. But working for him will change you, I think. Hopefully for the better. I just wanted to say that you should be very careful with what you learn from others and who you let into your life."

Her emotionless tone gave him pause. Mennie knew things, lots of things, before they happened. Her clairvoyance was unrivaled. "Is that your wicked psychic powers talking again?"

"Maybe it's my wicked overprotective ways." She kissed him on the brow. "You be a good boy for me, Nicholas. Always."

"Yeah, okay." He wasn't intending to be a bad one, since the last time he'd done that hadn't gone well for him. As it was, his shoulder was on fire and he had months of painful therapy ahead to get his arm to work right again.

Believe me, I'm done with this. Next time he saw

Alan and group, they were the ones who were going to be limping. *'Cause I'm gonna put my foot so far up their butts they're going to burp shoe leather.*

Or in the case of Nick's cheap shoes, man-made material, whatever *that* was.

He frowned as she stepped away to join his mother and Tiffany. There was something cold in the air that made his neck tingle.

Dismissing it, he ate his cake then joined the others, who kept playing old seventies songs. *Gah, could we please move the music forward to the correct decade? What is it with old people and their music?*

Well, at least it wasn't disco.

The party didn't last too long, since his mom was afraid of making him too tired. One by one they left until it was just him, his mom, and Mennie.

At his mom's urging, Nick headed to his bed while they cleaned up. He was on the verge of falling asleep when his mom disturbed him.

"You ready to go back to school tomorrow?"

Hardly. He'd really like a few more decades before he had to go back and face the mutant idiots. . . .

But he didn't tell her that. *Man up, Nick, and take it.* "I guess so."

"Okay, but if you don't feel like it, let me know. You're still healing and I don't want you to do anything to stress yourself."

Yeah, but he was already so far behind he wasn't sure if there was a shovel big enough to dig his way out of his back work. Any more days and he'd have to repeat a year.

Kill me first.

She brushed the hair back from his forehead before she tested his brow for a fever. "Mr. Hunter said that he'd have a car waiting to pick you up after school and take you to his house. He promised me that it was just an introduction for you and that he wouldn't make you do anything too hard. You okay with that?"

He reverted to his standard answer. "I guess so."

She rolled her eyes. "All right then. I'll let you get your rest. You let me know if you need anything. Oh, and I had to put those flowers your friends Bubba and Mark sent to you in the hospital out on the front porch. They didn't really fit in the house. Leave it to them to overdo it."

That was one way of saying it. Bubba had practically sent him a tree, with one little note.

Hospitals wig me out unless I'm the one being tended.
Sorry we're not there, kid. Get well soon. Remember
next time . . . Double tap.
    Bubba and Mark

Nick watched as she left and then closed his "door."
Rubbing his sore eye, he ignored her talking with
Menyara until he heard his name mentioned.

"You think this mess will stunt his growth, Mennie?"

Menyara laughed. "No, *chère*. Your boy's going to
be a fine, tall man one day. I promise you."

"I don't know. My dad was awfully short. Barely
five foot four. I know Nick's taller than that now, but
I'm scared to death he's going to stop growing and be
a munchkin like me."

"That's 'cause you're Cajuns, child. You're supposed
to be short. Be weird if you weren't. But Adarian's a
tall, handsome man and his boy's going to be just like
him in looks. Trust me."

Those words made Nick's blood run cold.

Adarian Malachai was his father and he was a monster. The mere mention of his name conjured up an image of a giant, hulking beast of a man in prison threads, covered in heavy tattoos. Nick had never seen the man when he hadn't been snarling at everyone around him and shoving people who got near him—including Nick's mom.

Angry, bitter, and rude, his father was a rare piece of work and he was glad his mother hadn't married him and given Nick his last name. Even though his Gautier grandparents didn't want anything to do with them, he still preferred having their name to Adarian's.

Malachai. Heck, he didn't even like the way it sounded. Bleh.

Nick raised his voice to speak so that they'd hear him. "I'd rather be short, fat, and ugly than take after that man."

His mother sighed. "That man is your father and you're supposed to be asleep, young man. Not listening in on our private conversation."

What did she expect when all that separated them was a thin blue blanket? "And you're not supposed to be talking about me where I can hear it. You always told me that was rude."

They laughed.

"Go to sleep, Nick."

Go to sleep, Nick, he mouthed, mocking an order that was easier said than done. Especially since his pain meds had worn off and his shoulder was throbbing like fire again. But he didn't want to take any more. That stuff made him too groggy and ill feeling. He'd rather hurt than be a zombie.

Besides, if he acted like a zombie, Bubba might mistake him for a hallucination and shoot him.

Rule One, boy: shoot first then ask questions.

Rule Two: Double tap just for good measure. Better safe than sorry.

Nick smiled at Bubba's laws until he looked up at their stained ceiling and wondered just how miserable tomorrow would be at school.

Blinking back the agony, he pulled Nekoda's Nintendo out of his front pocket. He didn't know why, but just touching it made him feel better. Like he had someone in the world watching out for him.

How stupid was that?

He turned it on and kept the sound off. His mom had no idea he had this. She'd probably flip out if she did and he couldn't really play it with only one hand anyway. Still, he liked the thought of having it. It made him feel special. Like he was connected to someone not related to him.

Like a girl might actually like him as something more than just a friend.

He wanted the courage to ask her to go and just have a beignet with him after school. But so far he hadn't been able to do much more than thank her for checking on him while he'd been in the hospital—which she'd done every time she had a shift. He'd looked forward to each and every one of those visits like a starving beggar getting his one meal a day.

It was hard, man, to get up the courage to ask her something so personal. He didn't want to be rejected and he knew better than to reach for the stars—

which was what she was. A bright, perfect star who made him laugh whenever she came near.

And he was a loser. *Don't put yourself out there unless you want to get shot down.* He'd been taken down enough by his classmates; he wasn't about to give Kody the chance to kick his teeth in. At this point, he was lucky she'd even talked to him in the hospital. No doubt tomorrow she'd be just like all the other cool, rich kids and pretend he was invisible.

Rolling his eyes at his own stupidity for even considering the thought of asking her out, he shut down the Nintendo and put it back in his pocket. Tomorrow he'd have to face the demon principal and the cretins of his school. To do that, he needed rest.

And maybe a flamethrower or two.

Nick was finishing up the leftover cake he'd eaten for breakfast when a knock at the door startled him. Since his mom and all of her friends except Menyara worked until dawn, he wasn't used to early morning visitors.

His mom went to open the door. In this neighborhood, he expected it to be cops wanting to know about
something that'd happened while they slept.

What was there shocked him to the core of his being.

It was Brynna Addams dressed in a pretty blue
dress and cream sweater. With her dark hair held back
from her face by a thin lacy headband, she looked like
an absolute angel. One that didn't belong in the run-
down crap hole that was their house.

"Hi, Mrs. Gautier. I'm Brynna—the friend of
Nick's from school who's been leaving his assignments at the hospital desk. Since it's his first day back
and all, my brother and I wanted to give him a ride . . .
if that's okay with you?"

His mother opened and closed her mouth as if she
was as stunned by their offer as he was. Turning
around, she met his startled gaze. "You know a
Brynna?"

Heat exploded across his face, partly because he
was embarrassed by their shabby house when he was
sure Brynna had never seen anything so run-down in

her life and partly because his mother had a weird look on her face that he didn't quite understand while she stood barely dressed in an open doorway. "Um, yeah."

"You want them to take you to school?"

"I guess so." His stock answer any time he was unsure of something.

He picked his backpack up from the floor but before he could shrug it over his uninjured shoulder, Brynna took it from him.

"Let me carry it. You're still healing."

Nick tightened his grip as he pulled it back. "No, thanks. I'm not having a girl carry my stuff. Wouldn't be right." And it would make him look like a mega wimp.

He could tell Brynna wanted to argue, but with a nod, she stepped back and let go of his patched and shoddy secondhand bag.

His mom moved forward to turn down the collar of the oh so lovely blue Hawaiian shirt he wore—at least this one wasn't so foul it glowed in the dark. "You have a good day, baby."

Yeah . . . She should have just burped him while she was at it. Anything to shoot down his manhood.

Without a word, he gave her a quick hug since his dignity had already been shattered, then followed Brynna outside to where her brother waited for them in a new black Lexus SUV.

He let out a low whistle of appreciation. It was an obscenely nice ride. "You know, a car like that in this neighborhood—people gonna think you're both drug dealers."

Brynna laughed as she opened the door to the front seat and stepped back. Nick ignored her invitation to sit up front and opened the back door.

"You don't want to be in the front seat?"

He climbed into the backseat and shut the door before he answered. "No offense, I don't know your brother and I don't want anyone thinking anything funny about us. I'm not even sure why you guys are here. How did you know where I live?"

Brynna buckled herself in, next to her brother. "Kyrian told us. He's the one who had me drop your homework off while you were in the hospital so you wouldn't fall too far behind."

He froze. "Do what?"

"Kyrian Hunter?" she said. "Your new boss? He's an old family friend of ours and you'll see us around at his place from time to time. He asked if we could take you to school and watch out for you, so here we are. This is my brother Tad, by the way. Tad, say hi to Nick."

"Hi." Tad pulled away from the curb.

Nick finished buckling his seat belt as he glanced back and forth between Brynna, who was turned around in her seat to look at him, and her brother, who ignored them while he navigated morning traffic. Dang, Tad favored her a great deal. He was just taller and hairier.

Brynna's eyes sparkled with warmth but for all that, she wasn't anywhere near as spectacular to him as Kody was. Brynna was pretty. Kody was sizzling. "You're really going to like working for Kyrian. He's a great guy."

"If you say so."

She smiled. "So how's your shoulder feeling? You excited to be going back to school? Is your physical therapy really hard? Did you get all the assignments done that I left for you? The math was really hard, but if you need a tutor, we can arrange one for you until you catch up."

Nick felt assaulted by her barrage of rapidly fired questions and comments. She didn't even give him a chance to respond until the very end. "You always this chatty in the morning?"

Tad burst out laughing.

Brynna slapped her brother on the arm, her face red. "Stop that."

Tad grinned. "Nice to know I'm not the only one your perky morning attitude annoys. I told you it was too much for a man to bear."

Nick felt his own cheeks heat again. He hadn't meant to offend her. "I'm not annoyed by you, Brynna." He actually liked her a lot. "I'm just not used to people like you talking to me with this much interest. It's kind of creeping me out. Feel like I've stepped into an alternate reality or something. You keep this up and I'm going to start looking for Raccoon City vans or something."

Brynna frowned. "Raccoon what?"

Tad snorted. "It's from the game Resident Evil, doof." He looked at Nick through the rearview mirror. "You have to forgive her, Nick. She doesn't play much. Just gabs on the phone with all her vacuous, self-absorbed friends."

She slid an offended glare to her brother.

Nick mentally kicked himself. *Why did I say that to her? I'm such an idiot.* Here he sat in the nicest car he'd ever seen, riding to school with one of the prettiest girls in his class—one who was really decent—and he'd offended her.

I'm never going to have a girlfriend. I'm too stupid for one.

And if that wasn't bad enough, Tad pulled up to a nice house and honked.

Three seconds later, the front door opened and Casey Woods came running out in her full black and gold cheerleader outfit that hugged every curve on her body . . . and for a fourteen-year-old girl, she had a lot of curves—unlike the rest of their female classmates. Her long wavy dark hair was pulled back from her face with a black and gold bow.

A bright smile curled her lips as she ran to them.

Oh, crap . . .

She was Brynna's best friend and, up until he'd met Kody, the one girl at school he'd sell his soul to have as his girlfriend. Unfortunately, Casey didn't know he even existed.

Something brought brutally home as she opened the door to the car and paused with a frown on her beautiful face.

Brynna didn't miss a beat. "Morning, Case. You know Nick?"

Casey turned her head to look at him from the corner of her eyes as if trying to remember him. "Should I?"

Yeah, why should you know me? We only have four classes together . . . and he sat directly in front of her in two of them.

I might as well be invisible.

Nick caught the sight of Tad rolling his eyes in the rearview mirror. "We're going to be late, Case. Get in or step back into your yard and close the door."

Tad's hostile tone caught him off guard. What magic pill did Tad take to be immune to her looks?

Glaring at him, Casey shrugged her Prada back-pack off and tossed it into the SUV before she climbed in and sat next to Nick.

Why didn't I sit up front with Tad?

Why, Lord, why?

Casey scowled at Brynna. "So is he like a new student or something? Does he speak English?"

Brynna slid a puzzled stare to Nick. "Nick's been going to school with us for the last three years."

"Oh . . . well, I'm in all advanced classes."

Nick bit back a snort at her snotty comment. *What am I? Special ed?*

Then again, at the moment, he felt like this was the short bus to hell and that he had a reserved seat on it.

Brynna opened her mouth to say something else, but Nick held his hand up to stop her from correcting Casey's mistaken conclusions about him before Casey made him feel any more worthless. "So, Tad, how 'bout them Saints?"

Tad laughed at his switch in topic. "You know, Gautier, you might actually grow on me."

"Yeah, that's me. Kudzu Gautier."

Casey didn't get it, but Brynna did. Obviously the tenacious vine must have invaded Brynna's yard and taken it over.

"What's kudzu?" Casey asked.

Tad ignored her. "What the . . ."

Nick looked out the window to see a boatload of police cars at the school as they slowed down. There were two ambulances and even a fire truck. "What's going on?"

Tad shook his head. "Not sure . . ."

Casey's face lit up. "Does this mean no school? Oh thank God, I didn't finish my social studies home-work."

The police wouldn't let them park in the school lot. Instead, they waved them down the street and away from the crowd. Tad went over to Royal and parked outside of Fifi Mahoney's. "I've got to know what's going on."

Nick concurred. Leaving his backpack in the SUV, he walked over to the school with Tad and the girls.

Many of the students were milling around in groups while reporters asked a few of them questions. Brynna and Casey broke off to join their friends.

Nick followed Tad as he headed over to Ms. Pantall, who was standing with three other teachers.

"Hey, Ms. P," Tad called, "what's going on?"

She let out a slow breath before she answered. "You won't believe this . . . Brian Murrey tried to eat Scott Morgan."

Nick's eyes widened at the unexpected explanation. Had he heard that right?

Tad gaped. "What?"

She nodded as she gestured toward the school's entrance. "They were in the cafeteria before the bell, acting completely normal, when all of a sudden Brian attacked him for no reason. He started chewing on his arm and tearing at his skin like a rabid dog with a steak. I've never seen anything like it in my life. It was so gross."

Tad passed a wide-eyed stare to Nick. "Is Scott all right?"

In perfect timing to the question, Scott came out of the school on a stretcher with two EMTs watching over him.

Nick drifted away from them so that he could listen in on a few other conversations, including that of a female reporter who was talking on her cell phone. There had to be more to this story than what Pantall was saying to Tad.

"I'm telling you, Bob, something's going on. What with the attacks last night and now this . . . How many cities have six cannibal attacks in twelve hours?"

Well, it was the Big Easy where they had a slack attitude over most things. But even the stoutest New Orleanian usually drew the line at eating human flesh.

Most days, anyway.

Then again, Halloween was just around the corner. If not for the cops, he might think it a prank.

"They're questioning the kid now. He seems out of it. Like his brains are rattled or something. But you should have seen the vic's arm. He tore it down to the bone and his classmates said he ate all the flesh like he was starving for it. You think it could be something voodoo related?"

Yeah, any time something freaky happened, blame the Goth or the voudoun communities—'cause normal people could *never* be insane. Maybe he should remind the reporter that the infamous serial killer and cannibal Jeffrey Dahmer hadn't been a voodoo worshiper either and Brian, until this, had been a normal jock like the rest of the team. A little dumber than most, but he was a poster child for normality.

Until he tried to eat Scott . . .

Nick moved away from her, closer to the ambulance where they were loading Scott. There was a white bandage over his arm that was red as more blood seeped through it.

Scott was sobbing. "All I did was reach for his milk. He could have just said no. He didn't have to eat my arm. . . . God, I'll never be able to throw a ball again. I'm gonna lose my scholarship, I know it. We'll never make the state championship now. Terry can't throw for squat. Man, the season's over. Why? Why did he do this?"

That seemed to be the question. . . .

"Hey, kid! Get back behind the barricade."

Nick nodded to the officer before he obeyed.

"Hey, Nick!" Frank McDaniel ran up to him. "Hear what happened? Brian ate Scott. How cool is that? Man, I wish I'd seen it. That's what I get for being late to school. I miss all the good stuff that happens."

Jason laughed in agreement. "I just hope whatever got into him isn't catching. I don't want no one coming up and trying to gnaw on my flesh or me going after someone else. Sheez. My mom's a vegan. She grounded me for six months last summer when I ate a cheeseburger at McDonald's. Can you imagine how long she'd ground me for eating a person?"

Frank cast a hungry look over to the group where Brynna and Casey were standing. "Oh man, if it is catching, I hope Casey Woods gets it and comes for me. If you gotta die, no better way to go than to get eaten by the head cheerleader."

Jason high-fived him. "Yeah, all right. Sign me up for that too. I definitely want to be her chew toy."

Nick ignored his friends as he caught sight of his lab partner Madaug St. James, who seemed to be muttering to himself as he stood off to the side of the ambulance. An almost stereotypical nerd, Madaug had a black gamer T-shirt on underneath his blue button-down that had been left open. His dishwater blond hair was cropped short and he had large blue eyes that were always covered with thin-rimmed glasses.

Even though Nick knew the name was pronounced "Mah-dug," he, like most of the people in his class, usually pronounced it "Mad Dog." But that always irritated Madaug and right now he looked agitated enough.

"Hey, dude. You all right?"

Madaug froze at his question. "Uh, yeah. It's terrible, isn't it?"

"Epically gruesome."

Madaug nodded. "I can't believe it. I just can't believe it."

Neither could Nick. "Well, I guess the bright side is you don't have to worry about Scott or Brian picking on you today in gym class, right?" Last time Nick had been in school, Brian had worn Madaug's gym shorts and then forced Madaug into them after he'd sweated all over them.

Gross and nasty.

Madaug didn't respond to his question as he continued to fret.

Out of the crowd, one loud voice suddenly drowned the others out. "I'm telling you people, it's a zombie attack. Z to the O to the M to the B to the I, E. Zombie. Open your eyes, people, before it's too late and he eats someone else. Any of you could be next on the Zombie Apocalypse Menu. Heed my words and stock up on ammo! I got a new shipment coming in today!"

Nick knew that voice. He just wasn't used to hearing it this early in the day.

Big Bubba Burdette, the owner of the Triple B store.

Wow, and Bubba hadn't burst into flames by getting up this early in the morning. Who knew? He'd have sworn the man was half vampire.

Standing well over six feet tall, Bubba was an interesting mix of redneck and Goth. Case in point, he had on a *Dawn of the Dead* T-shirt with a red flannel shirt pulled on over it. His baggy jeans were complemented by a nice pair of black Doc Martens that were decorated with red skulls. With short black hair and a goatee, Bubba was terrifying to behold. But the minute he opened his mouth and that thick Southern drawl came out, he looked less like a threat and more like a giant fluffy panda bear.

At least so long as you didn't interrupt his watching Oprah in the afternoon. Bubba said anyone dumb enough to do that deserved to have his entrails spilled.

And that thick drawl made most people underestimate a man whose IQ was off the charts. In fact, Bubba had graduated at the top of his class from MIT with degrees in both computer science and robotics. Now, he owned the Triple B—a gun and computer store where you could hire Bubba to hack anything in the world, legal or otherwise, and if that didn't work, he'd shoot it for you just to put it out of your misery.

The reporters left Bubba as they tried to interview more students.

Bubba spat a bit of his chewing tobacco onto the pavement. "That's right, troglodytes, ignore the only one who knows what's going on. The only one who knows how to save your putrid, insignificant lives. Go back to your media-induced comas where you believe all the crap spieled by greedy politicians who control you with ill-conceived lies and consumer-driven distractions."

"Aren't those consumer-driven distractions what keep you in business, Bubba?" Nick asked as he approached him.

Bubba narrowed his dark brown eyes on Nick with disgust. "Don't sass me, Nick. I'm not a morning person and I might take my ill mood out on you."

"Yeah, I know. So what are you doing up at this hour, anyway?"

"Haven't slept. Got a call from Fingerman at oh dawn thirty telling me there were zombies on the loose and that he needed reinforcement. So I grabbed my gun and we went hunting in the bayou." Normal people might find this conversation odd, but then all conversations with Bubba were odd, and zombie hunting was just another service he offered at his store.

"Mark get eaten?"

"Nah, the little wuss fell asleep on the way back to the store. He's cuddled up in the front seat like an infant girl, sucking his thumb and holding his jacket tucked under him like a pillow. Don't know what I'm going to do with him."

Nick opened his mouth to make another comment when he realized that conversations had stopped. The hair on the back of his neck stood up. Turning his head, he saw Brian being led out of the school in handcuffs.

Except for the blood marring his letterman's jacket, he looked normal. Completely. Totally. Normal. Yeah, his skin was a little pale and his eyes sunken like he hadn't slept well. But other than that . . .

No one could tell he'd tried to eat his best friend.

Brian slowed as he neared the captain of the team. Their gazes locked in such a way that it seemed like they were communicating without speaking.

The cops shoved him forward.

Brian kept his gaze on the captain until he was forced into the police car.

Nick looked at Bubba. "Is it just me or was that weird?"

SHERRILYN KENYON

Bubba gave him a droll stare. "Is there any part of this day that hasn't been weird, boy?"

Good point.

"So what do you think caused this?" Nick asked.

Bubba scratched his head. "That I'm trying to figure out. Normal zombie attacks—"

That made Nick wonder what would qualify as an *ab*normal attack.

"—are done by dead people brought back from their graves. They're under the control of their masters and attack humans to get a taste of blood. But this . . . the kid wasn't dead yet. Makes no sense to me."

"Maybe someone spiked his Wheaties?"

Bubba shook his head. "Well, there is some chemicals what can give a human zombie-like symptoms. But none of them make a person eat another one. Maybe it's some bioterrorism test being run by the government. Don't be drinking no tap water or seafood until I do some testing."

Nick grinned. "I don't normally drink my seafood, Bubba, but—"

"Don't get smart with me, Gautier. I still got loaded weapons from last night."

Nick opened his mouth to speak, but a hysterical scream silenced him.

"Oh my God! The coach just ate Mr. Peters! Someone help! Help!"

The police went running into the school as the secretary came dashing out, screaming in terror and tearing at her hair.

Nick froze as those words about Peters seeped into his brain. On the one hand he was horrified the man had been eaten. On the other . . .

He was strangely happy. The sanctimonious pig kind of deserved it.

Nick, that's so wrong. He heard his mom's voice in his head. Yeah, maybe it was, but he still couldn't help thinking it was some kind of divine payback.

The police forced the crowd back as the media rushed the school, trying to get photos and footage.

Suddenly, the vice principal was outside with a bullhorn. "School is canceled for the day. Students go home. We'll be calling later in the day with information. Please . . . disperse and leave. Any student found on campus will be suspended. Now go home and don't come back here today."

"And hopefully tomorrow too," one of the students shouted.

Bubba spat more tobacco out. "It's good to be you today, huh?"

"Yeah, as long as I don't get eaten by my football team. . . . Can I come hang in your store and do some research on this?"

Bubba nodded. "Sure, but you've got to open it for me and watch it while I catch some Z's."

That sounded fair to Nick. "Let me get my backpack and I'll head straight over." He left Bubba to find Tad, who was standing in a large group of seniors.

Intent on their discussion, none of them saw him.

"I'm telling you, we need to notify the council and the Dark-Hunters. This has Daimon written all over it."

"Not in daylight, it don't. Daimons can't attack until the sun goes down and you know that. They'd be toast if they stepped one foot outside right now."

"But there were more attacks last night and this is spreading. My money still says it's Daimon related. They're doing something. Mark my words."

One of the seniors rolled his eyes. "A Daimon can't convert a human. That's the first lesson we're all taught."

"Then what do you think it is? It has to be related to them. There's nothing else it could be."

Tad narrowed his eyes on his friend Alex Peltier, who'd been silent the whole time. "Can a Were-Hunter bite turn humans into werebeasts?"

"What's a Were-Hunter?" Nick asked before he could stop himself.

They faced him and clammed up immediately.

Russell Jordan, who'd been doing the most talking, curled his lip as if Nick disgusted him. "What are you doing here, Trailer Park?"

Tad cleared his throat. "He's working for Kyrian now. Be nice, Russ, or Kyrian won't be happy." He faced Nick. "What can I do for you?"

"I wanted to get my backpack out of your truck."

"I'll be right back," Tad said to his friends before he led Nick away from them.

Nick scowled as he followed after Tad. "So what's a Were-Hunter?"

"It's a . . . a gamer's term. Somebody who hunts animals."

That didn't make any sense and it was a term he'd never heard before. "If it's just a game, why did you ask if they could turn a human?"

Tad didn't answer. Instead, he led Nick to his SUV, pulled out his backpack, and then left him there to watch while Tad went back to his friends.

Thanks for all the nonanswers. Tad was going to make a great parent one day.

But in the meantime, "Something weird is going on here."

Something half the people in his school seemed to know about. And if it was the last thing he did, he was going to find out what this secret was.

Even if it killed him.

Most of all, he was going to find out some way to protect himself, 'cause he had no intention of losing what little brain matter he had.

New Orleans was definitely getting weird and Nick wasn't about to be added to anyone's menu.

Except maybe Nekoda, who was strangely missing from the crowd. . . .

Had something grabbed her last night and added *her* to its menu?

CHAPTER 5

Nick let out a frustrated breath as he tried typing another search. This one-armed crap was for the birds—except they wouldn't be able to fly any better than he could type. And they'd probably crash into a wall and get a concussion . . . which would probably hurt a lot.

Growling at his shifting ADD thoughts, he tried to focus on what he was doing.

Finding info on zombie attacks.

I am insane. . . . Since there were no adults around anywhere, he should be searching hot babe sites, not this.

He hissed as he spelled out "chemacil zmobies."

Gah, how did people manage with one hand? He kept making typos all over the place and reaching across the keyboard was really starting to tick him off.

Worse, his pain meds had vaporized in his system and since his school had a strict no-drug policy, including Tylenol or Advil, he hadn't brought more for fear of being strip-searched in Peters's office for it. And if the pain wasn't bad enough, he couldn't find anything online about diseases that would make someone crave human flesh. Well, not unless they were werewolves. Flesh-eating demons. Demonic parasites . . .

Yeah, right. As if such a thing were possible off a movie screen. . . .

He was dying to ask Bubba some questions about his theories, but the man had been explicit: "Wake me up, boy, and I will shoot you dead where you stand."

Now with most folks, that might be considered an idle threat. But when the person making the threat slept on more weapons than a terrorist training camp and had the temperament of a psycho killer, it was wise to believe he would actually do it and laugh while he gutted you.

As Bubba so often said: "I got a shotgun and a backhoe and no one looks under a septic tank for a dead body." Which made Nick wonder how many of Bubba's enemies had faces on milk cartons.

But that was another story. . . .

The bell over the door sounded. Sighing in aggravation, Nick left the computer to wander back to the counter to wait on whoever was there.

He stopped dead in his tracks, bug-eyed.

Holy . . .

Every male hormone in his body fired as he saw what had to be the sexiest chick in New Orleans. A couple of years older than him, she was amazing. The good news was she totally distracted him from his pain.

Decked out in tight black leather pants and a red halter top, she wore a studded black leather collar and bracelets. And a long, studded black leather belt that was wrapped around her narrow waist four times. A huge rhinestone-covered silver cross fell from the belt, banging against her thigh as she walked with a seductive gait he was sure had given a few old men heart attacks from hormonal overload. Her hair was cut short into a black bob. By the opaque color of it, he figured she'd dyed it that way. Her eyes were ringed by thick black eyeliner, giving them a decidedly catlike appearance. Like her eyes, her lips were also jet-black.

Normally Goth women didn't do it for him, but this one . . .

Yeah. She was h-o-t. Best of all, if he made out with her and got that lipstick on his collar his mom would think it was grease. Something that would definitely keep him from being grounded.

Shame on you, Nick. You're cheating on Kody.

Well, not really, since they weren't an item. It couldn't be cheating. Technically. Yet it did kind of feel that way.

How flipping weird. *I'm whipped and I'm not even claimed yet.* Dang, that sucked.

She sauntered up to the counter, leaned over it almost spilling her breasts onto the glass top, and looked toward the back room where he'd been. "Where's Bubba?"

"Sleeping. Can I help you?" He tried his best to keep his eyes on her face and not on what he really, really wanted to look at. That might get him seriously bitch-slapped and since she was wearing spiked rings . . .

It could really hurt.

She popped the gum she was chewing as she gave him an amused once-over. "What about Mark?"

"Also asleep."

She straightened up. "You new help?"

"Just filling in for the morning. They had a late night."

"I'll bet." She shrugged her backpack off, set it on the floor by her feet, and opened it.

Nick stood up on his tiptoes so that he could get a better view of her shapely butt as she rooted through her pack. Dang, she was fine. . . .

I could so go for an older woman. . . .

Think of Kody. Think of Kody. . . .

After a few seconds, she stood up with what ap-peared to be steel stakes in her hand.

"I need Bubba to sharpen these, and tell him that I need a new batch of shurikens. ASAP. Or sooner."

Nick's eyes widened as he realized there was blood on one of the stakes. "Should I ask?"

"Not if you want to live to eat lunch. Name's Tabitha Devereaux, and you are?" Cool, another great Cajun like him.

"Nick Gautier."

"Nice meeting you, Nick. Tell Bubba I'll be back at dusk to get those and they better be sharp. I don't want no vampire surviving my attacks to come at me again. Understand?"

Man . . . Why were all the sexy women absolutely insane?

"Yes, ma'am."

She picked up the backpack and slung it over one shoulder before cocking her hip in a deadly pose that drained all the blood from his brain. "Where do you go to school?"

"St. Richard's."

"The school where the coach ate the principal? That's so cool. Wish we'd have something like that at

St. Mary's. Unfortunately, I'm the scariest thing there."
She winked at him. "Have a good day, kid."

Hoping there wasn't drool coming out of his mouth,
he watched as she went outside to where a black Night-
hawk motorcycle waited. Slinging one long leg over
it, she started the engine, then put her helmet on.

Ah man . . .

Nick didn't breathe again until she was gone.

Whew . . . that had been the most awesome experience of his life.

You know, Bubba, I need to pay you to work here.
'Cause if women like that came by often, even if they
were total head cases, he definitely wanted a job. Forget Liza and her store that was usually frequented
by little girls and their moms. He wanted to work in
Hot Woman Valhalla until he died of testosterone poi-
soning.

Letting out a low whistle of appreciation, he pulled
the stakes off the counter and wondered who or what
had bled on them. With Bubba's friends, there was no
telling.

He put them in one of the plastic bins Bubba used

for intake items and left a note with her name and the instructions she'd given him.

As he started back to the computer, the door jingled again. Reversing course to return to the counter, he tried not to be frustrated with the interruption.

It was Madaug from school.

"Hey, bud, what's up?"

Madaug also leaned over the counter to look into the back room—it just wasn't as cool as when Tabitha had done it. Which was probably a good thing from Nick's way of thinking. "Is Bubba around?"

"Nah, he's sleeping upstairs. Can I help you with something?"

"No, I guess not."

Nick noticed the fact that Madaug was really distracted and fidgeting. Like something heavy was on his mind. "You wigged out about what happened at school?"

"Wha—no . . . not exactly. Well, maybe. Kind of. Look, I really need to get a hold of Bubba when he gets up. It's really important."

Nick gently scratched at his injured arm. "Yeah,

okay. Want to leave your number and I'll have him call you?"

Madaug reached for the pad and pen by the register. He quickly scribbled his number on it, then handed it to Nick. "Please don't forget. It's *really* important."

"You got it."

Madaug hesitated before he let go of the paper and stepped back. He cast one last wistful stare to the back room, then left.

Okay, the boy was even more insane than Tabitha had been. Too many sniffs of the formaldehyde jar in their biology class. His brain must be pickled. Either that or Stone and crew had bashed him against the lockers one time too many and given him a massive head injury.

Whatever . . .

Nick tucked the note into his pocket and started back for the computer.

He'd barely reached it when the door chime rang again.

"Son of a . . ."

What now? He growled low in his throat before he headed back to the counter to see who needed Bubba this time. No wonder Bubba was so cranky. If this was a taste of Bubba's typical day, it explained much about the surly redneck.

Nick paused as he saw three members from his football team walking around the store like they were looking for something. He didn't know their names, but he recognized their faces. Second-stringers like Stone, they were even more aggressive against "nerdy" kids. The kind of pricks Nick spent all of his time avoiding and the kind who slammed poor Madaug into lockers, then laughed about it.

But the weird thing was they were sniffing the air like dogs chasing prey. It was epically creepy.

"Can I help you guys?" Nick asked.

The tallest, a guy with brown hair and a smile that ought to be used to sell toothpaste, stepped forward. His jacket had the name BIFF on it.

Nick bit his tongue to keep from baiting him over *that* name. His parents must have really hated him. *I'm here to serve Bubba, not get my butt kicked by oafs.*

Biff stepped closer. "Nerd boy? Where he?"

Okay . . . sad that they couldn't even form a complete sentence. *See what happens when you abuse steroids?* Dudes should have read the warning label. First the penis shrinks, then the sentence structure deteriorates. Next thing you know, you're climbing to the top of the Empire State Building, swatting at planes with your oversized fists.

Granted you'd be there with a seriously attractive blonde, so even being a monster freak had some perks. . . .

But that was neither here nor there.

"You looking for Bubba or Mark?" Nick asked. Nerd definitely applied to either-or since they were the kings of computers, B-movies, video games, and science.

"Nerd boy!" He grabbed Nick by the shirt and hauled him over the counter to stand in front of him.

Cursing as pain shot through his injured arm, Nick slugged him hard across the face, but he didn't seem to even feel it. "Let me down, you animal. So help me . . ."

The jock buried his nose against Nick's neck and inhaled.

Nick screwed his face up in distaste. "What are you? A pervert? Get your sick hands off me." He kicked him hard in the groin.

Biff doubled over. "He smells like nerd boy. Get him!"

They moved forward, licking their lips. Oh crap! They were zombies, too.

Nick jumped the counter and ran for the back room where Bubba kept an ax . . . just in case. Bubba had never said what that case was, but this seemed like a really good time to grab it. Not to mention it was the only weapon in the store that Nick could use with one hand.

He angled it at the first jock to reach him—this one named Jimmy according to his jacket. "Dude . . . back off 'cause I will chop you. Hard."

Jimmy hesitated.

Feeling cocky about holding him off so easily, Nick strutted. "Yeah. That's right. You don't want no piece of me. I'm bad ah—"

His bravado ended when they attacked en masse.

Crappola...

Hefting the ax, he swung at the first jock to reach him. The ax landed in a case, shattering it. Glass fragments flew all over them as Nick pulled it free for another strike.

But before he could angle it at them, Biff bit him in his good arm.

He cried out in agony, then head-butted the jock. He used the top of the ax to shove Biff back into his friends. Then he turned in one graceful arc and cocked his arm for another ax swing.

"What in tarnation is going on here?" Bubba snatched the ax from Nick's hand. He angled it at Nick like he was about to use it on him. "Boy, have you lost your ever-loving mind? Tearing up my store. Smashing my things ... You're lucky I'm not beating you with the ax handle."

Nick gestured to the jocks. "Bubba, they're zombies!" He held his arm up for Bubba to see the blood. "And they're trying to eat me!"

Bubba cursed. "Well, why didn't you say so?"

Biff sank his teeth into Bubba's hand—something that was the equivalent of stepping into a den of rattle-snakes.

Bubba punched the jock so hard, Nick swore *he* could feel it.

Biff stumbled back as the other two opened their mouths to hiss at them.

"Freakin' zombies!" Bubba returned the ax to Nick's hand, then grabbed a shotgun off the wall. He pumped a bullet into the chamber and took aim for the head of the jock closest to him.

The jock's eyes widened as he realized Bubba was about to blow him into his next lifetime. Shrieking, all of them turned and ran out of the store with an inhuman speed and a freaked-out gait.

It was like something out of *Resident Evil* mixed with zombie chimpanzees.

Bubba ran toward the door to get a better shot at them.

Before he could think better of it, Nick grabbed the shotgun right as Bubba fired. The barrel swung wide and instead of hitting the jocks, the shot blasted a huge hole right through the eyes of the picture of Bubba's mama that hung on the wall near the register.

Nick stared at the hole in absolute terror. *Ah God. I'm so dead.*

Bubba really loved his mama.

And he'd shot her right between the eyes. . . .

The look of Satan's wrath on Bubba's face nauseated him. "Bubba . . . I'm so sorry."

He stalked Nick like a hunting lion out for dinner. "Not half as sorry as you're gonna be. Make me shoot my mama. Boy, what are you thinking? What the hell's wrong with you?"

Nick had to stop retreating as he backed into the wall and had nowhere else to go. He held his hand up to stop Bubba from slaughtering him. "I couldn't let you kill them."

"Why ever not?"

"For one thing it's illegal . . . hello? You think the police are going to buy it was a zombie attack? I don't think so. And for another they're my classmates. Crappy classmates, but still. I have enough trouble coping at school. I'm pretty sure killing three members of the football team when we're coming up for a champion-ship would ruin my rep forever."

Bubba snorted. "So what? In case you didn't no-tice, boy, your classmates are zombified. Had I not come down here when I did, they'd be ripping out your entrails and chowing down. So you ought to be thanking me, not shooting my mama in the head."

Nick swallowed his panic as he realized Bubba wasn't choking him. Yet . . .

"I know. But . . . they weren't dead. How can they be zombies if they're not dead first? Ain't that the first step?"

Bubba hesitated. "Well, that does pose a dilemma to us technically. . . . But only in the traditional sense of the word."

"How do you mean?"

Bubba scratched the whiskers on his cheek. "We're assuming their bokor raised—"

"Their what?" Nick hated whenever Bubba used one of his freaked-out words.

"Damn, boy, don't that school of yours teach you anything useful? Bokor. The person who creates and controls a zombie. What rock you been living under not to know that?"

Some people would probably call that rock "reality," but Nick valued his life enough to keep that sarcasm inside. It was hard . . . but after shooting Bubba's mama, he needed every advantage.

Bubba rolled his eyes before he continued his explanation. "Most times bokors use corpses, but they don't have to. There's been lots of studies of chemical-induced zombies who weren't dead first."

Maybe that was true. But Nick wasn't buying it. "Yeah, but what if this is like *Resident Evil* and it's the Mother Virus coming to take all of us out? What then? Huh?"

Nick stared at his bite mark as reality sank in and his panic overtook him. The virus always started with a bite . . . Zombie Zero. The first mark who started the apocalypse.

And he was *the* one.

"Man, first I'm shot, now I'm going to be a friggin' zombie. At this rate, I'll never live to have my first date or a driver's license. Ah, gah! I've come too far to

die a pedestrian virgin. Bubba, you can't let me die . . .
I only have seventeen more months and three days to
my sixteenth birthday!"

Bubba cuffed him on the back of his head. "Man
up, boy, and stop with that Hollywood crap. Zombie ain't contagious. You live in N'awlins, Nick, and
I've been fighting them for decades. The only way to
become a zombie is to be made one by your bokor."
Bubba paused as if another idea occurred to him.
"Now demon bites . . . that's a different story. But
them weren't demons in here. They were zombies.
Plain and simple. So stop freaking out before *I* shoot
you."

Nick took deep breaths to calm his racing heart.
"Are you sure I can't catch it?" He couldn't even believe he was asking that. This had to be the most bizarre conversation of his entire life, which, given the
usual weirdness of Menyara, was saying a lot.

"I'm positive. Believe me, I know my zombies."

Nick scoffed. *Is it just me or is that like saying I know
my elves and fairies?* If it wasn't for the fact Bubba
might kill him, he'd say that out loud.

"I still think we ought to disinfect the bites. Just in case it's some military-designed bioweapon."

"Disinfect what? What did I miss?"

Nick turned to see Mark entering the store. Yawning and scratching, he joined them from the door that led to Bubba's upstairs apartment where he'd been asleep on Bubba's couch.

Nick sighed in agitation. "See what you miss by sleeping late? Me and Bubba got bitten by zombies. I say they're contagious. This morning only one of the kids in my school had it. Now, I just got attacked by three more. It's spreading and it's going to infect us all. We need to do something before it takes out all the good-looking women and leaves us with only each other. Call out the National Guard or the CBC or something."

Bubba scowled at him. "The CBC? Is that one of those new anime people?"

Nick rolled his eyes. "No. It's that place where they talk about diseases and quarantine people when they're contagious."

"Bubba, Nick means the CDC in Atlanta."

Bubba made a sound of disgust that originated in the back of his throat.

Mark, who was barely a head taller than Nick, was still dressed in his zombie-hunting ghillie suit. Fluffs of Spanish moss jutted out from all the places where he'd tucked it in his clothes so that he'd blend in with the bayou. His face was streaked with camouflage paint and he wore yellow-colored contact lenses that had a rim of red around them.

Zombie eyes.

Also for camouflage.

But that wasn't the worst of it. As he stopped next to Nick, there was an odor so foul it took his breath.

Nick covered his nose to keep from being sick over it. "What is that smell?" It was like three-day-old cat vomit mixed with rotten asparagus.

Mark scowled at him as if he was crazy for even asking. "Duck urine. It keeps the zombies from thinking I'm human."

Nick snorted. "Yeah, well it keeps me from thinking you're sane."

"Give it up, Mark. The boy don't know nothing

about surviving. He actually kept me from shooting zombies who were in the store trying to eat him."

Mark cuffed Nick on the back of his head. "Are you out of your mind, kid?"

"Ow!" Nick rubbed the back of his head where they kept slapping him. If they didn't stop, he was going to get brain damage. "And no. I was keeping Bubba from committing a felony. No offense, but 'he's a zombie, Your Honor, don't electrocute me' isn't a viable excuse. Believe me, I know. My dad's doing three life sentences 'cause he killed, and I quote, 'a crap load of demons who were trying to kill me and if I hadn't killed them, Your Honor, they'd have taken over the city and enslaved all you petty, pathetic humans.' The court's not real understanding of that excuse. They wouldn't even let my dad plead insanity because of it. So trust me, 'zombies needed killing' isn't a legit defense."

Mark shook his head in supreme annoyance. "Well, it ought to be."

"Hey, Bubba? You in here or are you dead?"

Nick cringed as he heard the newcomers.

Bubba handed the gun to Mark and whispered to the two of them. "It's Officer Davis. Don't say anything."

Clearing his throat, he ambled toward the counter up front as if nothing had happened.

Nick hid the gun behind a curtain, amazed by how well Bubba could act. He slid his gaze to Mark, who was finally peeling off his camo suit. Seven years older than Nick, he had shaggy, light brown hair and bright green eyes. His features leaned toward pretty, except for his squared jawline. He also had three days' growth of beard on his face, which made him look a lot older. But it was his build that Nick envied. No matter how much he worked out, he just couldn't get the kind of muscle definition that Mark had without even trying.

It was so unfair.

"Can I see your bite wound?" Mark asked.

"Could you bathe first?"

Mark glared at him.

Sighing, Nick held his arm out so that Mark could inspect it.

SHERRILYN KENYON

He let out a low whistle as he touched the vicious bite, which was still throbbing. "Yeah, we might want to disinfect this."

Nick cringed. "It's going to turn me into a zombie, isn't it?"

"I don't know about that, but the human mouth is the germiest part of the body. You might get parvo or rabies or something."

Nick scowled at that unexpected response. "Isn't parvo a dog disease?"

"Yeah, but who knows what's happening in your school, kid. Could be loup-garous on the loose and that, my friend, is definitely contagious."

Nick jerked his arm back. "I'm not going to turn into a werewolf, Mark."

"Go ahead and mock, but I'm telling you, I've seen them down in the bayou. Many a night. A whole pack of them that shifted into humans. Walking in daylight, they could be right next to you and you wouldn't know it."

It took all of Nick's self-control not to belittle him for that load of horse manure. He wasn't sure what was more pathetic, the fact that Mark was comfortable enough with him to talk about it or that his friend actually believed it.

Deciding on the latter, he let Mark lead him to the bathroom, where Bubba kept alcohol and peroxide.

As Mark cleaned and wrapped the bite, Nick ground his teeth against the pain of the stinging alcohol. "Man, I look like a total goob with both arms wrapped."

"Nah, man, they're war wounds. Chicks dig scars. Means you're a manly man able to protect them."

Nick lifted one disbelieving eyebrow. "Then why don't you and Bubba have girlfriends?"

"I don't want the drama of it. After the last one burnt up all my clothes with my Jack Daniel's Black Label collection and tried to decapitate me with my CDs, I decided I'd take a hiatus for a bit. As for Bubba . . . I better not talk about that. Let's just say I don't think he wants to go through that again."

Nick wanted more clarification. "Go through what?"

"That ain't none of your business," Bubba said as he joined them. He narrowed his gaze on Mark. "You should learn to be quiet sometimes."

"Yeah, well, I always say that marriage is fine for others, but remember that it only leads to one thing."

Nick grinned. "Lots of naked party time?"

"Nah, kid. Alimony." Mark stepped back to put away the alcohol.

Wow. They were both rays of sunshine that broke through the darkest cloud . . .

In hell.

Nick turned to Bubba. "So what did the police say?"

"That if any more of my neighbors report a gunshot over here, they'd yank my business license and throw me under the jail for it. Nosy biddy bodies."

Nick scowled. "Isn't that busybodies?"

Bubba gave him a droll stare. "Have you seen Ms. Thomas next door? That's the ugliest witch on the planet. I swear she's a Gorgon."

"A what?" Nick asked with a frown.

Bubba snorted at him. "Get your head out of comic books and read some Greek mythology. Gorgons . . . women who were so ugly just looking at one could turn a man into stone."

"Ahh . . . in my high school that'd be my English

teacher, Ms. Richard. She's such a snotty jerk, I swear she thinks the school's named after her."

Bubba didn't say anything as he started picking up glass from the shattered counter. "So why were the zombies here, anyway?"

"They said they were after . . ." Nick's voice faded off as he put everything together.

Madaug freaking out.

Nerd boy . . .

Holy dog snot. He looked up at Bubba. "Madaug St. James. You know him?"

"Geeky little kid who reminds me a lot of Mark?"

"Hey!" Mark said indignantly.

Bubba ignored him. "What about it?"

"He said it was imperative that he talk to you. He'd just left when the jocks came in, looking for him."

Mark shot a glance to Bubba. "You think he has something to do with this?"

Nick dug the number out of his pocket. "I don't know. But I'm beginning to think that's a real good start." And the more he thought about it, the more sure he was.

Madaug had to be behind this. Nothing else made

sense. And if he was and Nick turned into a zombie because of him, brains were going to be spilled.

Lots of them and Madaug was the first person on his list. (Not that he had a list because that would get him thrown out of school and probably jailed—but should said hypothetical list exist, not saying that it did currently, or would in the future, Madaug was definitely target number one.)

CHAPTER 6

They tried for several hours to reach Madaug but he wouldn't answer the number he'd left.

Flippin' figures . . .

Nick watched as Mark hung up the phone again before he spoke. "I'm telling you, Fingerman, he was eaten by the jocks. They could smell him from the few minutes he was here and they were hell-bent to get him. I think they ran him down and had a banquet."

Mark smirked. "Zombies have dulled senses, Nick. They're not bloodhounds or werewolves. You don't move, and they'll walk right past you, never seeing you. Believe me, on the scale of scary monsters, they rank way down the 'crap in my pants 'cause they're after me' list. I'll take a zombie over a vampire or werewolf any day."

"What about the duck urine then?" Nick reminded him.

"I was sweating in a swamp and the wind carried my scent. That's different. Their senses are dulled, not nonexistent."

Nick started to argue the point, but really . . . wasn't whether or not a zombie could smell you the most ludicrous thing on the planet to fight about? Werewolves weren't real and he still wasn't completely sold on the whole zombie thing either.

Something was up with the jocks, no doubt, but he didn't believe in the supernatural. He never had. It was bunk made up by moms to scare kids, and Hollywood to make a profit. The true monsters in this world, the people like his dad, were real and human through and through. Which was what made them so dangerous.

You didn't see them coming until it was too late.

Bubba, who'd been ignoring them, stood up from his stool to tower over both of them. He pointed to the clock over the door. "It's four o'clock, guys. I'm going up to watch *Oprah*. Unless the shop catches fire or we're under massive zombie invasion, I don't exist for the next hour." He took a step, then paused. "On second thought, don't even bother me if it's zombies— I'll deal with them later. Today's a special episode on how to make peace with people who piss you off. And I definitely need to find my Zen."

Mark snorted. "Your Zen's shooting stuff, Bubba. Embrace your inner violence."

"Fine, then. My inner violence says I'll cut your throat if you bother me until *Oprah* ends, so sod off."

Nick laughed until the time sank in. "Ah, man, I gotta run."

Mark furrowed his brow. "For what?"

"My new boss was supposed to pick me up after school." Which was thirty-five minutes ago and he'd forgotten all about it. "Ah, geez . . . hope I'm not fired my first day."

Bubba hesitated. "Want me to write you an excuse?"

Nick shook his head. "Nah. I better run. See you guys later. Let me know when you find Madaug." Grabbing his backpack from the floor, he hit the door at full speed.

Luckily he was used to running for streetcars, and his school was only five blocks away. Something he made in record time.

There was still police tape cordoning off the front yard of the school and a couple of officers there to enforce it. They watched him closely as if expecting him to start biting on them or something.

Ignoring them, Nick slowed as he studied the cars that were lined up on the opposite side of the street. Only one had someone in it, and it wasn't Kyrian.

I am so fired. . . .

Crap.

My mom will kill me. More than that, he'd probably have to pay the hospital bill—which at last check had already added up to more than his first two years of college tuition combined—out of his own pocket.

Why couldn't Alan have shot him in the head and ended it all?

I was cursed from birth. Couldn't he *ever* catch a break with anything? Disgusted, he hung his head and started back toward Bubba's store.

"Nick Gautier?"

He turned at the unfamiliar voice to find the man he'd seen sitting in the black BMW, now stepping out of it. He was probably mid to late thirties. With dark blond hair and extremely clean cut (in other words he stank of serious money), he reminded Nick of someone, but he couldn't quite place it. "I don't know you."

The man smiled. "No, you don't. My son, Kyl Poitiers"—gah, he said that name like a true snotty blue blood: "Pwa-tee-aa"—"is one of your classmates. Kyrian asked me to pick you up after school and take you to his house. So here I am."

Yeah, right . . . "How do I know any of that's true?" Other than the fact that he did look like Kyl, which was why he'd seemed familiar. That still didn't make him safe or friendly.

"You don't trust me?" Mr. Poitiers asked.

"I don't trust nobody. My mama ain't raised no fools. I don't get in cars with people I don't know.

Ever. You could be a pervert or psycho or something. No offense."

Mr. Poitiers laughed. "None taken. Tell you what . . ." He pulled out his wallet. "I'm going to give you fifty dollars for a taxi and write down Kyrian's address. I'll see you at his house."

Nick hesitated. The offer did nothing to alleviate his suspicions. "How do I know you're sending me to his house and not someone else's? For all I know that's the address where you take all your victims."

"God, I hope my son's as streetwise as you are." He pulled out a cell phone and dialed a number. After a few seconds, he spoke. "Hey, Kyrian. Sorry to bother you. I'm here with the kid, but he won't get in the car with me. He's even more suspicious than you told me he'd be." He held the phone out to Nick.

Nick narrowed his eyes on the man as he placed the phone to his ear. "Yeah?"

"Hi, Nick. Phil won't hurt you. Get in the car and you'll be over here in a few minutes."

Uh-huh. Nick still wasn't sold. The voice was familiar, but . . . "How do I know you're Mr. Hunter?"

"Because I'm the only person, besides you, who knows you were helping your friends mug those tourists when you changed your mind and saved them."

Nick's stomach hit the ground at those words. He hadn't breathed a word of that to a single soul. Not even his priests. That was a secret that was supposed to be between him and God and no one else. "How did you know that?"

"I was there longer than you suspected and I saw everything. Now get in the car."

Nick hung up the phone and handed it back to Mr. Poitiers. "Okay, I believe you." He held the money out to him too.

Phil refused to take it. "Keep it."

Nick shook his head. "I really can't take this."

"Yes, you can. Just consider it a reward for being a smart kid."

Unused to people not being angry at him, Nick was still reluctant to accept the money. "You're not mad at me?"

"For protecting yourself? Not at all. I tell Kyl all

the time to behave just like you did. It does me proud to see a kid with a brain. Now get in."

Nick hesitated. How weird for someone like Phil to not look down on him. It felt really weird.

He got into the car and buckled himself in.

Phil pulled away from the curb then turned his radio down so that he could talk. "I should have brought Kyl with me to ease your mind."

"It wouldn't have eased it. My mom says pervs use other kids to lure vics too." Not to mention Kyl didn't exactly travel in Nick's circle of friends. He was a stuck-up snot who annoyed him almost as much as Stone did.

That being said, his father seemed to be decent enough in spite of his perfect speech. Made him wonder where Kyl got it from.

They didn't say anything else as Phil navigated traffic. It didn't take them long to reach Kyrian's house that was down in the Garden District. This was the coveted highbrow area where antebellum mansions went on row after row like hulking beasts from a bygone era of gentility and manners that most people nowadays lacked.

Nick and his mom would sometimes come walking down this way . . . mostly 'cause his mom's favorite author lived here and she wanted to catch a glimpse of her whenever she could.

His jaw went slack as they pulled up to a gate that opened into what had to be the biggest house he'd ever seen. It was a huge Grecian-style home with Doric columns supporting what seemed to be a never-ending porch. Top and bottom.

Phil pulled around the circular drive until he got to the front steps. "We're here." But he didn't turn off the engine.

Nick frowned. "Are you staying?"

"My orders were to deliver you to the door. Mission accomplished."

Weird, but okay . . .

Nick had no idea why he was so intimidated, but something about the house seemed eerie and forbidding. It wasn't like he hadn't known Kyrian had money, but knowing something and seeing such obvious proof were two different things.

What in the world would it be like to have this kind of wealth?

For that matter, he couldn't even imagine not having to count pennies to eat at McDonald's.

Gathering his courage, he got out of the car, grabbed his backpack, and headed up the stairs to the front door. Made of mahogany and etched glass that reminded him of cut crystal goblets, it looked like something out of a movie. He lifted his hand to ring the bell, but the door opened to show him a tiny Hispanic woman who eyed him like a warden greeting a new inmate. Dressed in a coral shirt and jeans, she had her dark hair pulled back into a tight bun.

"Nick?" It sounded more like "Neek," which was a much prettier version than the normal drawl he was used to.

"Yes, ma'am."

She stepped back to let him enter. "Mr. Kyrian is waiting for you upstairs in his office." She reached for his backpack.

Nick shied away from her.

"You no trust me?" Her tone was offended.

"No disrespect meant to you, ma'am, but I don't even know your name."

Her face went completely stoic. "I am Rosa and I

keep Mr. Kyrian's house for him. Now would you like me to put your bag away while you're here?"

He felt foolish for not letting her have it. It just wasn't in him to let anyone take anything from him without a fight no matter how worthless it was. It was the same reason he hadn't wanted Brynna touching it earlier. "I guess." He shrugged it off.

She umphed as he surrendered the full weight of it. "Goodness, you're much stronger than you appear. How you carry this without being hunchback?"

Nick shrugged. "It's what I have to have for school."

She gestured at the mahogany staircase that curved up to the second floor. "Third door on the right. No need to knock. He will hear you coming."

Yeah, okay, that was creepy too.

Nick headed up, taking his time to scan every inch of the impeccable palace. The banister had what he was pretty sure were gold medallions in the center of the black iron railing and the polished floors were some kind of something really expensive—like marble or tile or . . . whatever. Part of him wanted to run back to the street.

I so don't belong here.

He felt like a fraud or unworthy. Until he realized what really made him so uncomfortable.

There was no daylight. . . .

Every window in the house was covered with shutters and heavy drapes. Every single one. Not so much as a tendril of sunlight came in. How weird was that? His mother was always yelling at him for burning electricity in the daytime.

Stop shaming the daylight, boy. Turn out the lights. Have you any idea how much money you're wasting?

Pushing it out of his mind, he reached the door Rosa had mentioned and opened it.

Kyrian sat in front of a computer with a headset covering one ear. "Talon, I hear what you're saying. I'm just not listening to it. Look, the kid's here. I'll talk to you later." He hung up the phone and pulled the headset off before placing it on his desk.

"Talon?" Nick asked.

Kyrian smiled without showing his teeth—another peculiar habit Nick had noticed about him even back when he'd come to the hospital. "A friend I'm sure you'll eventually meet." He inclined his head toward Nick's sling. "How are you feeling?"

"Cranky. Pain meds wore off and it hurts like a mother."

Kyrian ignored his curt tone and semi-profanity. "Heard you had some problems at your school today."

"I didn't have no problems at school 'cause they wouldn't let me on campus. Makes it a great day if you ask me."

Kyrian rolled his eyes, but didn't comment on Nick's irritable tone. "Have you called your mom?"

"No. Why?"

"Don't you think she might have heard about the attacks at school and been worried?"

"I don't see how."

"Nick . . . She's your mother. She's going to be worried. Honestly, you have no idea how much your parents love you until something happens to you—then it's too late." There was a note in Kyrian's voice that Nick couldn't quite define. Something like buried pain from a bitter memory that still bothered him. . . .

But that didn't matter. Nick wasn't being stupid or disrespectful. "I know she'd be worried if she knew about it but I know she hasn't heard anything. We don't have TV or anything. Heck, we don't even have a phone. You have to call Menyara and she takes messages to us."

The shock on Kyrian's face set his temper on fire.

"We don't need your pity," Nick growled. "We get along just fine without it and them other things too. You don't need electronic crap to live. You know, people lived for thousands of years without it. There's a big difference between stuff you want and stuff you need."

Kyrian held his hands up in surrender. "Settle down, Nick. I don't feel sorry for you. I didn't have any of that when I was a kid either and believe me, I know how people used to live."

Nick looked around the expensive furnishings that belied those words. It was hard to imagine Kyrian having ever done without anything. "You've come a long way, huh?"

"In some ways . . ."

"And in others?"

Kyrian shrugged. "Let me put it to you this way . . .

money doesn't solve your problems. It just brings new ones to your door."

"Meaning what?"

"Meaning I hope you never know the betrayals I've had. My father once told me that no friend would ever be loyal to me because of what I had and who I was."

Nick's dad had told him basically the same thing. Trust no one at his back, 'cause all people did was betray. And that they usually laughed while they did it.

But he didn't want to be so jaded. "Was he right?"

"Absolutely not. There was one friend I had who was loyal. But when he died, it left me with others who more than proved my father a wise man. I know it's hard to listen at your age. The gods know I never did, but—"

"The gods?"

Kyrian chuckled, again without showing his teeth. "You'll have to forgive me. I'm a little eccentric sometimes."

"Is that why all the windows are closed?"

Kyrian arched a brow. "You're observant. Impressive. Most people don't catch that."

"Yeah, well, few things escape me. I tend to watch silently from the shadows. You learn a lot more that way."

"I'll keep that in mind then." Kyrian stepped from around his desk and handed him the phone. "Go ahead and send a message to your mom. In the event she's heard about your school, I don't want her to worry."

Nick screwed his face up. "Boy, with that kind of uberconsideration, your parents must really *love* you." *Mr. Goody Two-shoes.*

Kyrian hesitated before he responded. "My parents died a long time ago. And you know the sad thing? I still miss them every day. I spent my entire youth fighting with my dad over every little thing and damned if I wouldn't sell my soul to see him one more time and tell him I was sorry for the last words I said to him. Words I can never take back that should have never been said. So call your mom. No matter what kind of relationship you have with your parents, I swear to you, you'll miss them when they're gone."

Nick wasn't so sure about that. He barely knew his dad. His mom was another subject though—he would never intentionally hurt her. Dialing Aunt Mennie's number, he put the phone to his ear.

"Hello?" Mennie's Creole accent was thicker than normal.

"Hey, Aunt Men, it's Nick. Can you—"

"Boy? Where you been? Your poor mama done sick with worry over you. She's sitting right here, right now, all tore up and crying. She ain't slept or had a minute's peace since this morning when she heard about your school. Shame on you for worrying her like this. We went to the school and everything looking for you and couldn't find a trace of you anywhere. No one would tell her anything and there you sit all nice and fine. Shame on you, boy! Shame on you."

Nick felt like the lowest form of dog spittle as his mom took the phone. It wasn't like Menyara to fuss at him for anything. She usually left it to his mom to do. That more than anything told him how worried his mom was.

"Baby Boo?" Those words wrung his gut. It was

his childhood nickname that she seldom used any-more. "You all right?"

"Yeah, Mom. I'm good. I'm really sorry I didn't call. I—I just didn't think you'd hear about it."

"It's okay, Boo. I'm just glad you're all right. It's so good to hear your voice. The police wouldn't tell me nothing about the victims. They said they hadn't no-tified the families so I was waiting for them to come to my door and . . ." She broke off into sobs.

Nick cringed until he was sick. "I didn't mean to scare you, Mom."

"It's okay. It's all good. You're safe and that's all that matters to me. Where are you?"

He looked at Kyrian, who was giving him an "I told you so" glare. "I'm at Mr. Hunter's now. I was at Bubba's store, helping him out this morning since they canceled school. He said he'd pay me double time for it."

"But you're safe?"

"Yeah, I'm safe."

"Oh, thank God."

Kyrian took the phone from his hand. "Mrs.

Gautier? It's Kyrian. I wanted to let you know that I'll feed Nick and have him home about seven if that's all right with you?" He paused to listen to her. "Yes, ma'am. I'll take good care of him and won't let anything happen to him. Promise." He hung up the phone.

Nick scowled at him. "Why do you call her 'ma'am' when she's younger than you?"

"It's a sign of respect."

That he didn't understand, but he was grateful for it. "Not many people have shown my mom the respect she deserves. I really appreciate it that you do."

Kyrian put the phone in his pocket. "I learned a long time ago not to judge people by what they look like, sound like, or by the clothes they wear. Just because a house is nice and shiny out front doesn't mean it's not rotting on the inside. Your mom's a good woman with a good heart and I'm glad you're mature enough to appreciate that about her."

Nick found a whole new respect for him. "You know? I think I can work for you."

Kyrian gave him a tight-lipped smile. "Glad to hear it. Now shall I show you around?"

He liked the formal way Kyrian spoke sometimes. He went back and forth from typical slang to some old-world expressions that were tinged with an accent Nick couldn't place. "You shall indeed."

Kyrian rubbed his eyes at Nick's bad English accent. "Your duties here will be light. Nothing too strenuous, and if anything aggravates your arm until it heals, don't do it. Last thing you need is to set your therapy back."

Nick followed him to the staircase. "Why are you doing this, anyway? You know what I was into that night and yet you'd let me in here around all your stuff? Aren't you afraid I'll steal something?"

Kyrian turned around on the stairs to give him a harsh glare. "There's nothing you can steal from me that I can't replace. Things mean very little to me." He took a step closer to Nick.

"As for why I'm helping you . . . I believe in you, Nick. You remind me of a kid I knew once. Hard-headed to the point no one could stand him. He wouldn't listen and had a massive chip on his shoulder because he wanted to show the world how tough he was—that he didn't need anyone hand-holding him through life, or doing anything for him. Everything had to be learned by his own hand . . . the hard way."

"What happened to him?"

"He rebelliously joined the army against his father's wishes and met a man who changed his life. For whatever reason, that man had patience. And where others would have justifiably killed the arrogant snot-nose for his attitude, his commanding officer saw potential in him. He changed that kid's life and I'd like to pay that debt forward with you."

It took Nick a second to realize what exactly he was saying. "You're the kid?"

Kyrian inclined his head.

"And this dude who changed your life?"

He looked down at the ring on his hand that rested on the shiny banister. "A man named Julian."

Nick shivered at such a god-awful moniker. "Isn't Julian a girl's name?"

One corner of Kyrian's mouth twisted into a sardonic smile. "Trust me, Nick. He was the toughest SOB you've ever met on a battlefield. No one *ever* defeated him in a fight. He made Jackie Chan and Chuck Norris look like poseurs."

"Is that how you learned to fight like you did when you saved me?"

"Yes."

Nick had to give him credit. Kyrian could definitely handle himself. It was something he'd love to have. "Could you teach me some of that?"

"When your arm's better. For now, I promised your mom I wouldn't tax your strength."

Nick growled. "Yeah, but—"

"No buts. Today is only an introduction. I want you to get the lay of the land. Rosa is your direct supervisor. Whatever she says goes. Since I usually work at night, she'll be the one you deal with most when you're here." He turned around and descended the stairs again.

Nick skipped down behind him. "So how many people work for you?"

"Just Rosa and George the groundskeeper. . . . And now you."

"What about Mr. Poitiers?"

"He's a friend. I have many who do favors for me from time to time."

Nick could respect that. "Must be good to be king."

A flicker of sadness flashed across Kyrian's face before he hid it. "Why don't I show you to your office first?"

That announcement stunned Nick. "I have an office?"

"Yes." Kyrian led him to a room off the kitchen that was bigger than Nick's entire condo. Shelves of books lined the walls. And there were two desks and computers in it, along with nice black leather office chairs. It was an impressive layout. "Rosa has the bigger desk. Yours is there."

Nick walked over to it with his jaw slack as he ran his hand across the top of it. Made of rich cherry wood, it was pristine and beautiful. But it was the large monitor on the desk that really made him smile. "I have my own computer?"

"Yes, and you can do homework on it if you need to. It's hooked online so . . ."

Nick's eyes widened even more. "It's online and everything?"

"Yes. There'll be times when I'll need you to get information or order things online for me."

"Really?"

"Really."

Nick didn't know what to say. This was more than he'd ever imagined. When Kyrian had offered the job, he'd figured it was walking the dog, cleaning toilets, or something equally as crappy. Not in his wildest dreams had he thought he'd have his own desk or computer.

In fact, Rosa had already put his backpack there. It made him feel like an adult with a real desk job.

Most of all, it made him feel respectable.

Lifting his head high, he met Kyrian's gaze. "So how much money will I be making?"

"Since you're only part time, we'll start you out at a thousand a week."

Nick about choked on the amount. A thousand what? Lira? Yen? Rubles? "Excuse me?"

"That's before taxes, of course. And we do have work performance bonuses so you can increase that if you need more. I believe in rewarding hard work and—"

Nick held his hand up to stop him right there. "Go back to make sure I heard what you said. A *thousand* a week?"

"Yes."

"A thousand *American* dollars a week?"

"Yes."

"Not Monopoly money or anything?"

Kyrian gave him an irritated glare. "No, Nick. Real, hard cash, and you'll have your own credit card too."

Nick couldn't believe it. He was still aghast over the amount, never mind the other stuff. "And I don't have to do nothing illegal or perverted?"

"You just have to watch your tone, especially to Rosa."

Well, dang. That made him wonder one thing. . . . "How much you paying her if she's full time?"

Kyrian laughed. "A lot more than I'm paying you,

but it's not enough to put up with your smart mouth. So if you want to keep this job, you'll have to show her respect."

"Don't worry. I don't mouth off to women." But that rule didn't apply to men or really to anyone who tried to push him around.

However, Nick did have one major concern. "Um, how much will you be deducting out of that for the hospital bills?"

"You keep your grades up, your attitude in check, and show up for work on time for six months and we'll forget about it."

If something sounds too good to be true, it probably is. And though he was young, he hadn't been born yesterday. "I don't know about that. My mama says we don't take charity from people. We pay our own way."

"Nick . . ." Kyrian's voice was strained. "Look around. I'm not going to miss it. You were headed the wrong way down the street, when, for whatever reason, you made a right turn. No one made you do it. You did it by yourself. My goal is to keep you on the right path. And I know that desperate people do desperate things, so this job will help eliminate some of that temptation. You're a good kid and you deserve a break, which I'm sure life hasn't given you much of."

It was true. Life had pretty much battered him and his mom from the moment he'd been born. "Yeah, but that's a lot of money to be paying a kid for doing basically nothing."

"You won't be doing nothing. You'll be part of a vital support staff I rely on to do my job. Not to mention, you keep your grades up and that's nothing compared to what you can make working for me when you're grown."

Still, Nick was skeptical. "And I don't have to strip naked?"

"Oh God, no. Please keep your clothes on. Neither Rosa nor I need to go blind. There's a pool in back though, that you're free to use whenever you like. However, I would encourage you to always have trunks on when you swim. Last thing I need is for my neighbors to start complaining or George to quit."

Kyrian moved over to a small box on Nick's desk and picked it up to hand it to him. "By the way, this is for you."

"What is it?"

"Cell phone so that I can contact you when I need you."

Nick couldn't believe it. "No friggin' way."

"Part of the perks of the job. But don't abuse your minutes or texts. I get a ten-thousand-dollar bill in one month and I will choke you for it." Kyrian turned it on and handed it to him. "It's already hooked up and the number for it is on the card. Make sure your mom has it too. I programmed my number into the auto dial under two. Just press and hold it."

Nick was overwhelmed by the generosity. He didn't know what to say. "This is just so cool. Thanks."

"You're welcome." Kyrian's phone rang. He pulled it out of his pocket and checked the ID before he answered it.

"No, I've been up for a while. Why?" He frowned as he listened.

Nick played with his own phone. Man, this thing was really awesome.

"What do you mean there were more attacks?"

That got Nick's attention. Was Kyrian talking about the zombie stuff?

"Yeah. I'll head out as soon as I can and I'll keep my eyes peeled for, and I cringe as I say this, things out of the ordinary for us." He listened a few more minutes before he hung up the phone.

"Is something wrong?" Nick asked.

Kyrian didn't exactly respond to the question. "Is there someone at your school with an ax to grind against football players?"

Had the man never gone to high school? "Depends on the football player. Why?"

"There's been two more attacks."

Nick was stunned.

"All of them were against football players. How many guys are on the team, anyway?"

Nick had to stop and think. "I'm not exactly sure since I don't play anymore. Probably around fifty total, counting JV and V."

"JV and V?"

He was surprised Kyrian didn't know what he was talking about. "Junior varsity and varsity."

"Ah . . . Why don't you play anymore?"

Nick shrugged, as that brought up a memory he didn't like thinking about. He'd been really good at the game, but that hadn't saved him. "Got thrown off the first week I made the team for fighting when Stone mocked my shoes. In case you haven't noticed, I'm not exactly a people person."

Kyrian laughed. "I noticed. Look, I need to make a few more calls. Wander around the downstairs here and get acquainted with it. Don't get too tired. If you need anything to eat or drink, it's in the kitchen. Make yourself at home."

Nick waited until Kyrian left before he tried to call Madaug again on his new phone.

Still no answer.

Sighing, he had a bad feeling about this. If what Kyrian had said was right, they were down about a quarter of the team.

There won't be any state finals for us this year.

Stupid concern given everything going on, but it was the first thing that popped into his mind.

What he couldn't figure out was what had started it. Yeah, the jocks picked on certain people and now that they were becoming zombified, it would only get worse. Now they'd pick on everyone.

How could they stop this?

Aggravated with the lack of details, he made his way back to the kitchen, where Rosa was making something that smelled unbelievably good.

Licking his lips, he went to investigate the pot while Rosa chopped shrimp and onions on the cutting board. "What are you making?"

"Gumbo."

Nick's brows shot up at a dish that he'd eaten most of his life, but this didn't look anything like his mom's. "Huh . . . so this is what rich man's gumbo looks like."

"How do you mean?"

"It ain't got leftovers in it and you're putting real meat into it and not bacon bits or roadkill."

Rosa laughed. "I'm sure you've never eaten road-kill."

He wouldn't bet on it. His mom might have denied it, but some of the meat she brought home . . . he was sure it'd been scraped off the street. Maybe even plucked out of the tread on tires.

Rosa handed him a spoon. "Feel free to sample it."

"Really? Thanks." He dipped the spoon in and stepped away for it to cool before he took a bite. Man, it tasted even better than it smelled. His stomach growled so loud, it sounded like a monster was about to pop out.

Rosa turned to stare at him.

"Sorry. I didn't have lunch." Bubba hadn't given him permission to take money out of the till for it, and since school lunches came with his tuition, he didn't have money to buy lunch somewhere else.

Rosa's jaw went slack. "Why didn't you say something about being hungry?" She pulled him over to the island where two tall stools were set. "You have a seat and I'll make you a sandwich."

"I can wait for dinner. I'm used to it."

"No one goes hungry in this house, *m'ijo*. You just sit there while I make it."

This was seriously creeping him out. No one was ever this nice to him. Had he fallen into the Twilight Zone or something?

I'm going to die. It had to be an omen of doom. *Yeah, I'm going to turn into a flesh-rotting, flesh-eating, no-dating-'cause-I-stink demon.* His body parts, especially the really important one, were going to fall off like in that movie he'd seen. . . .

And all because he'd helped an old couple escape his friends.

Stop being stupid.

But it wasn't stupid. It was a fact. Something was wrong with the world. It'd skittered sideways and nothing was like it should be.

He was doomed. No if, ands, or buts about it. He was going to die.

And no sooner had that thought finished than he heard something scratching around the back door. There was a low growl and the rattle of a pretty large creature. Vicious and guttural, the sound reminded him of a dog cornering a cat. It must be a Rottweiler or something.

He frowned at Rosa, who'd frozen to stare at the door too. "What kind of dog does Kyrian have?"

She shook her head. "No dog."

"Then what—" His words ended as the back door flew open and two members of his team rushed in to tackle him.

CHAPTER 7

In a move he hadn't used since he was a running back, Nick went to the left, turned sharp, and sidestepped them, leaving them to slam into the wall. He grabbed Rosa and pushed her toward safety as he looked around for a weapon.

Rosa grabbed the cleaver in her right hand before he could. His jaw went slack as she took the carving knife into her left and held the two of them like a pro as she faced their intruders.

Nick was aghast. "Rosa?"

"Stand back, Nick. I wasn't always a housekeeper and any *hijo de puta* dumb enough to come in here to attack us deserves to die on the floor, butchered like a pig."

The zombies charged.

Rosa caught the first one with a slash to his arm. He didn't so much as grunt. Instead, he shoved her back and went for Nick, who grabbed one of the pans from the stove.

So much for dinner.

He slung the piping hot food into the football player's face. This time, the jock zombie screamed and stumbled back. Nick whacked him with the pan, then turned to help Rosa battle the other one. He barely reached them before the one he'd bashed grabbed him from behind. Zombie number one locked a hold on him that was like steel.

Nick let out a snarl as his injured shoulder was jostled. "No you din't!" Head-butting the zombie, he broke free.

Two seconds later, something so bright it blinded him ripped through the kitchen.

Nick shielded his eyes as he heard the zombies screaming in agony. When he lowered his hand and could finally see again, he staggered back in shock.

The zombies were gone and in their place was what had to be the tallest man he'd ever seen.

His mouth fell open in stone-cold shock.

"Are you all right, Rosa?" the man asked in flawless Spanish.

"*Sí, Acheron. Gracias.*"

The door behind Acheron slammed shut without anyone or anything touching it. Acheron moved toward him with the deadly gait of a ferocious predator. With long black hair streaked with green, he wore a pair of opaque sunglasses that kept Nick from seeing his eyes. Dressed all in black with a glow-in-the-dark vampire skull on his T-shirt, he had a black backpack slung over one shoulder. A backpack that had an anarchy symbol painted on it.

"Nice meeting you, Nick."

He tensed at Acheron's strange lilting accent. He'd never heard anything like it in his life. "How do you know my name?"

"I know lots of things."

Yeah . . . and that thought seriously creeped him out. Was the dude a stalker?

Nick looked around the room. There was no trace left of their attackers. "What happened to the jocks?"

"My demon ate them." Acheron said that with such a deadpan tone that Nick could almost believe him.

"Riiiight." Nick nodded his head in an act of brazen sarcasm. "And I suppose the Big Bad Wolf will be coming in right behind you to finish up? Or is it the Gingerbread Man I need to fear?"

Acheron gave him a lopsided grin. "Kyrian was right, you are a smart—" He glanced to Rosa before he amended what he'd started to say. "Aleck." He pulled his cell phone out, which looked freakishly tiny in his huge hand, and called someone.

Nick frowned at Rosa, who'd gone over to the sink to wash the blood from her cleaver and knife like nothing out of the ordinary had happened. Why was he suddenly hearing the *Addams Family* song playing in his head?

What kind of bizarre crack-house lunacy was this?

"Am I the only one weirded out by what just went down? You two are acting too . . . too . . . normal about it all. I mean this . . . is definitely *not* your typical day."

Acheron snorted. "Depends on the neighbor-hood. . . ." He paused to talk into the phone. "Hey, Kyrian, you might want to finish that shower and get down here. Your home was just invaded by zombies while Rosa and your boy fought them off. Just FYI."

Well, that explained why Kyrian hadn't heard the commotion and come down to investigate it.

Hanging up the phone, Acheron walked over to Rosa and whispered in Spanish. Nick wasn't sure how he understood, since he personally didn't speak Spanish, but he did. "Forget everything that happened. The food spilled on the floor by accident and nothing out of the ordinary took place. No attack. Just another day. . . ."

He looked at Nick, who took a step back in severe trepidation of what this stranger was going to do to him. When Acheron lifted his hand, Nick bolted for the front of the house.

Get out of here. Now! That was a crazy demonic-sounding voice in his head, but he didn't question it. He just ran like mad.

Rounding the staircase, he skidded to a halt as Acheron appeared directly in front of him out of thin air. Only this time, Nick didn't see Acheron in the body of a young man.

He saw . . .

Someone with fangs, mottled blue skin, black lips, and horns. The image was there in a flash and then gone. Like a freaked-out hallucination.

What had been in that gumbo?

It's supernatural.

I don't believe in that. Yet how could he deny what he was seeing? This wasn't normal. This wasn't chemical-induced, bioweaponed zombies. . . . There was no logical way for Acheron to have gotten in front of him and just appeared like that. Just like the door slamming shut when he entered the kitchen, or the flash of light.

It was impossible.

Utterly impossible.

No longer sure what he could believe, Nick swallowed. "What are you?"

Acheron scowled. "Completely perplexed. You remember everything that happened." It was a statement of fact and not a question . . . as if Acheron was inside his head.

"Yeah. Duh. Not like you're going to forget the killer zombie stalkers and psyched-out kitchen staff. What kind of freak show is this?"

Acheron gave an evil laugh. "You have no idea, Nick. But my question is: Why are the zombies after *you?*"

"Oh heck no, bud. The question is: Why you got horns on your head and black lips?"

Acheron's smile faded. "What?"

"I saw you a minute ago when you freak-flashed in here. You had horns and blue skin. What are you?"

Acheron returned that question with one of his own. "What funky vegetables you been eating? Meth is death and inhalants can kill you, kid. You should stay away from them before they destroy your last three brain cells."

Yeah, right. "I'm stone cold and you . . . you're not human. I know you're not human."

That irritating grin returned to Acheron's face. "Very few people are."

"Ha, ha. I saw you, man. What you did to the zombies when you arrived and with Rosa. . . . I know you're not human. Are you going to kill me because I know?"

Acheron paused as he considered his options. Nick Gautier was a lot more than he seemed. At fourteen, Nick's mind should have easily been wiped by his powers, like Rosa's had been. Not that Acheron liked to use those powers on anyone. As a rule, he seldom did, but there were times when circumstances demanded it.

Killer zombies exploding in a kitchen happened to be one of them.

And it wasn't until someone was older that they developed the ability to block that particular talent of his. And even then only the stoutest of wills could stand against his powers.

Come to think of it, no mortal human being had *ever* stood against his powers. Only gods and a handful of demons could fight or circumvent him against his will.

More than that, somehow, some way, Nick had glimpsed his true god form.

How?

Kill him and be done with it.

That was probably the most logical thing to do. But Kyrian, for whatever misguided reasons, had his heart set on saving the kid. Closing his eyes, Acheron used his powers to see into the future—to what would happen if he killed Nick.

Nothing was there.

Just a vacuous space of nothingness.

Crap . . .

Two weeks ago, when Nick had been injured, he'd seen the kid's entire life from start to finish as clear as a summer sky. Now he couldn't even glimpse what Nick had bulging in his front pocket.

This is so not good.

Because that meant only one thing—this kid was going to significantly impact his life somehow and the Fates had blinded Acheron to him to prevent him from interfering with Nick's choices.

I hate it when this happens. It was why he tried to never let anyone near him. Why he had no real friends other than his demon companion.

This little bugger in front of him was destined to alter his future. No wonder he couldn't use his powers against him.

Sighing, Acheron opened his eyes. There was no need to fight destiny. He'd learned centuries ago just how useless it was to try. *Might as well embrace the inevitable and introduce myself.* Because any time someone had tried to alter his future, it'd only made things worse. Much worse.

"I'm Acheron Parthenopaeus."

Nick snorted. "Dang, and I thought my name sucked. Your parents must have really hated your guts."

If he only knew. . . .

"Call me Ash. It's easier and takes a lot less time."

Nick held his good hand out to him. "Nick Gautier. Now what are you again?"

"He's the best friend you'll ever make or your last enemy."

Nick looked up to see Kyrian coming down the stairs. "Oh, I get it," he said sarcastically. "'Cause he'll kill me if I tick him off. Ha, ha, ha."

Kyrian rolled his eyes.

Acheron let out a long-suffering breath. "I'm not saying a word, General. I told you the kid was going to be more trouble than he's worth. So far, I'm right."

Nick took a step closer to Acheron and said in a low tone, "Does Kyrian know about . . . you know? Your particular weirdness?"

"He does indeed. Rosa, not so much. So let's keep that on the down low around her."

"Gotcha."

Kyrian paused beside Acheron. "I take it Nick saw something unusual?"

"Not too unusual," Nick said. "If you live in a friggin' video game."

Acheron shook his head. "He handled it well for the most part."

Nick scoffed. "Ash is omitting the part where I freaked out and ran like a girl. Did you know your housekeeper can handle a knife like a street fighter and has no qualms about hacking people up with it?"

"Well that was a random switch in topic," Acheron said to Kyrian.

Kyrian laughed. "Yes, Nick. I know all about her

knife-welding talents. It's why I hired her. And if I were you, I'd keep that in mind should you ever feel the need to lip off to her. She doesn't take it well."

"Don't worry. That desire . . . effectively quelled." Nick put his hand in his pocket as he digested everything that had happened over the last few minutes. "So you have a psychotic housekeeper with some serious ninja knife skills and Acheron would be what to you?"

There was a sudden awkwardness between them, so thick it permeated the air around them. "Ahhh," Nick said as he understood why they weren't explaining it. As the old saying went, opposites attract. "You two are *special* friends."

Kyrian frowned. "How do you mean?"

Acheron passed a peeved look to Kyrian. "He thinks we're a couple."

Kyrian took a step away from Acheron. "No. No. No. Definitely not. Not that Acheron is not an attractive man, not that I've ever really noticed whether or not he's attractive, but male is not my type."

Nick looked back and forth between them. On the surface, the two of them had nothing in common other than they were both badasses. "Then how do you two know each other? 'Cause aside from the money thing you seem really normal and Ash . . . really not."

Acheron cocked a brow. "Are you telling me that you have no oddball friends?"

"Uh, not like you. Mine just do weird things like eat Jell-O through straws and get thrown out of Kroger for eating samples. They're nowhere near as weird as you."

Acheron tsked. "I would disagree. I don't drown myself in Eau de Duck Urine or look for werewolves in the swamp, unlike some people you know."

"Yeah, okay, so Bubba and Mark walk off the beaten path into Planet I Don't Know. But they don't do that creepy mind wipe stuff or slam doors without touching them."

"How do you know the wind didn't catch it?" Acheron asked.

"Would that be the same wind that somehow blew you through the house to land in front of me?"

"Could be. Hurricane force. It is New Orleans, after all. It happens."

Nick gave Acheron a droll stare. "No offense, I ain't Dorothy and I didn't see no house land on a woman in striped socks. But if you believe all that, I have a house on a hill in the bayou to sell you. By the way, how do you know about Bubba and Mark?"

Ash got really quiet.

Kyrian's face was completely stoic.

"What?" Nick prompted.

Ash cleared his throat before he answered. "I get bored sometimes. Infinite power . . . local lunatics. There's just times when you really need to screw with someone's head and Mark is such an easy target. He wants to see, and a few well-placed shadows go such a long way in making him happy, and me entertained."

"Dude, you're so wrong." But Nick could almost understand that. "And the zombies? You plant them too?"

"No. I'm as clueless about them as you are. In fact, I came over here to warn you"—he turned to Kyrian—"about them. Believe it or not, I don't know how many are infected. But it seems to be mostly teenagers, and Nick's school's the nucleus for it. Ground zero as it were."

Kyrian looked as confused as Nick felt. "How can you not know, with your powers?"

"As hard as it is to believe, even for me, there are things I can't decipher. This would be one of them. Someone else is shielding them—probably whatever entity created them. And I don't know who that is, but the bokor seems to be targeting school officials and nerdy students."

Nick stiffened. "Why you look at me when you say the word 'nerdy'?"

Ash flipped up the tail of Nick's hideous blue Hawaiian shirt. "Normal people don't dress like that."

Nick brushed his hand down the front of his shirt and gave a confident tilt of his head. "Hey now, I make this look good. And you're a fine one to talk. Why you wearing those sunglasses inside when it's dark, Geek boy?"

Ash let fly a cocky grin. "'Cause no matter where I go, the sun is always shining on me."

Nick was completely unamused.

"Nick?"

He turned at Rosa's call. "Yes, ma'am?"

"Didn't you tell me you hadn't eaten?"

"Yes, ma'am."

"Then you come in here and have something before you waste away." She paused as she entered the doorway of the kitchen and saw Ash. "Acheron? When did you get here?"

Ash indicated the door over his shoulder with his thumb. "I came in the front door a few minutes ago."

Rosa's brow was creased with a stern frown. "Strange. I didn't hear the bell."

Ash smiled. "You know me, Rosa. Silent like a ghost."

A chill went down Nick's spine at what Rosa was saying and about her lack of memory where Ash was concerned. He should probably be running for the door, but there was something about Acheron he actually liked. And while the guy looked like he could sweep the floor with Rambo, Nick sensed a kinship with him. Almost like they were long-lost brothers. It was so strange and yet . . .

Stay away from him. Ash is evil to the bones. He will destroy you. Nick shook his head at the deep voice that echoed in his ears.

For a second, he felt like he was losing his mind.

"Are you coming, Nick?" Rosa asked.

"Yes, ma'am." His stock answer for most women since his mom really didn't like the word "no." Dutifully, he made his way to Rosa and to the food he was starving for.

Acheron watched while Nick made his way to the kitchen. He didn't know why, but his gut told him that Nick was somehow key to what was going on. It was like a presence was here. One he couldn't see, hear, or touch.

He could only feel it like a hidden shadow. Malevolent and cold, it sent a shiver down his spine. It was pure hatred, but he couldn't tell who it was directed at.

Him.

Or Nick.

Kyrian lowered his tone so that neither Rosa nor Nick would hear him. "What aren't you saying?"

"Ever have one of those feelings you can't shake?"

"Every damn night."

Ash gave a short laugh. "Still planning to set Nick up as your Squire?"

"He's not old enough yet. But when he is, that's my plan. Why? Is there something about him I should know?"

Ash felt the tattoo on his biceps shift down toward his elbow. The burning sensation was Simi's way of letting him know she was getting restless and wanted to come off his body and take human form, or maybe she just had indigestion from eating the zombies so fast.

Rubbing his hand over his demon, he stopped her for the moment. "He seems like a good kid."

"But?"

But there's something about him not quite . . .

Right.

If only he could put his finger on it. Not wanting to worry Kyrian when there was no reason to, he shrugged. "I have nothing to add. Other than don't let the zombies eat you while you're on patrol tonight. Be a damn waste of a good Dark-Hunter."

Kyrian flexed his foot so that one of the knives shot out from the toe of his boot. "I think I can take them."

Ash wasn't so sure about that. Kyrian always had a hard time harming anyone under the age of consent. Not that he was cold-blooded himself.

Simi was another matter. She'd eaten the zombies in the kitchen before he'd had a chance to corral her. It was why he'd blinded Nick and Rosa. His little demon had a mind of her own and when she smelled nonhuman delicacies, which she claimed weren't on her banned food list, there was no stopping her.

Soon he'd have to let her loose again or she was going to crawl all over his body until she had him doing St. Vitus' dance. "The sun's setting. You want me to take Nick home for you?"

Kyrian nodded. "Thanks. While you do that, I'll rendezvous with Talon in the Quarter and see if we can get a handle on this zombie outbreak."

"Good luck."

"Back at you." Kyrian headed for the door that led to his garage.

Ash waited until he was sure Kyrian was gone before he went to the kitchen. He paused to watch Nick joking with Rosa. There was something extremely charismatic about Nick. Like an aura that warmed people and made them want to listen to him.

Some would call it glamour—a power certain creatures were born with while others learned it later in life. It was more than charm. More than a good personality.

Ash had a similar ability, only it pulled people toward him for an entirely different reason. One that kept him on guard against people constantly lest they lose control of themselves.

Funny thing was, Nick seemed immune to that too. And for that, Ash was extremely grateful. Very few people didn't react to the curse his aunt had given him at birth. In fact he could count on one hand the number of people over the centuries who'd been immune.

There's something not right about this kid.

You're being paranoid.

Was he?

You were human once too with no knowledge of your true birth or destiny. Another curse given to him by his family. Until his twenty-first birthday, he'd had no idea that he was a god. No idea that his real mother had been the Atlantean goddess of destruction.

And when his powers had been unleashed, it'd almost destroyed the entire world and had driven mankind back into the Stone Age.

What if that innocent kid eating the gumbo Ash had repaired was a creature like him?

You are *being stupid.*

Or was he? When Ash had been human not even other gods had been able to detect his real nature. Artemis herself had stood right beside him and proclaimed him human.

He narrowed his gaze on the boy. The zombies had been here for Nick and Nick alone. He was sure of it. There was no other reason for them to have attacked.

The only question was why. . . .

CHAPTER 8

✹

Nick froze in front of Ash's shiny black car. . . . No, not car. Friggin' Porsche 911 Turbo! Talk about epic. His heart actually started pumping like a freight train at the prospect of riding in it.

"How can this be your car?"

Ash shot him a "duh" stare. "Well, I wrote a really big check that didn't bounce to the dealer and then the most amazing thing happened. . . . The salesman gave me the keys and let me take it home. It was like magic."

Nick gave him a peeved glare. "Only I'm allowed to be that sarcastic."

"Trust me, Nick. I've got many more years of practice at it than you have. Now hop in."

"Hop in? Dude, are you out of your ever-loving mind? I can't touch this. I might leave a fingerprint or something."

"Oh the horror. Guess I'll have to trade the piece of junk in and get a new one if that happens. By the way, don't breathe on the upholstery or I may have to gut you." Ash slid into the car without missing a beat.

Even though Ash had been kidding, Nick hesitated. He'd only seen cars like this in posters and online. The price tag for it was more money than his mom made in . . .

Fifteen years.

At least.

People lived in houses that cost less. *He* lived in a house that was probably cheaper than the tires on this thing. Dang, what would it be like to own something so fine?

"Nick, get in. I don't have all night."

Biting his lip, Nick pulled his shirttail up so that

he wouldn't tarnish the pristine black paint with a paw print. Ash had already put his backpack in the floorboard. Man, this was such a cool car. Careful not to leave a shoe mark on the tan interior, he got in and shut the door. "Are you a drug dealer?"

"No." Ash let out a short laugh. "I'm a wrangler."

"A what?"

Ash started the engine with the key on the left side of the steering wheel. How weird was that? "I manage people."

"What kind of people?"

"People like you. Hard-headed. Stubborn. Irritating and smart-mouthed." He shifted into high gear and kicked it.

Nick grabbed the door handle and held on for his life as Ash pulled into traffic at supersonic speed.

"Relax, kid. I'm not about to dent this car."

Nick wasn't so sure about that. "You like to drive fast, don't you? How many tickets have you gotten, anyway?"

Ash didn't answer. Probably for the best since Nick didn't want to end up as a hood ornament on someone else's vehicle. Last thing he needed to do was distract Ash while he was driving at warp speed.

Or attempting to anyway.

Nick cringed as Ash weaved between two huge semis. "Gah, do your parents know how you drive? And where did you get your license anyway? The Blue Light Special at Kmart?"

Ash laughed. "Who says I have a license?"

Nick let out a cry of alarm.

"Relax, Nick. Remember, I have evil Jedi powers. Nothing's going to touch us." He downshifted and they shot forward like a bullet.

"I think I'd rather take my chances with the zombies. Stooop . . ." He swore the car actually left the ground to avoid being slammed by a car pulling out.

Yeah . . . evil Jedi powers indeed.

He looked over at Ash, who was driving through the dark night with his sunglasses still in place. "How did you get those powers anyway?"

"They were a gift on my twenty-first birthday."

"You're that old?" Nick would have sworn he wasn't any older than eighteen or nineteen.

Ash laughed again. "Somewhat older than that."

"So what did you do for the gift? Sell your soul or something?"

The humor fled his face. "Something like that."

This was getting good. Nick would kill to have the kind of powers Ash did. "Who'd you sell it to? The devil?" Now, with anyone else, that would be a stupid question, but since Nick had seen what Ash could do, he knew Ash had gotten them from somewhere, not the local Walmart.

Ash paused before he answered Nick's question. He didn't like talking or even thinking about his past for a multitude of reasons. But his ownership wasn't something that was that big a secret, since most of the people he knew had sold their souls to the only person who could control *him*. "I'm owned by a goddess, Nick."

"Which one?"

"Artemis. Ever heard of her?"

Nick scratched his ear. "Greek goddess of the moon, right?"

"The moon's associated with her, but Selene is ac-

tually the goddess of the moon. Artemis is the
dess of the hunt."

"And what does she hunt?"

"Most days, me," Ash said under his breath. Clearing his throat, he spoke louder. "She's basically retired
now. Most of the ancient gods are only powerful
when they're worshiped by followers."

"Most?"

Yeah, some, like Acheron, didn't need followers to
charge their powers. They were the really dangerous
ones because their powers never waned. And unfortunately, Artemis could and did tap into his powers
when it suited her to. But lucky for the world, she
really didn't care about using them except against
Acheron himself.

When he didn't clarify, Nick asked another question. "Are you one of the ones who's weak?"

"I never said I was a god." But somehow Nick seemed
to sense what he was. Another thing that made him
different from everyone else.

Nick fell quiet as he digested Ash's comments.
Ash didn't say it, but there was something about him

was so powerful he could almost feel it in the
rrow of his bones. If he wasn't an ancient god, he
was something . . .

Equal to it.

"Well, you know, you haven't told me what you
are, Ash."

"Just think of me as a powerful immortal and you'll
be fine."

Nick cocked his brow as he zoned in on one word
in particular. "Immortal?"

"Yeah."

"So how old are you? Really?" He must be totally
ancient. "Two, three hundred years?"

Ash gave a testy smirk. "Over eleven thousand."

Nick's mouth fell open in disbelief. It wasn't possible. He could *not* be *that* old. "Bullshit!"

"Watch your language, kid."

"Okay, bullcrap. There's no way. We didn't even
have people back then. You're yanking my chain."

Ash shook his head. "I assure you, we did. I was
even on a first-name basis with some of them."

Nick remained still as that sank in and he tried to

imagine the world Ash must have come from. What would people have been like back then?

Was Ash just full of total garbage?

"You're really not kidding, are you?" Nick asked.

"Dead serious."

Still, he couldn't believe it. Could people really be immortal? He'd seen the movies and read the books, but . . .

"How? Are you a vampire or something? What made you immortal?"

"Really good DNA."

Nick rolled his eyes. Ash's glib answers were starting to irritate him. He wanted an answer and he wanted one now. "Oh, come on. I have to know about the who-do voodoo that you do. Most of all, I want to know how I can become immortal . . . well, not at my age 'cause that would suck. But in a few years when I'm filled out and in my prime." He grinned at Ash. "Make me immortal."

Ash wasn't charmed. "Look, Nick, I don't like talking about my powers and not a lot of people know what I can do. I'm trusting you with a secret and I expect you to keep it. If you can't . . ." He tilted his head down as if he was looking at him over the rim of his sunglasses. "Well, I'm sure your mom's going to miss you."

"Not half as much as I'd miss me if you killed me." He blinked like a girl and leaned against Ash's shoulder. "Please don't hurt me, Ash. Please. I don't want to die while I'm still a virgin. At least let me get laid before you kill me—which according to my mom I can't do until I'm married and I can't do that until I finish college. So you have to wait a good ten years before you snuff me. Deal?"

Ash shoved him back onto his side of the car. "You're really not right, are you?"

"Yeah, I know. It was all the paint chips I ate as a kid. They were good, but chromosomally damaging."

Ash let out an audible sigh as he forced himself not to laugh at Nick's antics. He was really beginning to like the kid a lot more than he should. There was just something about him that was infectious. "Ten years, huh?"

"Yeah, you can kill me when I'm twenty-four, provided I'm not still a virgin, but not a day before that."

"All right. It's a deal . . . provided you keep your trap shut."

"Trap nailed shut, sir."

"But at twenty-four . . ." Ash let his voice trail off.

"I'm all yours, babe."

Ash shook his head. "I don't intimidate you at all, do I?"

"Well, when you chased me through Kyrian's house, I did wet my pants a bit. Guess I'm not housebroken after all. My mom will be so disappointed after all she went through to potty train me. But once you let me live . . . your big mistake . . . now I know you think I'm too cute and fluffy to kill."

It was really hard to be agitated at someone with that kind of humor. And in all honesty, it was nice to be around someone who wasn't trying to prove himself, wet himself, or posture. It'd been a long time since someone who knew he wasn't human had treated him like one.

"You are cute and fluffy, but never forget, kid, that

I'm a carnivore from a time and place where we had to kill and skin our food in order to eat it."

Nick's eyes widened as he tried to imagine Ash dressed like a Goth caveman in a studded black loincloth chasing down saber-tooth tigers and killing them with a spear. . . . Did they have saber-tooth tigers eleven thousand years ago?

Did people have loincloths or did they hunt naked?

Dang, his teachers were right. Some of that trivial crap could come in handy.

But that wasn't the point of this conversation. Nor the point of what Ash was telling him. "You just like to scare people, don't you?"

"As much as you like to annoy them and for the same exact reason."

It kept people from getting too close. Nick did it so that others wouldn't mock him or so that when they did, it didn't hurt as much.

What was Ash trying to protect himself from? It was definitely something to think about.

Ash pulled up to the curb in front of Nick's house,

which looked all the more dilapidated after he'd been in Kyrian's neighborhood.

To Ash's credit, he didn't react to the ramshackle house in any way.

Nick gave a low whistle as he saw a couple of people on the street stop and stare at the car. "Man, my neighbors must be freaking out. First I get picked up by a Lexus and now I'm being dropped off in a Porsche. It's a wonder they're not calling New Orleans' finest to report suspicious activity."

Ash scoffed as he turned the car off. "I think the LEOs have more important things to worry about to-night than the cars coming to your house."

Nick frowned at the word he didn't understand. "LEOs?"

"Law enforcement officers."

"Ah . . . cool anagram."

"Acronym," Ash corrected. But this time when he spoke his accent was extremely thick with the first part of the word coming from deep and low in his throat—like a growl. It was a really cool sound.

"Wait . . . Say that word again."

"Acronym." And poof, Ash now sounded like anyone else on the street.

"That's so awesome that you can toss out your accent. How do you do that?"

"Lots of practice. Now if you don't mind, I need to
dump you out so I can get down to my business."

"Which is?"

"Wrangling people . . . which right now is you. Get
out, Nick."

Nick opened the door and rolled out of the car.
Ash grabbed his backpack and followed him up the
short, crumbling walkway that was overgrown with
grass and littered with pebbles.

Not to mention a few cockroaches that scattered
out of his way. Some of them ran up under the plant
Bubba had sent to him.

Trying not to think about the roaches, Nick barely
made it into the door of his house before his mom
threw it open and grabbed him into a tight hug. "Arm!
Arm! Arm!" he said quickly as she hurt him.

She released him immediately. "I'm so sorry, Boo.
I was just so scared and then to see you . . . I could

beat your butt blue, boy. Don't you *ever* worry me like that again. You hear me!"

Nick rubbed his hand over his injured arm, which was still stinging from her hug. "You know, I hear they have medication for those kind of vicious mood swings, Ma. Maybe you should consider taking some?"

She scoffed at him. "Don't you dare get lippy with me after what you've put me through today. You're lucky you're not grounded over this stunt. If you'd been any place other than work, you would be." She turned back toward the door to close it and froze as she saw Acheron on the porch. Her face went white as she took in the size of him.

"It's okay, Mom. He's a friend of Mr. Hunter's who brought me home."

Acheron held up Nick's backpack for her to see. "I was just carrying this in for him, Mrs. Gautier. Sorry I startled you."

His mom smiled as she caught herself gawking. "It's okay. I just . . ."

Ash smiled. "Yeah, I know. It's a hazard of the height and clothes. I tend to freak out a lot of people."

Not to mention that lethal aura that sizzled in the air around him. But Nick was beginning to get used to that.

"Do you work for Mr. Hunter too?" his mom asked.

Ash set his backpack down by the door. "No, ma'am. We're just old friends."

She smiled. "You don't look old enough to have old friends."

Nick snorted at her making the same assumption he had. "Trust me, Mom, he's a lot older than he looks."

"Well, thank you for bringing my baby home. I appreciate it."

"No problem." Acheron turned toward Nick. "Keep your nose clean, kid. I'll see you around."

"Thanks, Ash."

He inclined his head before he left.

His mom locked the door and moved Nick's backpack away from the threshold so that they wouldn't trip over it. "He's a bit peculiar, isn't he?"

"You don't know the half of it."

"So how did your first day with Mr. Hunter go?"

"It was all right." Aside from the zombies, Rosa's lunacy, and Acheron, but no need to completely terrify her. Only one of them needed to freak out at a time.

"Good. Now I better get ready for work." She headed for her room.

Nick pulled her to a stop. "I don't think so."

"What do you mean?"

"I mean I want you to quit tonight."

Sighing, she twisted her arm out of his hold. "Stop with the nonsense, Nick. You know I can't quit. We need the money."

"No, Ma, really. Mr. Hunter's going to pay me four thousand a month to work for him."

Her jaw went slack as her eyes narrowed in anger. "Doing what?"

"Running errands, like he said."

"Oh no, no, no. I'm not having any of that. No one pays that kind of money for running legal errands. I want you to quit first thing tomorrow."

"No, Mom. It's all legal. I promise."

Still she refused to believe him. "Not for that kind

of money it's not. What kind of fool do you take me for? I wasn't born yesterday. I—"

"Mom, listen. Please. He really is loaded like you've never seen before. Ash told me that Kyrian thinks I'm underpaid. The guy has no concept of how much money he's paying me. Really."

"No one is *that* loaded, Nick, that they'd just throw forty-eight thousand dollars a year at a kid for running errands. Think about it."

A day ago, he'd have been right there with her. But after today . . . for some reason he believed in Kyrian and his intentions. "Yeah, he is. Trust me. I saw the house and you ain't never seen nothing like it. So you can quit dancing. I'll be making enough working part time that you won't have to do anything but stay home." Just like they'd always dreamed of.

His mom hesitated. "I don't know."

"Please, Mom. Trust me."

Her features softened as she cupped his cheek in her hand. "Tell you what. You work for him for a couple of weeks and after you get your first paycheck then we'll see, okay?"

Nick curled his lip as he realized her tactic. She was shutting him down and not really listening to a word he said. "Why don't you believe me?"

"I think you misunderstood him."

"I didn't."

She brushed his hair back from his face. "We'll see, Nick. We'll see."

God, he hated that tone she used. It was so condescending and what she was actually saying is that he didn't know what he was talking about. He wasn't stupid.

Whatever. He was too disgusted to keep arguing when it was obviously futile.

She went to go dress. "I left you some eggs and cheese on the stove in case you're hungry."

Nick cringed at her words. He should have thought to bring her some of Rosa's gumbo. She wouldn't have forgotten about him.

Next time . . .

"I'm full if you want some more. Kyrian's housekeeper fed me about an hour ago."

"Was it good?" she called from her room.

"Yeah."

She poked her head out of the door. "Better than my cooking?"

He started to say yes, which was the truth, but self-preservation kicked in. He'd made the mistake of saying Menyara made better biscuits once and his mom hadn't taken it well. "No. No one's gumbo can touch yours."

She winked at him before she closed the door.

Nick let out a relieved breath that he'd sailed past that land mine without getting his butt kicked over it. It wasn't often he passed those tests. *I'm getting better at dealing with women.*

Today his mom. Tomorrow an actual girlfriend. . . .

Like Kody.

Maybe I should call her? Since he hadn't seen her at school, he still had her Nintendo in his pocket.

You know you don't have her number.

Oh yeah. That was a problem. One he'd fix first thing tomorrow when he went to school. And this time, he wouldn't wuss out. He'd actually ask her to go have beignets with him.

Nick headed to the counter and picked up his

worn-out copy of *Hammer's Slammers,* then headed to his room to read. He was just skipping ahead to where he left off last night when his mom pushed back the blanket.

"I'm heading out. You need anything before I go?"

"I'm good."

"Okay. Mennie said she'd come by later and check on you. I'll be home a little after dawn."

Nick set his book down as he thought about her taking the streetcars to and from work while more zombies could be out on the street. His mom would barely be a snack for them. "Would you mind if I went in to work with you tonight?"

"You need to rest."

"Yeah, but with all this weird sh—" He caught himself before he said something she'd ground him over. "—stuff going on, I'd feel better if you weren't by yourself."

A slow smile spread across her beautiful face. "You going to be my protector?"

"That's my job, isn't it?"

"All right. Grab a jacket and I'll tell Mennie."

Nick did as she ordered. She didn't often let him go to the club on school nights, but he'd meant what he said. He didn't like his mom out by herself. New Orleans could be dangerous on its best nights and since she was all he had . . .

He'd guard her with every breath in his body.

By the time he had his jacket on over his bad arm and had reached the porch, Mennie was outside with her.

"Why don't you borrow my car, *chère?*"

His mom hesitated. "You know I don't like being responsible for other people's property. Besides, it's hard and expensive to park it in the Quarter. Bourbon Street's already blocked off."

"Then park it on Royal. Please, Cherise. I'd feel better if you two weren't roaming the streets in the wee hours of the night by yourselves. Think of poor Nicky."

His mom looked at him before she nodded.

Menyara handed her the keys, then kissed Nick on the cheek. "You watch over your mom."

"Always."

His mom smiled at her. "I'll leave the keys on the counter so that you can get them in the morning."

"Sounds good."

His mom turned and led him down the steps to where Menyara's dark blue Taurus waited next to their beat-up red Yugo that needed repairs they couldn't afford at present. Nick got in first. It was weird to be in Mennie's car without her. Normally they only rode in it whenever there was a hurricane coming and they needed to evacuate when their own car was broken down.

Or Nick needed stitches.

Not wanting to think about that, he buckled himself in while his mom started the car.

She ruffled his hair. "You know, since I have the car, you could stay home."

"Nope. You still have to walk from Royal to Bourbon."

She shook her head. "My fierce little bulldog."

"I'm bigger than you."

"I'm meaner."

She always said that, but it wasn't true. His mom

was the kindest person he'd ever met. It was one of the reasons why he was so protective of her. In many ways, she was still a doe-eyed innocent who only saw the good in people.

Impossible to believe, but she even defended his dad and there really was nothing good to be said about that man. He was like the devil himself.

Closing his eyes, he listened to the zydeco playing low on the car radio. That and Elvis were his mom's favorite kinds of music. Zydeco, she said, because it spoke to her Cajun roots. Elvis because it reminded her of being a little girl and playing with her cousins and sister. Apparently they used to get together and try to out-Elvis each other. And that thought made him grimace as the Mojo Nixon song "Elvis Is Everywhere" started echoing in his head—it'd take him days to get that to stop torturing him.

And it didn't make sense that they impersonated Elvis since they were all girls, but far from him to interject sanity into anything, especially after the day he'd had.

They reached Royal Street and parked two blocks

from her club. Nick got out and scanned the street where tourists were walking, some stopping to browse in the windows of the antique and jewelry stores that lined the street. They were only a few blocks away from Liza's store. She should be closing up right about now and getting her receipts together for her deposit.

He walked his mom to her club, then hesitated at the back door as she knocked for admittance. "Do you mind if I go check on Ms. Liza?"

She gave him a suspicious scowl. "Is that really what you're doing?"

"I promise. I don't like her dropping cash at the bank alone."

His mom kissed him on the cheek. "I don't know how I raised such a great son. Go on, but don't be gone long."

"I won't." He nodded to John as he let his mom in, then reversed his tracks back to Royal Street and over to the doll store.

Just as he thought, Liza was at the counter batching her credit card machine. She looked up and smiled at him as he knocked on the window.

Crossing the shop, she came to the door to let him in. "Well, isn't this a surprise. What are you doing here, sweetie?"

"I came to work with my mom and just wanted to see if you needed me to walk with you to the bank."

She locked the door behind him. "How thoughtful of you and yes, I'd love to have company. I'm just about done. You want a cola or something while I finish?"

"You got any cookies?"

"Always."

Nick skipped around her to go to the back room where she usually kept her fresh-baked cookies. Oh yeah, now this is what he was talking about. . . .

He didn't know what she put in them, but they melted in his mouth and left him aching to eat his weight in them.

"By the way," he called out as he grabbed a handful. "Thanks for sending some to the hospital. They made my day."

"You're quite welcome, Mr. Gautier. Have you been to Kyrian's yet?"

"Was there earlier." He came out of the room to stand with her behind the counter. "Met a friend of his named Ash Parthen-something I can't pronounce."

She went completely still.

Nick wondered what that meant. "You know him too?"

"I do." She tucked her bills into the blue envelope she used to hold the deposit money.

"Any idea how to say his last name?"

"With great respect." She winked at him. "It's Pahr-thin-oh-pay-us. Ack-uh-ron Pahr-thin-oh-pay-us."

"Yeah, that's a mouthful. I don't think I even want to know how to spell it. Can you imagine having to learn that in kindergarten? And I thought Gautier was hard. I was almost ten before I stopped putting an 's-h' in it."

She laughed.

Nick had just finished the last of his cookies when she reached for her jacket. Shrugging it on, she went to set the alarm while he waited by the door. As soon as it was beeping, she led him out and locked it tight.

Liza wrapped her arms around his good one. "You know, I miss these walks with you. Any chance I can steal you back from Kyrian?"

"You'll have to talk to him about it. Since he paid for the hospital, he kind of owns me."

"I'm sure he pays better too."

"A little bit. But he doesn't bake me chocolate chip cookies."

Laughing, she stopped at the ATM and made her drop.

Nick escorted her back to her car and waved to her as she got in and left him on the street in front of her store. He was just about to head back to the club when he heard a strange sound coming out of the alley that cut between her store and the one next to it.

It sounded like a dog. . . .

No, it was the same sound he'd heard outside of Kyrian's house earlier. The sound of zombies hunting him.

A chill wind blew against his skin and he could swear the sky darkened.

All the lights on the street failed as several car alarms went off.

"What the . . ."

Something came out of the alley so fast he couldn't even identify it as it rammed into him and knocked him back.

CHAPTER 9

It struck him hard in the chest and knocked him down. Rolling with it, he came to his feet, ready to fight, even though his shoulder was throbbing again. Dang, would it never stop hurting?

His stomach knotted as he recognized Stone. At first he thought Stone was a zombie, but as he looked at him, he realized he was . . .

As normal as Stone could be. Which really wasn't saying much.

"What are you doing?" Nick had to force himself to stop there and not let fly the particularly nasty insult that was stinging his tongue. But he wouldn't give Stone the satisfaction of letting him know how rattled he'd made him.

Stone laughed, shoving Nick back. "Did I scare you, little girl?"

All right, gloves off. "You're such an epic dork."

Stone grabbed him in a grip so fierce it didn't seem human. "I'm going to make you eat those words, Gautier. Along with your teeth."

Nick tried to break free. Stone increased the pressure on his neck until his vision dulled and his ears buzzed. What kind of Vulcan, kung fu death grip was he using? Nick was like a puppy someone had grabbed by the scruff of his neck. His body had just gone limp and he couldn't do anything other than dangle in Stone's grip.

It was highly embarrassing and it seriously pissed him off.

"Let him go, Stone. Now."

Stone's grip tightened as Caleb Malphas stepped out of the shadows. The quarterback and star of their high school football team, Caleb had all the power and popularity Stone craved.

And luckily none of Stone's stupidity or cruelty.

Stone shoved Nick away. "I was just having fun with him."

Caleb's dark hair was brushed back from his face, showing just how perfect his features really were as he eyed Stone with malice. "Really? Well, why don't you run along before I decide to have some fun with *you?*"

Stone's gaze narrowed. "We're not at school, Malphas. I'm not the same person out here that I am there."

Caleb invaded his personal space. He stood so close that their noses were almost touching. "Neither am I, Blakemoor. Trust me, the animal in you is no match for the demon in me. Now move along before I give you a taste of what I can do to you without the football pads to dull my blows."

Curling his lip, Stone blinked and stepped back. He raked a sneer over Nick that promised him another round whenever Caleb wasn't here to interfere. "You're not worth getting my knuckles busted anyway."

With one last sullen glare, he put his hands in his pockets and crossed the street.

Nick glared at the punk. "You better be glad my

arm's in a sling. Otherwise you'd be missing some teeth . . . buttmunch."

"Is that the best insult you can deal?"

Nick turned his fury toward Caleb. "You want a taste of it?"

Caleb laughed. "I like your spirit, Gautier. It's a shame you're not still on my team."

Nick scowled as he sensed Caleb meant something other than football. "What are you doing here?"

"I was on my way to the Triple B. It's almost time for Mark and Bubba's class on Zombie Defense and Execution. It's the most entertaining thing since that time Stone set himself on fire in chem class."

Nick laughed at the memory. Stone had been trying to show off for Casey when he knocked over a beaker full of something highly flammable that had exploded and ignited his sleeve. Unfortunately, Ms. Wilkins had been fast with the fire extinguisher and all Stone had lost were his eyebrows and some dignity.

Half the class had been rooting for a Freddie Kruegering of Stone, but luck hadn't been on their side

and he'd survived to continue being a waking nightmare for all of them.

"You want to come along?" Caleb asked him.

As much fun as it sounded, he hesitated. "I'm supposed to head back to my mom's job." 'Cause she
would absolutely kill him if he didn't.

"And miss Bubba's Zombie Roadkill Recipes?
C'mon, Nick, you know you have to see this. It's must-
view entertainment on an infinite scale of epic awe-
someness." Caleb pulled out his phone and handed it
to him. "Give her a shout and ask her if you can go."

Nick wasn't so sure about this. Caleb hadn't exactly been overly friendly to him these last few years.
In fact, he'd basically ignored him.

So why would he care if he went or not? Unless
this was a trick moment like when the cool guy asked
Carrie White to the prom just so they could drench
her in blood and laugh at her.

Yeah, I'd look stupid in a prom dress. Worse, he didn't
have the psychic powers to attack them back.

Caleb frowned at him. "What are you waiting
for?"

Lightning to strike him, 'cause let's face it, that was much more likely to happen than the most popular guy at school inviting him to watch an infamous Bubbisode.

"Why are you being so nice to me?"

A sly grin curled Caleb's lips. "My enemy's enemy is my friend."

"Who's your enemy?"

Caleb shrugged. "You wouldn't believe me if I told you . . . and I know what you're thinking. How can a guy as popular as me have any enemies or problems, right?"

Yeah, basically. "I haven't noticed you being slammed into anyone's locker lately."

"That's because you're not around me all the time. Trust me. Life's not easy for anyone. Everyone has scars they're afraid to show and we all get slammed headfirst into a proverbial locker from time to time by someone bigger and badder."

Riiight. He was more than sure that Caleb's idea of a bad day was no match for his. "What? Your parents ground you for driving your mom's new car or did you forget to tell the maid to pick up your room?"

Caleb didn't respond to his sarcasm. "You going to call your mom or not? No real sweat off my nose, one way or another. I'm just trying to be neighborly."

I swear if I get drenched in pig's blood, I'm going after you with an ax. Taking the phone from Caleb's hand, Nick punched in the number at the club.

Tiffany answered on the sixth ring.

"Hey Tiff, it's Nick. Is my mom nearby?"

"Sure, sug, hang on."

While Nick waited on his mom to get to the phone, Caleb went to stare into one of the store windows. He still wasn't sure why Caleb was willing to do this. Even though he knew Caleb, they'd never hung out before. Caleb had transferred into school not long after Nick had and though they'd had many classes together, Caleb hadn't really spoken to him in school except on rare occasions. Such as to tell him to move his punk butt out of the way so Caleb could get to his locker.

An extreme loner in spite of being popular and

playing on the football team, Caleb ignored most people. No one knew much about him. He never talked about his home life or parents. If anyone ever asked a question about it, he changed topics. But it was obvious from his clothes and bearing that his parents had more cash than most, and the rumors around school said his dad was one of the richest guys in town.

Of course rumors also claimed Caleb was an ex-con who'd learned to play football in juvey. One rumor even claimed he'd killed his dad and then sold his liver on the black market.

Given what Caleb had said a minute ago, Nick figured it must be bleak at his house. Why else would a guy with his kind of looks, money, and popularity be wandering the streets on his way to see two lunatics give lessons on fighting off nonexistent creatures?

Then again . . . after all that'd happened today, zombies weren't so fictional after all.

"Nick? Are you all right?" his mom asked as she came to the phone.

"I'm fine. I'm just a couple of blocks away. I

dropped off Liza and met a friend from school on the street—"

"Hi, Ms. Gautier," Caleb called into the phone.

Nick ignored him. "It's Caleb Malphas. He wanted to know if I could go with him to Bubba's store and attend one of Bubba's classes."

"Oh Lord, what's he teaching tonight?"

"Zombie survival."

His mom let out a tired sigh. "Is he going to have dynamite there again?"

"I doubt it. The ATF was pretty strict after the last incident. Any time the authorities step in, Bubba usually lays low for a while."

"And how long is it going to last?" she asked.

He looked at Caleb. "How long is it?"

Caleb flashed a mischievous grin. "It's supposed to be an hour, but usually Bubba or Mark has a serious injury about thirty minutes in and we have to break for a hospital run. Sometimes they come back if they can get in and out of the emergency room fast enough or the burns aren't too bad. Most times it ends early. I'd tell her an hour though 'cause we need to factor in the time it takes to stop laughing so hard we can walk again."

The sad thing was, Caleb wasn't joking. "About an hour, Ma."

"And you won't be alone?"

"No, ma'am. Caleb's with me and he's a good-sized guy."

"How old is he?"

Nick clenched his teeth in frustration. Why did he have to play this game with her all the time when it was only a matter of a simple yes or no? Dang, his mom should have been a lawyer. "How old are you?"

Caleb paused as if he had to think about it. "Fifteen."

"Fifteen," Nick repeated into the phone.

"What do his parents do for a living?"

This time his temper snapped and he spoke before he could stop himself. "What does that matter?"

"It matters to me and if you want to go, I want an answer."

Nick rolled his eyes at the response that grated on his last nerve. "What do your parents do?"

There was a strange look on Caleb's face. When he spoke, his tone was completely stoic. "My dad's a broker and my mom is his eternal unwilling concubine who sold her soul to him to buy the equivalent of a Ferrari."

Nick let out a long breath. Caleb definitely had a way with words. "His dad's a stockbroker."

"His mom?"

"She's a housewife."

His mother hesitated before she continued grilling him. "Is he a good boy?"

"No, Mom, he's Satan incarnate. In fact, once it's over, we're going to get liquored up and tattooed, then find some cheap hos and have a good time with his trust fund."

Caleb laughed.

His mom, however, did not share that sense of humor. "Don't you take that tone with me, Nick Gautier. I'll ground you till you're old and gray. Now answer my question."

Would she never appreciate his sarcasm?

Realizing he had to play nice, Nick took the attitude out of his voice. "Yes, he's a good boy. Never been in trouble at school and he's on the honor roll. Captain of the football team. All-around psycho serial killer who hides bodies in the fridge whenever his parents go out of town."

Well . . . he'd tried to remove all sarcasm. Thing was, for him, it was an impossible task.

Caleb laughed again, then leaned in to speak so that Nick's mom could hear him. "I also eat babies for breakfast and torture small animals for fun. My therapist says that I'm making real progress though."

His mother responded with a sharp note. "Don't you boys get smart with me."

Nick grinned at Caleb. "Sorry, Mom. We couldn't resist."

She spoke to her boss, then came back to Nick. "All right. You can go, but I want you here in an hour."

"Yes, ma'am. I'll be there."

"I love you, baby."

Nick felt his face turn bright red as he turned away from Caleb. "I love you too," he said in a low tone. Then he hung up the phone and returned it to

Caleb. "I don't want to hear no crap from you about that."

Caleb held his hands up. "Don't worry. Wish I had a mom I could love. Mine's a psycho hose beast who begrudges me every breath I take. Besides, you didn't make kissing noises at her. So what's to mock?"

This time. And it was only because Caleb was here that he didn't.

Caleb put the phone in his pocket and led the way toward Bubba's store.

As they walked, Nick's thoughts went back to Stone and the oddity of their meeting. "What do you think Stone was doing behind Liza's store?" It wasn't like him to be out alone. His brand of cowardice usually needed an audience to perform for.

Caleb jerked his chin in the direction of the full moon. "He was probably prowling around with his buds and found some Dumpsters with trash in them to sniff."

"Huh?"

"It's a full moon, Nick. I'm sure the animal in Stone took over. He was probably trying to teleport some-where and because of his young age, screwed up the jump. I think he landed behind the doll store 'cause Liza was summoning the gods earlier tonight and her powers called out to him or something. They might have even interfered with his."

Nick snorted at his worthless answer. "Ah, gah, you're not going to start with all that werewolf crap too, are you?"

"You don't believe in them?"

"I only believe in zombies and only because I've seen them today. The rest . . . total caca."

Caleb shook his head. "You live in New Orleans and you're Catholic, not to mention friends with Bubba and Mark, yet you don't believe in demons, were-wolves, or vampires?"

"The only vampires I've ever seen are the Goths trying to get a glimpse of Anne Rice's house, who drink strawberry sodas and tell each other it's blood."

"You're such a skeptic."

And Nick took a lot of pride in that too. He didn't like the idea of anyone putting anything over on him. Better to be jaded than a victim. "I take it you're not."

"I believe in it all."

"Why?"

"C'mon, Nick, haven't you ever been walking down the street and just felt the hand of evil brush down your spine? You know that tingle. That sense that something isn't right, but you don't know what it is. That's a demon by your side, boy. He's sizing you up to toy with."

Nick didn't believe a word of what he was trying to sell. "You're just trying to mess with my head."

"I'm trying to prepare you for the real world."

"The real world is getting a good job, paying your bills, and keeping your nose clean." Staying off death row.

Caleb gave him an arch stare. "Wow. You've totally bought into that namby-pamby status quo."

"It's not status quo. It's the truth."

"Whatever you say." Caleb stepped up on the curb as they reached the Triple B. He moved ahead and opened the door to let Nick enter first.

"Store's closed. There's no classes to—" Mark's voice broke off as he came out of the back room and saw them. "Oh. It's you guys. Come on in."

Nick scowled at the strange welcome. "What's going on?"

Mark didn't answer as he walked past them and went to the door they'd just entered through, locked it, then turned the CLOSED sign around. "You won't believe this." He motioned for them to follow him into the back room.

Oh goody. He couldn't wait. Whenever Mark uttered those words, it was always a doozie.

But the minute he entered the back, Nick pulled up short. Bubba and Madaug were sitting in front of the computer—oh, that little wanker. How could Madaug be here after not picking up the phone all day?

Nick wanted to choke him.

Madaug's glasses were slightly askew on his nose as he tugged at his short hair while reading through the code on the screen.

"How did he get here?" Nick asked Mark.

Mark gave him a droll stare. "Walked."

Nick scoffed at him. "Seriously. After all we've done to locate him today, when did he pop back in?"

"Couple of hours ago." Mark stood opposite of Nick and Caleb.

Oblivious to them, Madaug pointed to a line of code. "See, Bubba. That's what I was talking about. This algorithm was designed to subliminally repress their anterior cingulate cortex while this one stimulated the orbital frontal cortex and amygdala, thereby raising their serotonin levels."

Nick scowled at Caleb, who, thankfully, looked as confused as he felt.

Bubba and Mark, however, seemed to be fluent in the geek speak that left him baffled.

"Yeah." Bubba scratched at the stubble on his chin. "But I don't see how that gave you control of the hypothalamus."

"It doesn't really. Only the somatic nervous system should be affected with a small byproduct of elevated stress in the hypothalamus that should have inhibited his aggressive behavior. What I can't figure out is how I lost control. What did I miss, Bubba?"

Nick cleared his throat. "I can tell you what I'm missing. A clue. What are you people talking about?"

Mark cut a sideways look to Nick. "Zombie Hunter."

Nick had to bite his tongue to not respond with *no, duh.* "And that would be different from all the other discussions you guys have had how?"

Mark let out an aggravated breath. "Not killing zombies, Nick, playing them."

Madaug turned toward Nick to answer. "I invented a video game called Zombie Hunter. That's what we're working on."

Nick smiled. "Oh, that's cool. Can I play?"

"No!" Mark, Bubba, and Madaug shouted all at once.

Bubba took a swig of his soda. "Trust us, Nick. This is one game you don't want any part of."

"Why?"

Madaug pinned a gimlet stare on him. "Because anyone who plays it gets turned into a zombie."

Oh yeah right . . . Nick didn't believe that for one instant. "Bullcrap."

"Nah, man, it's true." Bubba indicated Madaug with the can in his hand. "Your little friend here is quite brilliant."

Yeah, brilliant at getting shoved into lockers. . . .

Nick couldn't understand how Madaug could be bright enough to figure out how to program a game, but not fly under the radar of the people who wanted to abuse him.

Madaug pushed his glasses up on his nose. "I learned that a specific sequence of light and sound can actually alter brain waves and override them. See, the brain is like a computer and if you can bypass certain programming, you can hack in and change someone's core hard drive."

Nick had to give him credit, it sounded impressive. "How did you learn this stuff?"

"My mom's a neurosurgeon at Tulane and my dad's a research criminal neurologist. They have really boring conversations at the dinner table and force me to listen to them while I eat my mom's really bad cooking. My dad's doing a study right now on ways to inhibit violent behavior, which is what gave me the idea for the game. I took his notes, did some independent research, and then had Bubba teach me the core programming to build levels for the game that would alter their brain pattern."

Caleb hit Nick in his good shoulder. "See what you can learn when you listen to your parents?"

Nick scoffed. "That ain't what my parents talk about." But if anyone ever wanted to learn how to pole dance or gut a human being, Nick was the one to talk to.

That, however, was another topic and not helpful tonight at all . . . then again, the gutting *might* come in handy if more zombies came for him.

"So who has the game?" Nick asked Madaug.

"I gave a copy to Brian 'cause he was always messing with me. I wanted to see if I could reprogram him to stress out whenever he felt the urge to come at me. Instead of getting pleasure, bullying would increase his fear, and make him pull back. That was the plan."

Bubba took another drink. "He was Madaug's guinea pig."

Madaug looked sick over that comment. "Yeah, and now I can't find the game. I don't know who has it, but apparently other people have been playing it which is why we have zombies cropping up all over the place."

Bubba snorted. "Yeah, two and three at a time,

'cause God forbid kids should do what we did back in the old days and play in a room by ourselves. What kind of geeks are they raising nowadays? Geeks with friends who play video games together. Whoever heard of such? It's the end of days, I'm telling you all."

Nick was confused by his outburst. "But, Bubba? Aren't you and Mark friends?"

"Ah, hell no. Mark's not my friend, he's my minion."

Mark stiffened. "I prefer sidekick. I tried once for the title of Padawan, but Bubba wigged out saying that mentors are always killed off in books and movies and he'd be damned if he was going to die once he taught me everything I needed to know about killing zombies."

"Then why let you be his sidekick? Isn't that the same thing?" Nick asked.

Mark laughed. "Uh, no. In the movies, the sidekicks are the ones who die."

Nick wasn't about to touch that screwed-up logic.

Bubba ignored him as he continued speaking. "And because Madaug had it programmed to repel Brian from him, we think the programming is backwards and it's making them seek him out instead. So we need to rework the code to switch them back to normal."

That sounded good, but Nick only had one problem with this theory. "So why are they coming after me?"

Bubba and Madaug gaped at him. "What?"

"Two of them, a few hours ago, tracked me down at work," Nick explained. "They almost had me too."

Bubba shook his head in denial. "That's not possible. The programming only works around Madaug and his DNA."

Nick held up his good arm to show them the bandage where he'd been bitten. Again. "Possible or not, they tried to turn me into a Nick McNugget."

Bubba grabbed his arm, pulled the bandage back, and studied his two wounds. "Well, isn't that interesting."

Nick was aghast at his nonchalance. It might have been funny had it been happening to Stone and not him. But right now, he didn't exactly have a sense of humor about being a zombie chew toy. "I ain't your science experiment, Bubba. I don't want to be interesting and I definitely don't want to be a nubby treat for the zombies."

Bubba looked at Madaug. "Why would they try to eat Nick?"

Madaug shrugged. "I don't know why they're trying to eat anyone. Period. The program was to calm them down and make them passive. Not aggressive."

"Epic fail, dude," Nick said.

Madaug looked back at his code before he responded to Nick's outburst. "From what I've observed today, when the programming kicks in they attack whoever they're around. But I haven't seen them tracking anyone except me and I still haven't figured out why they're stalking me and not quivering in fear."

Caleb crossed his arms over his chest. "You turned them into zombies, Madaug. They're after your brains."

Nick laughed. "I'd say it's because they're all mindless jocks, but that might offend you."

"Yeah, and then I'd have to break your other arm."

Bubba set his drink down. "Don't make me have

to separate the two of you. I'm out of patience with kids today." He indicated the smashed cabinets from earlier. "I still wanna know who to sue to get my store fixed."

"I'm a turnip." Nick pointed to Madaug. "Sue the rich kid who started it."

Before Madaug could defend himself, there was a sharp thud against the door, followed by the sounds of someone moaning while trying to get in.

Mark leaned his head against the wall as if he were in agony. "Please let that be Tabitha playing a prank."

Bubba hefted his ax from its peg on the wall. "Guard the geek," he said to Mark. "I'm going to check it out."

Mark moaned even louder. "Please don't let it be another cop. I'm outta bail money." He looked at Nick. "Wait a minute. . . . I could sell you on eBay and make a killing."

Nick pointed to his busted arm. "Not in my current condition. You'd have to sell Caleb or Madaug. I'm sure there's someone willing to buy two perfectly good white boys." He leaned forward to look past Mark, who had thankfully bathed the scent of duck urine off him, to see who was at the door.

With the ax cocked on his shoulder, Bubba unlocked it and a group of Goths spilled into the store. They were so excited that they were talking over each other to the point Nick couldn't understand any of them.

The last one in let loose a whistle so piercing, it echoed. As she turned toward him, Nick recognized Tabitha decked out in pants so tight he was sure they were illegal in some states.

Probably this one.

She looked up at Bubba. "We need supplies, B. Lots and lots of supplies."

Bubba scowled. "Why? What's going on?"

"Who let loose the zombies?" one of the guys asked.

"Yeah, and they don't move slow," another inserted. "They're like super zombie mutants on speed."

The tallest of the guys pointed to his swollen and red eye. "They look like a rival football team that I swear we played a couple of weeks back. Which is how I got the black eye. I was trying to keep Tabitha from committing murder."

Madaug moved past Nick, his mouth hanging open. "Eric? Is that you?"

The one holding his eye turned with a stern frown. His black hair was teased to stand out all over his head like Rob Smith from the Cure. He wore even more makeup than Tabitha, which included black lipstick, guyliner, and black blush. Even his fingernails were painted black. A color that swathed him from head to toe. "What's my kid brother doing here?"

"Mazel tov, Eric!" Bubba slapped him on the back so hard he staggered. "Your brother is the one who gave us the zombies."

Eric's face was a mask of disbelief. "You've got to be kidding me. Madaug?" Eric turned on his brother then. "What the he—you doing? Mom and Dad are going to ground you for life."

"I know," Madaug said wistfully. "I'm trying to undo it. But . . ." He shook his head as if he'd had a thought and was banishing it. "Never mind. You're worthless. You haven't passed a science test since fourth grade."

Eric shoved him.

Madaug pushed back. "Don't start with me, you cross-dressing freak. I can't believe I share a common gene with you. I swear Mom and Dad found you at a rest stop."

"They found you in a toilet drain, jerk weed."

Tabitha separated them. "Quit, you two. Save your energy for killing what's important. The undead."

Bubba rested the top of the ax against the floor. "Hang on a minute, and I can't believe I'm about to say this . . . but since what we're dealing with is innocent kids Madaug messed with and a handful of really stupid adults who should have had a life other than playing video games, and you should consider that's coming from a gaming addict, we can't kill them." He passed a stern look to Tabitha. "These ain't the undead, Tabby. They're living, breathing morons and we have to save them."

Tabitha sighed in disgust. "I'd rather stake them all and let God sort them out."

"And I'd rather not go to jail for the rest of my life," Eric said sternly. "No offense, but I know what they do to good-looking guys in prison and I'm way too cute to be resisted."

Mark snorted. "Pah-lease. Your worse problem what with that black lipstick and long hair is that they'll mistake you for a woman. I highly doubt they'd lock you up with the men dressed in that getup. More like you'd go in with the prostitutes. Hey . . . you know, lockup might not be so bad for you."

"ADD applicants," Bubba snapped, "can I have your attention for a minute. We need to get out there and find these people before they eat anyone else. Bring them here so we can try to undo what Madaug did."

Eric pursed his lips. "Where we going to put them? The tub?"

Bubba glowered at Eric before he went to the wall, pulled down a gun, and showed a hidden . . .

Cell—one that was completely padded and with steel reinforcements and restraints hanging from the ceiling. Nick had never seen anything like that in his life.

Tabitha laughed. "Oh my God, Bubba has a sex dungeon!"

Bubba narrowed his glare on her. "You're too young to know about such things."

"Are you kidding? My aunt owns Pandora's Box on Bourbon Street. From the looks of those restraints, I think you went shopping there."

Bubba made a sound of deep aggravation as he glanced at Eric. "Can you muzzle her?"

"How you think I got the black eye? And for your information, she don't hit like a girl. She might be from an all-estrogen family, but some dude trained her well."

Mark arched one brow. "Looks like bad eyeliner to me. You sure you got hit by a girl?"

Bubba whistled. "And we've lost focus again, people. I swear it's like herding cats. For the next five minutes I want all of you to banish the sarcasm and focus. I know I'm asking for a miracle, but this is life and death. Okay?"

"A'ight," they said in unison.

Bubba nodded at all of them. "We have got to protect the city. I want all of you out there patrolling for zombies. When you find them—"

"Stake them!" Tabitha pulled out one of her steel spikes to illustrate her words.

Bubba snatched it from her. "No. Get them to chase you back here, where Mark and I will be waiting to tranq them. Is everyone clear? No murder. No bloodshed."

Tabitha rolled her eyes. "What a waste of a good night."

Madaug was aghast as he looked at his older brother. "Do Mom and Dad know you're dating a homicidal lunatic?"

"No, and if you tell them, I'll superglue your fingertips to your keyboard."

A tic started in Madaug's jaw as his cheeks turned bright red. "Mom said if you ever do that again, she's going to shave your head while you sleep."

"Children!" Bubba shouted. "There are dangerous creatures out there. Let's go get them."

Madaug took a step for the door.

Bubba pulled him to a stop and forced him back toward the storeroom. "Not you. We need you to stay here and keep working on a cure."

Caleb looked at Nick. "You ready for this?"

Nick checked his watch. "Only for the next forty-five minutes. After that I get grounded."

"C'mon, Cinderella. Let's get started before you turn into a pumpkin." Caleb led him out of the store and down the street, toward their high school, which made sense since it was where all of this started.

And my worst fear this morning was being late. . . .

Who knew he'd end up having to be afraid of having his brains ripped out and devoured?

Wonder if I should start carrying a chainsaw to school? That wasn't listed on their anti-weapons list. . . .

As they walked, his thoughts went to Madaug and his family. "Don't you think it's odd that Madaug's brother doesn't go to school with us?"

Caleb put his hands in his back pockets. "Probably too dumb to get in."

"You think?"

"Genetics doesn't always rule intellect. Believe me. I come from a long line of really stupid people. Scares me that I swim in their gene pool. Yet here I am, a hell of a lot smarter than they are."

Nick didn't even want to think about his gene pool for fear of the infection it might contain. He lived in constant terror that one day a switch would turn on in his head and make him the monster his father was. Every time he tried to talk to his mom about it, she told him he was ridiculous. And yet he couldn't shake the feeling that there was something inside him dying to get out. Something sinister, cold, and unfeeling.

"You have any sibs?" he asked Caleb, trying to distract himself from that line of thought.

"Not full-blooded. I really don't count the others. What about you?"

"No."

Caleb nodded. "So what does your dad do, Nick?"

"I don't talk about my dad." To anyone. Bubba and Mark were the only two who knew his dad was a felon. To the rest of the world, he never said anything.

"He's not part of our lives and I want to keep it that way."

"I understand. Don't have much to do with mine either."

"Why not?"

"You wouldn't believe me if I told you. But that's okay. That which doesn't kill us just requires a few centuries of therapy."

"Yeah, and usually a lot of Tylenol."

Caleb laughed. "Hey, I tell you what, if we spread out, we can cover more ground. Want to meet back up at the cathedral?"

"Sure."

"All right. I'll see you there."

Nick headed down the side street that would connect him to Bourbon, which was thronging with people who could be the next victims. *Like you could tell the difference between a zombie and a drunk tourist?*

That would be challenging. But if he were a zombie looking for business, that's where he'd head. And as he'd noted, they would blend in seamlessly there.

As he walked down the street, he noticed that the buzzing in the street lamps was getting louder. He slowed as he came even to the Lalaurie mansion—the most haunted and evilest place in all of New Orleans. If there was such a thing as a hell-mouth, this place stood on it. Ever since he was a kid, it'd given him the creeps.

Tonight more so than normal.

A sudden wind whipped down the street, stirring his hair and raising a chill on his neck as a huge raven flew over his head to land on the upper wrought-iron balcony where it seemed to stare down at him.

I know I sound crazy, but I swear that bird is watching me.

It cocked its head. *Yeah, that's eerie as all get out.* Just like the building itself.

In that house, dozens of people had been brutally tortured and murdered in ways his mom wouldn't even talk about. Every family who'd owned it since the Lalauries had reported seeing and hearing the ghosts of those who'd lost their lives to Delphine Lalaurie's psychotic cruelty. Something that had been so atrocious her own cook had set fire to the kitchen, trying to kill herself to escape the madwoman.

Even the seasoned firemen who were used to dealing with death and gore had vomited when they'd uncovered the mutilated victims Delphine had left behind.

Help me. . . .

Nick turned around, trying to see who had spoken. It sounded like a child's voice.

I'm so scared. Why can't I see? Is anyone there?

"I'm here," Nick called. "Where are you?"

Disembodied laughter rang out. The light above him shattered.

Cursing, Nick jumped back as glass rained down on him.

He saw the shadow of a little girl by the side of the house. "Help me find my mommy. Please." She walked through a door that was ajar, into the small alcove that led to the interior garden.

"Wait!" Nick closed the distance between them, wanting to help her. He reached out to pull her to a stop.

His hand passed right through her body.

What the?

All of a sudden, she turned around and his gut shrank. Her face was scarred, her large eyes were nothing more than an eerie shadow.

Baring a set of fangs, she attacked.

CHAPTER 10

Nick staggered back as the "little" girl grew to over six feet tall. Towering over him, she grabbed him by the shirt with hands made of talons and laughed in his face. "You should have done what your friends wanted you to, Gautier, and helped them rob and kill that couple. You made a big mistake by being nice. So long as you let your goodness weaken you, we can feed on you." She moved to bite his neck.

He kicked her back and sprinted for the street.

Just as he reached it, three more creatures appeared to block his way. They looked like men, but cold lightning danced in the sockets where their eyes should be. The courtyard's temperature instantly dropped twenty degrees to leave him shivering. Worse, these newcomers smelled like something that came out of the back end of the mules that pulled the carriages through the Quarter.

Dang, didn't they *ever* bathe?

The lead one tsked at him, flashing a set of sharp, jagged fangs. "Did you really think you could get away from us?"

Yeah, he did. . . .

Nick stepped back and looked for a way to get past them. They completely shielded him from the street. There was no way to reach it without coming into contact with them. And behind him was the closed-off courtyard.

Crap . . .

"What do you want?" Nick asked, trying to think of a third option.

The girl grabbed him from behind. "We want to kill you." She sank her teeth into his neck.

Hissing, Nick slammed his good arm into her midsection. She released him enough that he was able to twist out of her arms and scramble away from her.

The other three came at him.

Where's an ax when I need one?

Better yet, a rocket launcher.

The raven swooped down to land on his injured shoulder. The moment its talons touched him, something like electricity went through his body. It was so intense and painful that it sucked his breath out. For thirty seconds, everything seemed to stop. The wind, his attackers, the bird.

His heart.

When the world returned to normal, it came back with a rush that slammed into him so hard, he gasped. His senses sharper than they'd ever been before, he realized his arm was no longer injured.

Fight. The voice in his head sounded demonic.

From somewhere deep inside him, Nick felt a power rise up and radiate through his entire body. The bird launched itself back to the balcony to watch as the things attacked him.

Even though he knew they were moving at an inhumanly fast speed, he saw them as if they were in slow motion. It was like he was possessed by something else.

The first one struck.

Nick dodged the blow and returned it with one of his own. The creature staggered back. He spun to catch the next one with a head butt.

The third one screamed out in rage as he ran for Nick's back. Nick flipped him over and slung him to the street before he slammed his fist into his chest.

The female kicked him into the wall.

Nick turned around and blocked the punch she sent to his throat. Like something out of a movie, she punched him repeatedly and he countered every blow.

When did I learn kung fu?

And his mom said all those Jackie Chan movies were a waste. Apparently, he'd learned by osmosis—'cause there was no way he knew this otherwise.

He felt like he could take on the world.

Someone toss me some nunchucks.

Kicking her back, he caught another of the creatures and slammed him into the first. Within a matter of seconds, they were on the ground and he was standing over them without even breathing hard in a perfect sotobiraki jigo hontai dachi stance.

Take that, Chuck Norris!

The bird cawed as if in approval before it flew off into the night.

Nick straightened up. His shoulder didn't hurt at all. More than that, he had total control of it, which was something his doctor and physical therapist had said would take months to have again.

What is going on? He would think this a dream, but for the fact he knew he was awake.

The creatures evaporated into a fine mist that scattered into the shadows while the temperature returned to normal.

All of a sudden, there was a man in front of him. One who bore a striking resemblance to his father except this one had a strange double bow-and-arrow mark on his face. Dressed in black, he had on a long leather coat that fell to his ankles. With hair the same color as Nick's, only longer, he stood six feet four and had a well-trimmed goatee. And whereas Nick's eyes were blue, his were as black as his clothes.

Nick braced himself to fight. "Who are you?"

"Relax, Nicky. I'm just a friend who's here to help you."

"How so?"

The man held his hand up and a ball of light appeared in his palm where it danced and flickered in the darkness. His face grim, he closed his hand and the light vanished. "You have no idea how important you are. How many powers and creatures will be fighting over you. But trust me, kid, the only one who really cares about you, besides your mother, is me."

Nick wasn't so sure about that. "And you are?"

"Your uncle Ambrose."

Yeah, right. "I don't have an uncle."

"Of course you do, Nick. You're even named after me."

He shook his head. He was named after his father and grandfather—at least that's what he'd always been told. "My mom never mentioned you."

"Because I'm from your father's side and she doesn't really know about me. But that doesn't matter. My goal is to keep you from making some really bad mistakes."

"Such as what? Talking to you?"

Ambrose laughed. "The world is not what you see, kid. There's a veil over everything and it's blinding you the way it blinds most people." He brushed the hair back from Nick's eyes, and the moment he did, a jolt went through him. "That is perspicacity. The ability to see what's hidden. My gift to you even though you've already had a taste of it. Now it's more honed and reliable. I don't want anyone fooling you again."

Nick staggered back as he saw Ambrose not as a man, but as . . .

Something else.

His skin was mottled black and red. His eyes bright yellow. Ambrose wasn't human and that terrified him.

"What are you?"

"Your friend. Always. I'm the only being you'll ever be able to trust."

Bullcrap. The only person he could fully trust was himself. Words were easy and actions often lethal. Nick wasn't dumb enough to think for one minute that this guy was on the level. "Dude, I don't know you and I'm not about to trust you."

"You know me much better than you think. Look inside yourself and you'll know I'm telling you the truth."

Nick looked and what he saw there made his blood run cold. He refused to believe it.

Unable to stand it, he started to run, but couldn't. It was like an unseen power held him prisoner.

"I know you don't trust me. I don't blame you. But you will learn to listen in time. I've unlocked your powers early this time around—for your protection."

Ambrose was whacked. There was no other explanation.

"What powers? Are you high?" Nick asked him.

A wicked smile curled his lips, showing him a set of fangs. "No. But you must keep what I'm going to teach you quiet. Let no one, especially not Acheron, know."

"How do you know about Acheron?"

"Oh . . . it's not time for you to understand that yet. But my tampering isn't without problems. Those mortents who attacked you a moment ago are just a few such byproducts. Don't worry though. You'll have the ability to battle them and you'll grow stronger every time they attack you. I haven't left you defense-less in this."

"Look," Nick interrupted him. "I don't know what you've been sniffing . . ." He tried to move past, but Ambrose stopped him.

"I'm on your side, Nick. You don't have many friends, and even fewer you can trust."

"Like Nekoda?" He didn't know why her name popped into his head. But it did. Along with an image of her smiling face.

Bonus round was the look of shock on Ambrose's face. "Nekoda?"

Yeah, he wasn't as smart as he thought, and that gave Nick a new confidence that Ambrose might still be lying. "You don't know her?"

Ambrose tilted his head as if he was trying to listen to the cosmos. "How can you know someone I don't?"

"Probably easy since I don't know you at all."

He shook his head. "Something's not right. . . . This isn't possible." He vanished into nothing.

Nick looked around, turning in a small circle. There was no sign of anything.

I've lost my mind.

Perhaps, but his arm was still working and he felt no pain.

Then as easy as it'd come over him, the power vaporized. It flooded out of him and left every part of his body aching. The pain of his shoulder drove him to his knees. Wave after wave of agony cascaded over him until it dulled his vision.

One minute he was standing. The next, the street rose up to knock him down. And the last thing he heard was a deep female voice.

"You belong to us, Nick Gautier. And you will learn your place or we will see you dead. . . ."

CHAPTER 11

The raven left Nick and flew up to the sky, then vanished as it was summoned away from New Orleans. When it reappeared, it wasn't in the Quarter where it preferred to feed. It was miles away, flying over a razor-wire fence.

And because he was summoned here so often, the bird was as familiar with Angola prison as any of the inmates.

Buzzing past the guards' tower, he headed to the Reception Center—the building where the death-row inmates were housed. He slowed as he approached the correct window.

I really don't want to do this.

But he had no choice. When he was summoned, he had to obey. Those were the rules and any hesitation would only end badly for him.

One minute he was perched on the sill, the next a hand appeared out of nowhere to grab his throat and haul him inside.

Caleb manifested into human form as he stared at one of the most powerful demons ever spawned. Absolute pure evil, Adarian Malachai was incapable of any kindness or mercy.

Without a word, he drove Caleb headfirst into a wall. Then he pulled Caleb up and held him by the hair of his head. "What do you think you're doing?" he snarled in Caleb's left ear.

Caleb grimaced as he tasted the blood that was seeping from his nose. He knew better than to fight. It would only make Adarian more cruel and worsen his beating. "Training Nick like you ordered."

He tightened his grip in Caleb's hair. "With mortents? Are you out of your mind? He could have been killed! Why didn't you stop them from attacking him?"

Those words stunned him on more levels than he could count. Why would Adarian care if some snot-nose bought the farm? "I didn't know he'd run into them, but since they showed up, I thought it would be a perfect opportunity for him to start learning to fight. I was there the whole time, watching. He was never in any real danger. Besides, if he dies, you live. What's the crime in that?"

"You're so stupid." He released him.

Caleb turned and shoved him back as he took his true form. He knew he shouldn't, but it wasn't in him to not fight back. At the end of the day, he was a demon and he never swallowed crap from others without vomiting venom back up. "Stand down, Malachai. You're not as powerful as you think."

Adarian laughed. "And I own you. So don't even try to intimidate me. I've picked my teeth from the bones of demons stronger and older than you."

That was probably true. But it didn't change the fact that Caleb would give anything to have the power to destroy Adarian. *How did I become enslaved to this . . .* There was no word foul enough to describe him.

Unfortunately, Caleb knew exactly what had led him here and he hated that as much as he hated Adarian. "I've done exactly what you've asked. I've watched over your sniveling spawn for these last few years while not interfering with anything he's done."

"You should have befriended him before now."

Caleb was stunned by those words. "You told me not to."

Adarian seized him by the throat. His eyes glowed a deep, deadly red. "And now I'm telling you to guard him with your life. There's a new power here. One I can't discern, but it's following him and I want you to keep him safe. So help me, if anything happens to my son, I will come for you, and when I'm through, you'll wish you could crawl back to the slime hole where I found you."

Caleb felt his teeth sharpen and elongate in response to that threat. "I command legions."

"And I command *you*. Never forget that."

If only he could. "One day I'm going to break free of you, Malachai."

"And until you do, you will do exactly as I order.

Now guard my boy and his mother. Let nothing happen to them. Do you understand?"

"I understand. But how am I to train him if I can't have him attacked?"

Adarian's lips curled into a sardonic smile. "You're resourceful. Find a way. And remember, I'm in this jail because I choose to be. I can leave it and come for you anytime I want to."

It was true. Adarian lived here because he fed off the cruelty and evil of others. This prison was like living in an Energizer factory as far as he was concerned. It kept him superstrong and able to deflect anything that came at him.

Except for his son. Nick's presence could weaken him instantly. Little prick had no idea that by avoiding his father, he was allowing Adarian's powers to remain at full strength, which put the rest of them at a major disadvantage.

Adarian pulled him closer. "You better not betray me, Malphas. Not in this."

Caleb would accuse him of loving the boy, but he knew better. This wasn't about love. It was about power. If Adarian could keep Nick alive and away from him, he could rebuild his army through Nick and there would be no power on this earth or beyond that could stop him.

None.

Other than Nick, the only one who was capable of bringing down the Malachai army was now imprisoned and kept as weak as a sick kitten. While Adarian's powers grew, Jared's deteriorated under the care of a vicious guardian who had no idea just how important her prisoner was.

The balance of power was shifting, just as it'd done in the days before recorded history. Then the bloodiest of all battles had raged. One of the fiercest soldiers, Caleb had barely survived it and the memory of it burned inside him. The fight with Adarian's father had cost him everything.

Now he was servant to his son.

Life really sucked.

"I will obey you . . . master." That title stuck deep in his craw.

Adarian smiled. "Good boy. And remember, my

son must be evil to the marrow of his bones. You have to turn him. No matter what it takes. Do you hear me?"

"What if the only way I can turn him is to kill the mother?"

Adarian seized his throat again. "You touch one hair on her head . . . you allow anyone else to, and I will make you pay in ways you can't imagine in your wildest nightmares. Cherise is mine and no one else is to ever lay a hand on her."

That was the one order Caleb couldn't understand. Again, he would attribute it to love, but there was no way the Malachai could love anything except himself and his quest for power.

Bowing low, he backed away from Adarian.

Caleb had to force himself not to sneer as he retook his raven form and flew through the wall. But once he was out of sight, he used his talons to flip off the demon lord.

Protect the boy, my arse.

What irony, really. The fate of the entire world, of humanity and demonkyn, was in the hands of a fourteen–year-old boy who had no idea of the untapped powers he'd been born with.

A fourteen-year-old boy whose biggest fear was getting grounded by a mother who wouldn't even be a decent snack for Caleb and his kith. What a waste of power.

And I'm the schmuck who has to protect him.

Not just from the demons, but also from the werewolves like Stone, and others who had a natural inclination to pick on Nick because they could sense that he wasn't quite human.

Caleb let out a tired breath. Would his indignities never cease?

CHAPTER 12

Hello? Mr. Human Boy Person? Can you hear the Simi? Or are you dead? Hello?"

Nick came awake to someone poking a hole in his upper arm with her fingertip. "Ow! Would you stop poking on me?" He opened his eyes to find one of the prettiest girls he'd ever seen leaning over him.

Dang . . .

Teach me to be rude before I find out who's assaulting me. 'Cause this girl was f-i-n-e and he was more than willing to be her victim any time she wanted to invade his personal space, even if it was with nothing more than her fingertip.

Her long black hair hung in pigtails and was streaked with bloodred. She had on a studded leather choker that matched the black leather corset she wore. Probably around the age of seventeen or eighteen, she had a pair of red eyes (must be some of those weird contacts) that were ringed with black eyeliner. Her lips were also bright red, like her fingernails. And her features were absolutely perfect. Dressed in a really short black and red skirt, she had purple leggings and a pair of bright red Doc Martens that were accented with a skull-and-rose motif.

She cocked her head in a gesture that reminded him of a bird as she eyed him with consternation. "Why you sleeping on the ground out here, Mr. Boy Human? The Simi don't think this is a safe thing to do. Comfortable either. Someone might think you dead and steal something or they could kill you. Maybe not if they think you dead already, but then again, people do weird things all the time—like killing dead people even though they're dead. Is that overkill or is that just dumb? Never mind. So you should probably get up soon and not sleep here. Did you lose your bed? Or are you one of them special people who don't have a bed but sleep outside instead? Some of them can be real nice. Some even offer the Simi drinks, but akri says I can't have any 'cause it'll give me indigestion. Not like rubber does, but worse. So says akri." She had a strange singsongy voice that was endearing and adorable.

But it made understanding her a little difficult, especially with the headache he had.

"What?" Nick asked.

She let out a long-suffering sigh. "You one of them humans can't follow Simi speak. That's okay. This why the Simi don't bother talking to most humans 'cause, no offense, you all weird. Some of you even stupid. Real stupid. Like stump stupid. It's the lack of hornays, I say. See, only really smart creatures have hornays . . . except for them moo moo cows—they not bright. But akri says there's always an exception to every rule. So they would be the exception to the hornay one. But they taste really good so the Simi will forgive them for bringing down her bell curve of superior intellect over all the other nonhorned subspecies."

She narrowed her eyes on his head. "Hmmm, I bet

you'd be really cute with hornays. Not that you're not cute right now, but you're a bit young. You're only what? Four in human years? Oh wait, that's wrong, isn't it? You ninety?"

Was she serious? "Fourteen."

"Oh." She put the tip of her finger to her lips as she considered something. "I wouldn't have guessed that. Still, you're young. So can the Simi help you find a place to sleep that's not dangerous? My akri can help if we need him to. He always does."

Nick shook his head. "Who are you?" *What planet are you from?* Obviously Planet Insanity was missing a local, long-term resident.

She held her lace-covered hand out to him. "I am the Simi, and who are you, Mr. Boy Human?"

He shook her hand carefully in case her lunacy was catching. "Nick."

Letting go of him, she picked at the edge of his sling. "You gots a wound, don't you? Did you have that before you went to sleep on the street?"

"Uh, yeah." Nick pushed himself up and Simi sprang to her feet beside him.

Dang, she was tall. At least six feet. Of course some of that was augmented by the platform boots.

Frowning, she leaned forward and touched his neck. "You bleeding, Mr. Nick. Are you supposed to do that?"

Nick brushed her hand away so that he could feel a cut there. He tried to remember what'd happened, but for his life he had no memory of it. The last thing he remembered was leaving Caleb and heading toward Bourbon. "Is it bad?"

"The Simi wouldn't suggest being around no Daimon with that 'cause they might be hungry and it look mighty tempting to drain your blood out and feast on your soul, but it not gushing or anything. I think you'll live." She paused again as if thinking about it. "Yeah, that's right. People only die when it gushes and don't stop. If you don't live though and drop dead from it, can the Simi eat you? Akri says the Simi can't eat no living people, but he never said no about them newly dead people. Maybe that's why he don't let me near them fresh dead. But—"

"What are you talking about?" Nick interrupted her. "Are you for real?"

She blinked innocently. "What you mean?" Biting her lip, she looked at her hand. "The Simi's not turning invisible again, is she? Ooo, that would be bad. I promised akri I wouldn't do that no more in public places. But sometimes the Simi can't help it. Kind of like putting barbecue sauce on salads. It's just mandatory and reflexive 'cause you gots to kill the taste of the ick rabbit food."

Nick stepped away from her. She was nuts with a capital N. Was there any female left in New Orleans under the age of twenty who hadn't lost her mind?

Kody . . .

Yeah, he definitely needed a Kody shot right about now.

He cleared his throat as he looked at Simi. "No, you're not turning invisible and I'm sure I'm late so I better get going. . . ."

She stepped in front of him to stop his leaving. "Did you hear that sound?"

"What sound?"

"Zombies! They're coming for us. Wheee! Yum!"

* * *

Ian St. James was alone in his big brother Madaug's room. He wasn't supposed to be in here. Ever. Under penalty of severe mutilation and much shouting by their parents. But Madaug always had the coolest games, which he refused to share with his little brother.

The big poop head.

What he doesn't know won't get my arm frogged. . . . Yeah, Madaug had run out the door hours ago and he didn't seem to be coming back anytime soon. Which gave Ian plenty of time to sneak on Madaug's computer and play his brother's latest creation: Pokémon Death Trap Fever. His brother had taken all the characters from Pokémon and merged them with the ones from Mortal Kombat. Like Charizard now had acid spit and could rip the spine out of other characters while laughing at them. It was a bloodbath death match that would leave their mother fainting if she ever knew.

But what she didn't know wouldn't get Ian grounded.

Grinning, he booted up, then cringed at Madaug's

stinky manga wallpaper that bordered on hentai . . . another thing their mother would die over. The cartoon girl had so little clothing on she might as well be naked. And the way she had her leg lifted up, kicking . . . he gagged.

Ew!

"I just don't get it." Ian put his hand up to block the view of the girl as he went into the menu to find the games. His brother kept telling him that he'd get it in a few years, along with hair in weird places and body odor. Honestly, Ian liked being ten and had no desire to grow up and smell, especially if it meant smelling like Madaug.

He shivered at the thought as he read through the games. He paused as one in particular caught his eye.

"Zombie Hunter?"

Madaug hadn't told him about this one. Oooo, it sounded good. Double clicking on it, he waited for it to load. Rubbing his hands together, he giggled, knowing he was getting away with something that would really anger his brother if Madaug ever found out about it.

And Ian loved getting away with things he wasn't supposed to be in.

Suddenly, he heard a sound outside the door.

Ian jumped, terrified it was Madaug coming in to discover him in his room on his computer. *I'm dead. I'm dead. I'm dead.* His brother would beat him until he screamed like a girl.

Killing the power to the computer, he shot from the desk. His heart hammering, he went to the door and opened it.

It wasn't Madaug.

It was some tall and scary guy he'd never seen before. His eyes were bloodshot and swollen as he glared down at Ian. "Brains," he growled.

Ian rolled his eyes. Puh-lease. What was it with teenagers that they thought something that stupid would intimidate the big kids? "I'm not a baby. You can't scare me with that stuff." He lifted his chin defiantly.

Until the guy grabbed him and bit him in the shoulder.

Screaming out, Ian did what his mom had always

told him to do whenever a guy, not one of his brothers, grabbed him. He hit him in the nuts as hard as he could.

The zombie staggered back, but he was still in the doorway, blocking him from leaving.

Panic swelled as Ian's lips trembled. *I'm so sorry I'm in your room, Madaug. I'll never come into it again unless you tell me to. I swear. . . .*

That was, as long as the zombie didn't eat his brains.

Ian ran to Madaug's desk, looking for a weapon. Dang it, his geekified brother didn't even have a trophy to bash the zombie in the head with. All he had was a half-eaten ham sandwich, a Yoda bobblehead, an empty can of Dr Pepper, potato chip crumbs, a greasy two-day-old pizza box, a bunch of CDs, and a glasses case. All of that was worthless.

Think, Ian, think. . . .

The zombie grabbed him again.

Ian picked up the only thing he could reach.

A pencil.

Not just for doing homework. . . . They were good for all kinds of things. Resetting his Nintendo, undoing knots in his shoes, getting stuff out from under his fingernails, drawing on the wall. . . .

And stabbing zombies.

"Iiiiyaaa!" he shouted as he stabbed it into the zombie's arm as hard as he could.

The zombie screamed.

Like a frightened jackrabbit, Ian squatted between his legs and ran for the stairs. "Mom!" he called as he scrambled for safety. Luckily, he was used to running for his life from his two older brothers whose tempers and kill-the-little-brother mind-sets made the zombie look like a girl.

"Mom!" he yelled again as he entered the kitchen and rounded the island where she stood, making dinner. "Help! A zombie's after me!"

She let out a frustrated breath as he grabbed her about the waist. "What in the world is wrong with you, Boo?"

Ian tried to explain but before he could get more than a handful of words out, the zombie was in the kitchen, glaring at him.

The pencil was still protruding from his forearm as he growled.

Ian's mom scowled at the teenager. "Danny? What are you doing here? How did you get into the house? I didn't hear the door."

"He's trying to eat our brains, Mom."

She tsked down at him. "Ian, don't be ridiculous. Danny goes to church with us. Don't you know him?"

"No." He would remember if he'd ever seen a zombie at church. The limping and groaning tended to stand out.

His mom turned back to Danny. "Are you here for a donation? I heard your youth group was—"

Danny grabbed Ian's mom and bit her on the head.

She screamed.

"Don't you hurt my mama!" Ian ran at him with the whole of his weight, driving him back a few steps and causing him to let go of his mom. Ian clamped down on Danny's leg and bit him until he tasted blood.

No one attacks my mama!

Danny cried like a baby while Ian's mom picked up the pan where she'd been making biscuits.

She bashed Danny's head repeatedly with the pan, forcing him away from them. "Get behind me, Ian."

For once, Ian did as she told him.

She backed away from Danny, toward the front door.

Ian was feeling pretty good about their escape until he turned around.

There were more zombies on the front porch and they all looked hungry. . . .

Caleb's heart skipped a beat as he flew in as a raven and saw Nick and some unknown female completely surrounded by zombies while trying to fight them off.

Malachai's going to kill me. . . .

Because from his vantage point, it looked like the zombies were getting the better of them. Nick was covered in blood from various bite wounds while the female seemed to be doing a better job at keeping them off her.

Summoning his powers, Caleb sent a mental wave to the zombies to disperse them.

They didn't listen. If anything, it made them even more aggressive against Nick.

"What the crap?"

As a demon, one of their first learned powers was to be able to control the dead. It was the lesson Nick was supposed to be learning right now.

But Caleb's powers were useless against the zombies.

How could this be? It didn't make sense. Not that it had to make sense to thoroughly tick him off.

And then he realized why he couldn't control them.

They weren't dead. These zombies had been made from the living. The living he could possess or influence, but he couldn't control them without their cooperation.

Growling in frustration, Caleb flew toward the street, into the shadows, where he took human form. The demon in him wanted to blast the zombies into oblivion. But that would blow his cover and he'd already learned the hard way three years ago that his powers didn't work on Nick.

If he exposed his powers and Nick saw them, there was no way to undo it. He'd be screwed and Nick would never trust him again. Of course, he could try the clumsy and inexact human method of memory loss by bashing Nick on the head. . . .

It might work.

Or it might give him a concussion.

Worse, it might kill him.

And since Caleb's survival hinged on his . . . best not to chance it.

So instead, he rushed into the alley to help them, then drew up fast as he realized the girl with Nick wasn't a girl after all. She was a demon, too.

A Charonte demon, to be precise.

Oh Düsseldorf, this was getting complicated. He shielded his powers immediately. The problem with the Charonte, they were highly territorial and didn't tolerate other demons in their domain. Ever. To them, if you weren't Charonte, you were garbage, and all garbage should be eaten. Literally. Slowly and with relish—or, more often than not, with barbecue sauce.

Since the Charonte were one of the most powerful branches of demon, it served him best to stay off her radar.

And menu.

But why she was with Nick and not attacking him, he had no idea. Charonte didn't normally associate with anyone unless, as previously noted, they were on the menu.

"Nick!" Caleb shouted as one of the zombies went for Nick's neck. "Behind you!"

Nick turned around as he heard Caleb's shout to see Brett Guidry, one of his classmates, coming at his back. Grateful Caleb had returned, he indicated Brett with his chin. "We've got to get these guys to Bubba's. Anyone got a clue how to do it?"

Simi looked at him. "They gotta be breathing?"

"Yes," Nick and Caleb said in unison.

"Well, pooh." Simi poked her lips out. "That just takes all the fun out of it." She let out a dramatic sigh.

SHERRILYN KENYON

Nick was overwhelmed by the herculean task. How did three high school students get a dozen zombies to Bubba's store without getting eaten?

Why didn't I stay home?

Look on the bright side. . . .

Trouble was, he didn't see a bright side.

I knew I should have taken up lumberjackery and not the one where you shoot snot out your nose or the other one he didn't want to think about while fighting. 'Cause face it, both of those would be worthless right about now. Rather lumberjackery where you break Army of Darkness with a chainsaw all over the Deadites and send them into oblivion.

Or at least send them out of his sight.

The zombies closed in. Nick braced himself for more hand-to-hand (literally, in his case) fighting.

Suddenly, Simi grabbed him and Caleb by their hands and ran with them to the corner. She hesitated under the street sign. "Where's Bubba's?"

Nick pointed down the street toward the store.

"Okay." Simi released their hands. "You boys run on and I'll get them there right behind you."

Nick shook his head as all the lessons his mom had taught him roared to the forefront. "That's not right. I'm not about to leave a girl to be eaten by crazies."

Caleb looked over his shoulder to where the zombies were closing in fast. "Folks, we stand here arguing and we're going to die." He grabbed Nick and pulled him forward. "Let her be the bait. We need to get the doors open."

Nick would have fought him too, but Caleb's grip was too fierce, leaving him no choice except to follow or lose his other arm.

They only got half a block before two more zombies stepped out of the darkness to attack them.

Nick cursed as he pulled up short and kicked the first one back into the alley. "How many of these are there?"

Caleb shook his head. "I'm beginning to wonder if Madaug didn't license the game to Sony or something. Where are all of them coming from? Raccoon City Cloning Farm? What is going on here?"

Nick stepped back to avoid being bitten. "We're about to get our butts kicked. That's what's going on."

He scissor-kicked the zombie closest to him. Then he looked to see Simi leading the others closer. "I'm beginning to feel like Jim Bowie at the Alamo."

Caleb knocked the zombie in front of him back. "Yeah, but we're not going to die."

I wish I could be so sure of that. 'Cause right now, things were not looking good for him and if he was a betting man, he'd be betting on the zombies.

Even so, Nick pushed his fear and panic down and kept moving toward the store, drawing the zombies along behind him while he continued to beat them off. Gah, if one more of them touched his wounded shoulder, he was going to forget the ban on killing them and go hog wild—chainsaw or not. "I really don't like being the dangling carrot."

"Better than being the dead duck." Caleb smacked the zombie closest to him.

He had a good point with that.

Nick was the first one to reach the store. He opened the door and called for Bubba, Madaug, and Mark. "We got a group coming in. You might want to widen that room and be ready to lock it tight."

But getting them into the store was hard enough. Into the room . . .

Where were the X-Men when you really needed them?

Nick grabbed the cattle prod that Bubba kept hanging on the wall behind the counter . . . again for those "just in case" moments. He was beginning to not only understand Bubba's paranoia, but be grateful for it.

Bubba was right. You never knew when these things could come in handy. It did pay to keep a cattle prod and ax on hand. The necessity of the rocket launcher and blasting caps remained to be seen.

At least the cattle prod would make it easier to corral them. But the moment Nick touched the prod to the zombie closest to him, Brett, he realized Mark and Bubba had made some serious modifications to the voltage. This wasn't a typical cattle prod to move people along. This one was meant to stun and stun hard. The jolt was so severe, it drove the zombie to the floor like a million-volt stun gun.

"What the . . . ?" Nick gaped at Bubba, who grinned in all his unabashed glory.

"Neighbors don't complain when I shock people, only when I shoot them."

Mark agreed. "But the downside is it's a pain to drag them out of the store, and if you leave them in here, when they can move again, they're usually pretty pissed and looking for blood."

Madaug, Caleb, and Simi continued to try and beat the zombies into the holding cell.

Nick zapped another zombie that was going for Simi. It was actually kind of fun. He'd touch them with the prod. They'd scream and then flop to the ground like dying fish. Made him wonder what would happen if they were wet, but he wasn't sadistic enough to test that curiosity. Lucky for them.

He shocked another one who went for his head and sent the zombie flailing. A guy could get used to this, especially if he didn't go to jail for it.

By the time Nick had stunned the last one and Bubba and Mark were dragging the first one into the room, they made a "shocking" discovery.

As the voltage wore off, the zombies returned to normal.

"Get your hands off me!" Brett snarled as he shoved Bubba back. "My dad's a lawyer and I'm going to sue you for offensive touching."

Bubba arched a brow. "You might wanna rethink that, boy. 'Cause if I'm going to get sued for offensively touching you, I'm going to make it worth my while. Think about it."

Brett's face paled. He looked around the store as if he was waking up from a nightmare. "How did I get here?"

Nick angled the cattle prod at him, still not trusting that he was completely normal. He'd seen that movie too many times where the idiots think the monster's gotten over whatever had it possessed, only to turn back into the monster and kill them the instant they let down their guard. No way. He wasn't about to become intelligent-zombie kibble. "You were trying to eat my brains, you psycho."

Brett gaped at him. "What?"

Caleb nodded. "It's true, dude. You went for Gautier's throat, and mine too."

Madaug took the prod from Nick so that he could

examine the prongs on the end of it. "Wow, Nick. You found the cure. That's how we fix it."

"Electrocution?" Nick tried not to smile as he thought about seriously zapping Stone.

Madaug nodded. "The voltage works on the central nervous system. . . . I'm thinking it works like a power surge that causes the programming to dump and essentially reboot to the original that existed before they played my game. It reverses everything. Nick! You're a friggin' genius."

Nick rested the cattle prod up on his good shoulder. "Well, someone slap my butt and give me a hero cookie."

Simi stepped forward and slapped him on the right cheek.

"Hey!" Nick snapped, rubbing his offended buttocks.

She blinked innocently. "You told me to. Or would you rather have had one of them men slap your butt instead?"

Nick was horrified by the mere suggestion. "If someone is touching that part of me, I'd much rather it be you than one of them." Or better yet, Kody.

"Us too," the guys said quickly.

As they stood there, one by one the zombies came out of it. All of them were disoriented and baffled by what had happened to them.

And none of the twelve guys on the floor remembered having played Madaug's game.

None of them.

Nick scowled at Madaug. "You think when I shocked them that it caused some kind of memory loss?" Which really worried him since he had a memory lapse himself about how he'd gotten in that courtyard at the Lalaurée mansion. Had he been a zombie and not known it?

Please don't let me have eaten any brains.

That was the only thing he knew that could make his mom's powdered eggs taste good.

Madaug scratched his chin as he thought about it. "I don't know. We need a case study."

Bubba paused and turned toward him. "Case study how?"

"We have to get to Brian, shock him, and see," Madaug said. "It's the only way to know for sure since he's the only one I know for a fact was turned into a zombie after playing my game."

Not to be one to ever interject logic into anything, Nick laughed nervously. "You do know he's in jail, right? And that the police tend to get a little perturbed at people who show up there with cattle prods and stun guns. I'm just saying."

Simi jumped up and down. "We could get the police to shoot him for us!"

Mark scoffed. "Our luck, they'd shoot him with a real gun and kill him. Then we'd learn nothing."

Like that was the worst fear they had at the moment. . . .

Yeah.

Madaug didn't relent. "We've got to either get him out or we get in to see him and stun him. Otherwise we don't really know if this is going to work. It could be temporary and they could turn right back into zombies. Think about it."

Nick was thinking about it. He was thinking of spending the rest of his life in jail, provided his mother didn't kill him first. "I don't guess any of you former zombies would like to go into the holding cell until we sort this out?"

Brett seized him by the shirt. "I don't know what game you and geek boy are playing, Gautier. But you get in my way as I leave and I'll wipe my boots on your balls."

Nick cringed involuntarily at a threat that went down his spine like a shredder.

Before he realized what was happening, Simi had taken Brett's hand and squeezed it so hard Nick heard the bones break.

Brett cried out.

Simi held his hand in hers without letting up. "Nick is a friend of the Simi's. You threaten him and you make the Simi really unhappy and want to eat your head. Trust me, not something you want me to think about. Now go away mean person or the Simi will tell akri she don't know what happened to you and your masticated form. Not that I like to lie, but there are deceptions to every rule. And you're about to become one." She shoved him back toward the room. "Now get in there and be quiet."

By their faces, it was obvious none of them wanted to obey. But none of them had the backbone to stand up to Simi.

Bubba grinned. "I like your friend, Nick. She doesn't mince words, does she?"

"Not really." But then some of the words she didn't mince really didn't make sense, and who the heck was this akri she kept mentioning? He must be some serious badass to corral her.

Mark locked the hidden door and shut the wall so that no one entering the store could see their new prisoners.

Caleb frowned. "What if they start calling for help?"

"Won't do them any good," Bubba said. "It's sound-proof and made with enough metal that no cell phones will go through neither. They're there until we let them out."

Mark let out a nervous laugh. "Then let's not get killed and starve them to death."

Nick stared at him. "Mark, there are many, many reasons I don't want to get killed doing this other than just starving the ex-zombie hostages." He looked over to Madaug. "Or go to jail. I cannot stress enough how badly I do not want to go to jail and how badly I do not want to die."

But he had a bad feeling that they were all about to head to one of those places or the other.

CHAPTER 13

"Nick?" Mark called through the door as Nick was coming out of the shower. "It's your mom on the phone and she's hotter than Angelina Jolie lying in a bikini on the equator, covered in mud. . . . Not that I'm saying your mom is good-looking, not that she isn't, but I don't ever fantasize about your mom 'cause that would just be wrong to do to a guy—not that your mom isn't fantasy worthy . . . but— Ah, hell, all that sounded better in my head. My point is, she's angry. Just take the phone before she scalds my ears some more."

Nick paused. That was an interesting tirade and made him wonder about Mark's daydreams—Wait,

never mind. Knowing Mark, those had to be terrifying. Heck, he was lucky Mark's dream girl wasn't
zombified.

He opened the door only enough to reach through
it to get the phone from Mark before he put it up
to his ear and braced himself for her anger. "Hey,
Mom."

"What are you doing?" Yeah, she was totally upset
at him. That hot tone could melt polar ice caps. She
was yelling so loud, he pulled the phone about three
inches from his ear and still heard her perfectly. "Boy,
where are you? Do you have any idea what time it
is? You are so grounded when I see you, which, for
your information, had better be soon, as in right now.
If you're not walking through the door, which you're
not, you're busted. You understand? Nick? Are you
listening to me? What do you have to say for yourself? Huh, young man?"

He honestly didn't know what to say that wouldn't
make her twice as mad, which was not his goal right
now. The name of the game . . . survival.

I value my freedom, but I see severe restriction ahead.
Too bad there weren't lawyers out there willing to

represent kids with their parents. "Which question do you want me to answer first?"

"Don't you get smart with me, Nicholas Gautier. I'm too mad at you right now to take it."

He had to clamp down on his own temper. If he'd learned anything in his life, it was that his mom didn't react well to direct conflict. A nice, contrite Nicky was often one who avoided being grounded even when he deserved it. "I'm sorry, Mom. I'm not trying to be smart." He was trying to get her to stop screaming at him. "I got covered in—" He paused before he said the word "blood." That would flip her out even more. "—goo during the class." A small lie, but what she didn't know wouldn't give her a heart attack and him a restriction that lasted until he was bald and middle-aged. "I—um, I wanted to take a bath at Bubba's before I headed back and got goo all over the club, which might get you into trouble." Not to mention the sight of his bloody clothes would have panicked her into calling the police, and the last thing Bubba needed was another arrest on his record. "I should have called and let you know first.

I'm really sorry. I guess I spent more time in the shower than I meant to. Did you know Bubba has one of them steam things that comes down from the ceiling? You should see this bathroom, Mom. It's the coolest awesome ever."

She refused to let him distract her. "Are you all right?"

"Yes, ma'am." A little show of respect always went a long way in soothing her.

She sighed. "Then I guess there's no harm. But you did scare me, Nick. I just want you to know that."

"Sorry, Ma. By the way, Bubba said he'd walk me over to the club."

"That's mighty nice of him." Her voice was finally back to normal and not the I-want-your-butt-on-a-platter tone it'd been a few minutes ago. "Tell him I said thanks."

"I will. Is it okay if we stop for something to eat too?"

Her tone turned sharp again like she was accusing him of something. "I thought you ate at Mr. Hunter's?"

"I did. But I'm hungry again."

"Oh." She went from angry to calm so fast that he wondered if she wasn't the Ferrari of moms. Her top speed had to be .65 nanoseconds. Maybe less. "You must be growing again. You want to come get some money?"

"Nah, Mr. Hunter gave me some earlier."

"Why?" Boom! Her anger returned. Granted it was tinged with something he thought might be fear or suspicion, but the primary tone was definitely anger.

"Taxi money in case I needed it to get to work or home. He didn't want me on the streetcar after dark 'cause he said he didn't want me to get hurt." Which, when combined with what Mr. Poitiers had given him, was close to a hundred bucks. They kept this up and he might actually start making some progress on his ever-pathetic college fund.

"I don't know what I think about that, Nick."

What was there to think about? From his point of view if they were willing to throw money at him and he didn't have to do anything for it, he was more than willing to take it. "Well, while you figure that out, can I eat?"

She made a sound of aggravation. "I swear you're the lippiest child on the planet. Yes, Nicky, grab something to eat and I'll see you within the hour or I will come and get you myself. Do you understand? And you will be a very sorry young man if I do."

"Yes, ma'am."

"I love you, baby." Must be some mutant form of maternal bipolar disorder. There was no other explanation for the frightening mood swings.

"I love you, too, Mom, and I really am sorry I worried you."

"It's all right. It's what you're best at anyway. Remember to eat some vegetables, and neither french fries nor ketchup count."

"Yes, ma'am." Nick hung up the phone and dressed in his jeans and the Triple B BIG BALLS AND BRAINS T-shirt Bubba had loaned him. The best part of it was Bubba's logo on the back that featured a photo of Bubba holding a shotgun over his shoulder as he leaned up against an oversized computer that had smoke coming out of the top of it and a bunch of bullet holes in the monitor. It read:

Computer Problems?
Dial 1-888-Ca-Bubba
If I can't take care of your problems one way . . .
I'll take care of them anotha'

And in small print under it, it read: *We tend all manner of ills for you. Zombies, rodents, and vampires. If you got a pest, we got a cure. Just call us now. We will believe you.*

Yeah, Bubba really wasn't right in the head, but Nick loved the commercials he and Mark filmed for the store. They were hilarious. And always ended with that slogan. "Ca' Bubba."

Sad thing was, he knew for a fact that Bubba had used a few people's computers for target practice, and he didn't want to think about Mark and the anti-zombie duck urine.

Shaking his head, he toweled off his hair and went downstairs to where Bubba, Mark, Simi, Caleb, and Madaug were discussing the great jailbreak.

They are so going to get me arrested and my mom will kill me for it.

Simi pointed to the schematic Bubba had produced from memory of what he liked to call the numerous "unfortunate incarcerations" he'd had at the parish lockup. "See, now the Simi can napalm that and—"

"That might kill them, Simi," Nick pointed out.

She looked up innocently. "Your point?"

Nick was too stunned to answer her honest question.

So Madaug answered for him. "We need Brian alive to test him."

"Well, poo." Simi crossed her arms over her chest and pouted. "You just take all the fun out of it then. You sure you don't know my akri?"

They ignored her.

Caleb leaned back in his chair to study them. "Can't a lawyer get in to see him?"

Bubba nodded as he studied his diagram. "Well, yeah, but a lawyer ain't going to spring him."

Caleb smirked. "Depends on the lawyer."

Bubba looked up with a scowl. "How you mean?"

Caleb's eyes gleamed like a demon eyeing evil. "I know one who owes me a favor."

"You know a lawyer?" Bubba's voice was filled with disbelief.

Caleb rubbed his hands down his shirt. "Hey, beneath these . . . well, they're basically crappy clothes." Nick frowned at his choice of words. Only Caleb would consider his nice designer shirt and jeans crappy. "But beneath them beats the heart of someone who knows the right people willing to sometimes do the wrong thing for the right price."

Bubba wasn't completely sold on it and neither was Nick. "Yeah, but we need to do this before anyone else gets killed. We have to know if this is a cure."

Caleb pulled out his cell phone. "Can be arranged. Trust me."

Nick wasn't any more willing to buy into this than Bubba was. Not to mention, there was one really important, as yet unaddressed factor. "How much is this going to cost us?"

Caleb held his hand up. "Hi. This is Malphas calling to talk to Virgil Ward. Is he in?" He gave them a crap-eating grin as he waited.

Nick could hear the tone of a deep voice on the line, but he couldn't make out the words.

"Hey, Virg. Long time." Caleb laughed at something Virgil must have said. "No, it's nothing like that. We rather have a situation where we need to get *in*to jail, not have you get us out."

He paused again to listen. "Yeah, I agree. Stupid is my middle name, you know that. I'm pretty sure you're the one who gave it to me. So can you help a brother out?" He rolled his eyes. "No, you can't have my soul for it. *I* don't even have my soul. Yeah, I know you're a bloodsucking attorney, but you're going to have to placate yourself with money like the rest of the mundanes."

Nick passed a scowl to Mark, Bubba, and Madaug, who looked as puzzled as he felt. Caleb was definitely an odd duck.

"Is that really what you want as payment?" he flashed another grin at them. "Done. Can you meet us outside the jail in about twenty minutes? Yeah, we'll see you then. Thanks, bud, and yes, I'm well aware of the fact that I owe you." Hanging up the phone, he winked at them. "Let's go stun us a zombie."

Nick couldn't believe Caleb had accomplished it so fast. "I'm impressed."

"Don't be. One of you guys is going to have to feed the vampiric lawyer some blood and it can't be me."

Nick rolled his eyes at Caleb's bizarre humor. "Why? You afraid of a little bite?"

Caleb laughed. "I'm anemic."

"And I'm Catholic. Doesn't that knock me out of the running?"

Caleb shook his head at Nick.

"The Simi gots some barbecue sauce in her bag. It kind of looks like blood if you squint at it the right way. And it don't coagulate between your teeth like blood or give you them funky burps, not to mention it tastes a lot better too. Especially over that type A stuff. Bleh! I'd rather eat my shoes. But that

O-flavored blood . . . yum!" She straightened and held one finger up in a gesture that strangely reminded him of Smokey the Bear. "And just remember, kids, three out of four demons all prefer barbecue sauce over hemoglobin."

"Oookay." Bubba stepped away from her, which said something. When Bubba repudiated you, you knew you were the poster child for weird. "On that note . . . I guess we need to get into the truck."

Grabbing his keys and the cattle prod, Bubba led them outside to his giant dark green Armada, which he said he'd bought because it was one of the few things large enough to haul all of his zombie-killing gear.

And it was great for tailgate parties.

Nick cast a doubtful glance at the cattle prod before he got into the back of the truck while the others piled in. "So, out of curiosity . . . any ideas on how we're going to get a three-foot cattle prod smuggled into jail?"

Caleb buckled himself in. "That's why we need Virgil. He can smuggle in anything."

"You think a lot of him, don't you?"

SHERRILYN KENYON

Caleb shrugged. "I've known him a long time and have seen him do things that would put hair on your chest."

"Yeah, like what?"

Caleb refused to elaborate.

Bubba got in and drove over to the Orleans Parish intake and lockup. Nick fell quiet as old memories surged of the handful of times he'd visited his dad—not here, but prison, which was basically the same thing.

"You keep that brat away from me, Cherise. I don't even want to look at his ugly face. Don't bring him up here anymore to see me."

Love you, too, Dad.

Nick still had no idea how his beautiful, kind mother had hooked up with such a monster. It didn't make any sense. She'd told him once that she liked bad boys. But there was a difference between a guy like him who had attitude and a guy like his dad who had mental damage.

Why did women and girls find psychos so desirable? Even at his school, it was the vicious loons like

318

Stone who got all the girls while nice guys like him only got the finger when he asked them out. He'd never understand it.

Of course, in his case, his mother's insistence on him wearing these foully ugly shirts didn't help.

Whatever.

He just hoped that with his DNA linking him to the psycho killer that he never ended up inside something like this. That was the one promise he'd made to his mother he never wanted to break.

Bubba pulled around back and parked under a streetlight. "What now?" he asked Caleb.

"We wait on Virgil."

"How will he know which car's ours?" Mark asked.

Before Caleb could answer, someone knocked on the window next to Bubba. Bubba jumped a foot in panic. "What the hell?"

Caleb inclined his head to the . . .

Nick scowled as his gaze focused on his friend.

Virgil looked nothing like what he'd expected. A little over six feet tall, he couldn't be any older than sixteen or seventeen. Even though he was in a suit and dressed like an attorney, he looked like a teenager going to a funeral.

Surely he wasn't a real lawyer. . . .

Was he?

And as Nick watched him, something odd happened. Virgil suddenly looked older. Like he was in his late twenties. Nick looked around the truck, but no one else seemed to notice.

Caleb opened his door and got out to talk to him. "Hey, Virg."

Virgil eyeballed them while they stayed in the car. There was an insidious air about him . . . but that could just be the evil lawyer funk. "What exactly do you need me to do?"

Caleb glanced at Nick before he answered. "You know the kid who tried to eat his classmate this morning at St. Richard's?"

"Yeah?"

"We need you to shock him with a cattle prod and tell us what happens."

Keeping his lips closed, Virgil laughed—until he

realized Caleb wasn't joking. He sobered instantly. "Why?"

"We think we have a cure for his zombie programming."

Virgil's face went through a myriad of emotions. Astonishment, puzzlement, and finally an expression that said he thought they were all short a few monkeys in their cage. "You're out of your mind, aren't you?"

"No, seriously. The kid who programmed the game that turned him into a zombie is in the car." Caleb pointed at Madaug, who waved at Virgil.

Virgil frowned at Caleb. "It's a program that turned him? Not magick?"

"Nope, not magick."

"Too bad. There are a lot of people out there who would've killed for a potion. I could have made you rich."

Caleb shrugged. "They'll have to find another way to make living zombies. In the meantime, we want to make sure that the ones we've turned back to human actually had direct contact with the game.

The only one the kid knows played it for sure is the one sitting in jail right now. We gotta make sure this works." He passed the cattle prod to Virgil. "Warning, don't touch yourself with it. It's not low voltage like it's supposed to be. Bubba rigged it so that it actually lets loose over a million volts."

"All right," Virgil said slowly. "Let me make sure I have this straight. . . . The award-winning plan of intelligence that all ye brainiacs came up with is that I take an illegal, modified cattle prod into parish lockup, past the people armed with guns who are trained to kill, find a kid who's waiting to be arraigned for an attempted murder trial, and shock him until he turns normal again. Anything else?"

"Nope. That'll do it."

Virgil let out a slow breath as he eyed the cattle prod with a doubtful stare. "You seriously owe me."

"I know."

Without another word, Virgil headed for the front of the building.

Nick was dying to see this miracle up close and personal. "Hey, Bubba? Can you unlock the door? I need a rest stop."

"Sure."

Nick slid out of the SUV and made his way to the building to scope things out. Inside it, there were cops everywhere. No duh. Right? But what stood out most was the metal detectors. There was no way Virgil was going to get through all that without getting shot.

This ought to be entertaining.

Nick had just got into position when Virgil waltzed in like he owned the place. Several officers greeted him and acted as if they didn't see the cattle prod at all. In fact, Virgil fed it through the belt scanner before he walked through the upright one—all the while talking to the officers.

He was putting his shoes on when the cattle prod came out. One of the officers picked it up and held it out to Virgil.

"Don't forget your umbrella, Mr. Ward."

"Thanks, Cabal. I know it's not supposed to rain, but I believe in always being prepared."

"I hear you. Especially here in N'awlins. You never know when a downpour's going to hit. As I always say, you don't like the weather? Wait a minute."

SHERRILYN KENYON

Laughing, Virgil took the cattle prod and headed for the hallway.

Nick was aghast as Virgil disappeared from his sight without anyone saying anything about his weapon.

You know, if I did that, they'd body slam me down and shoot me in the head for good measure.

Stunned by what he'd seen, Nick made his way back to the SUV where the others were waiting.

Bubba arched a brow at him. "That was quick."

Nick buckled himself into his seat. "I mostly wanted to see if Virgil made it past security."

Caleb looked smug, but didn't say anything.

"And?" Mark asked.

"Don't ask me how, but he did. They didn't even see it. It was like the cattle prod was invisible or something."

Bubba frowned. "How?"

Simi let out a peeved huff. "He's a vampire, demon, human people. Jeez, didn't any of you notice?"

Mark scoffed, "Most lawyers are. Ain't never met one yet what wasn't a bloodsucker or a soulsucker. Of course, in my case, they're *all* money suckers."

Caleb's phone started ringing. He picked it up

and answered it. "Yeah?" He listened for a second, then said, "Wait. I'm putting you on speaker." He switched it on. "Now repeat what you just told me."

"What the hell's in this cattle prod? I about launched the kid through the wall."

Caleb snorted. "Not that part, Virgil. Move on."

"Okay, I shocked him and now's he's squalling like a girl, wanting his mommy. He says he has no idea of how he got here. I asked him about biting the kid and he has no idea what I'm talking about. Best of all, he's no longer trying to eat my brains, which have to be missing for me to agree to this. So to answer your experiment, I think it works."

Bubba looked skeptical. "Can we trust his report?"

"You do know I can hear you, right?" Virgil's tone was irritated.

"Yeah," Bubba drawled, "and I repeat, can we trust you?"

"Well, since I don't have a dog in this fight, yeah. Why would I lie? Not that I'm not beyond those ethics. I fully believe in whatever lie will set me free. But in this case, I'm being honest. The kid's now clean. Listen for yourself. . . ."

"I want to go home. Why am I here? I don't understand what happened. . . ."

Caleb turned the speaker off. "Thanks, Virgil. I'll get the payment to you later." He paused, then looked at Mark and Bubba. "You guys need your cattle prod back?"

"Absolutely," Mark said. "We got some people to shock."

Caleb nodded, then spoke into the phone. "If you don't mind, please bring it back to us."

Virgil appeared before he could hang up the phone.

This time, Nick was the one who jumped as Bubba got out to return the cattle prod to the back of the SUV.

Virgil eyed Nick closely as he studied him through the truck window. "Don't I know you?"

Nick shook his head as a strange chill went over his body that made his skin crawl. Virgil definitely wasn't what he seemed. "I don't think so."

Caleb cleared his throat.

Virgil glanced over at him and something strange passed between them. When he turned his attention back to Nick, his look was guarded and cold. "Nice to meet you, Nick."

"How do you know my name?"

Virgil didn't answer. "I better get back. I have night court in an hour and don't want to miss it. My first case is a doozie: Some guy beat up another on Bourbon with a hot dog before he tried to kill his victim by drowning him in a puddle." He literally vanished.

Bubba turned around in the seat to stare at Caleb. "Interesting friend you got there."

"You have no idea."

Mark scratched at his ear. "We need to let Tabitha and crew know how to fight them."

Madaug fished his phone out and pressed the auto dial for his brother. "I'm on it."

Bubba pulled out of the parking space and headed back to the store. "All right, we have half the equation. We know we can turn them human again. But the question is, how are so many getting their hands on the game?"

Mark shook his head. "Someone else has to be disseminating it."

Nick scowled at the unfamiliar word. "Dis-a what?"

"Disseminating," Mark repeated. "It means distributing it."

"Then why didn't you say that?"

Mark looked at Bubba. "Remind me to get him a word-of-the-day calendar." Then he pinned Nick with a shaming stare over the back of the seat. "You need to up your vocabulary, boy. You can't walk around letting people think you're stupid. Expand your horizons. Besides, it's fun to call people names they have to look up to realize they've been insulted."

Bubba laughed. "Yeah, that's a twofer there. You get away with it and then they're twice as mad when they realize how bad you really insulted them. Especially if they mistake it for a compliment when you say it and thank you for it."

"And," Caleb jumped in, "those insults keep you from getting grounded by your mom."

You know, they all had very valid points.

"And best of all, it'll help you with your SATs," Madaug said as he hung up the phone—*he* would think of that. He looked at Mark. "Eric and the zoo crew are heading to the store for supplies. Do y'all have enough stun guns for them?"

Bubba bristled as if Madaug had insulted him. "Does a bear defecate rurally? What kind of question is that for someone who owns the biggest gun store in town? Of course I got plenty. I got enough Tasers to light up New York City *and* Boston just for giggles."

Good, 'cause Nick had a feeling they might be needing them.

Ambrose grabbed the bookcase and slammed it to the ground, spilling the ancient books he'd carefully collected for centuries across the floor of his stygian office. It probably destroyed a few of them, but at this point, he really didn't care. Rage burned through him with the power of a thousand suns so raw and potent that he could taste it.

"Why can't I stop it?" he snarled. Why, with all the powers he'd mastered, all the elements he controlled, couldn't he prevent a mere fourteen-year-old boy from being an idiot? No matter what he did, certain events kept unfolding.

And he wanted blood.

He felt a calm, soothing hand on his cheek, covering his bow-and-arrow mark that she'd given him during a time so long ago he should have no memory of it. Yet it was forever carved deep in his mind. More beautiful than any other, Artemis, goddess of the hunt, put all women to shame. Her long red hair flowed to her tiny waist, which was accentuated by the white Grecian gown she wore. "Shhh . . . You shouldn't work yourself up to such a frizzy."

His anger tripled. "The word is frenzy," he corrected. Because of the differences between the English he spoke and her native ancient Greek, she constantly screwed up sayings and colloquialisms.

"What are you doing here, Artemis?" he demanded.

"I'm trying to calm you down, love. You shouldn't do this to yourself. It pains me to see you suffer like this."

And that dark power inside him wanted to strike out at her and make her beg for his mercy. It was an all-demanding power that was getting harder and harder to fight.

Soon there would be no way back from it. It would consume him and he would become his father. A mindless killing machine that lacked all compassion and humanity. A machine that wanted to end everything.

Kill everyone.

Ambrose stared at the wall, where he saw himself as a boy. Nick Gautier had no idea how the random small decisions he was making right now would turn him into the beast Ambrose had become.

I have to save myself.

More than that, he had to save the ones he loved. Before it was too late.

But how?

God, how could I have been so stupid, even at fourteen?
It was so hard to look back and see the faces of his
friends and loved ones, especially since he knew what
would become of them if he didn't alter history. It cut
so deep that it alone was almost enough to make him
insane.

How do I stop it?

Ambrose turned to Artemis. He hated her. She,
like Acheron, had played a major role in turning him
into the Malachai.

No, Nick, you did that to yourself.

But it was so much easier to blame them. They had
made it so easy for him to make the wrong decisions.
Decisions he was now trying to unmake before he
lost the ability to care.

Sighing in frustration, he met Artemis's gaze. The
gaze of the woman who'd brought him back from the
dead and unleashed his powers. Powers he was now
trying to unlock earlier in his life. Had he possessed
some of them as a kid, he could have saved the ones
who were most important to him.

He could have saved his mom. . . .

Nick flinched as he forced that memory away and turned his thoughts to something he'd said to himself earlier. "Who is Nekoda?"

Artemis gave him a blank stare. "Never heard of him."

"*Her*, Artie. It's a girl."

One of her perfect brows shot up as jealousy darkened her green eyes. "What kind of girl?"

"I don't know. Nick knows her."

"*You are* Nick." Her tone was testy.

"Exactly. How can *I* not know who she is?" How could he not have seen her as he looked back? For some reason, she was a complete ghost to him. No matter what power he used, he couldn't find this piece of his past. Even with certain aspects altered, he should still be able to hone in on her.

Yet he couldn't.

Why?

Artemis shrugged her thin shoulders. "You forgot her. It happens. You were human . . . once."

But he wasn't human now. Now he was the type of creature he and Tabitha had once hunted and put down like a rabid animal. More than that, he was hungry.

Starving.

Artemis took a chance by being here with him. Every time he fed from her blood, he grew stronger and deadlier. It was getting harder and harder not to kill her with his powers and absorb her godhood.

Harder to not destroy everyone and everything.

I won't do it.

Yes, you will. In time. You can't change what you are. Fight all you want. In the end, you are what you were born to be and nothing will ever change that.

But he refused to believe it.

He stared at himself on the wall as the younger him innocently rode in the back of Bubba's SUV toward a destiny that had been carved in blood onto his heart. *C'mon, Nick, don't let us down. I need you to be strong, kid.*

Smart.

Most of all, he needed himself not to make the same mistakes. Some things, such as meeting Simi while he was young, were already changed.

But others . . .

He ground his teeth as he saw the future as clearly as he saw his past.

Karnarsas, the final battle where he would command his father's army, was coming. And when it did, if he didn't change the past, he would destroy the rest of the people he loved. . . .

All of them.

CHAPTER 14

Nick got out of the SUV in front of Bubba's store and checked the time on his cell phone. Ooo, he was cutting it close. *So much for food. . . .*

"Hey, guys? I need to be heading up to my mom's club before I get grounded." Again.

Mark, who was standing on the sidewalk, shot his head up in a gesture reminiscent of a spooked deer. "Hey, Bub? You catch a whiff of that?"

What? Had someone ripped one in the car?

Nick was just about to blame Caleb when Bubba froze. Two heartbeats later, he tossed keys at Nick. "Kids, get in the store. Now!"

He started to ask them what was up when he saw
something that left him stunned.

Zombies.

Not like the ones who were his converted classmates. These were the real thing. Flesh rotting. Bad
smelling. Limb losing. Eye jelly oozing . . .

Zombies.

And they were coming at them with speed a
puma would envy. Madaug let out a yelp as he ran
to the door. Nick and Caleb followed while Bubba
and Mark pulled out two baseball bats from under the seats of the SUV in an act that strangely
reminded him of Mary Poppins and her bag of
goodies.

Simi came out of the SUV and acted like she was
going to head for the zombies until Bubba caught her
arm.

"Get inside with the boys, Simi."

She actually pouted. Nick could tell she wanted to
argue, but with a curt nod, she ran to them.

Bubba cursed. "Tell me again why I put the flamethrower up in the store?" he asked Mark.

Mark hefted his bat over his shoulder. "I'm pretty sure the cops had something to do with that."

Bubba popped the first zombie to reach him in the head with his bat. "Well, the next time I decide to do something so stupid, remind me it's better to be in jail than dead."

"Hurry, Nick!" Madaug pushed up against him as Nick fumbled with the keys and lock.

Nick ground his teeth. It was hard to do this with only one hand. "I'm trying. Dang, Bubba. How many keys you got on this ring, anyway?" He'd already tried a dozen and not a one worked. He only had ten more to go.

"It's the one with the green rubber piece around it." Bubba knocked the head from the zombie closest to him. "Green." Strike two. "Rubber." Strike three. "Piece."

Caleb pulled the keys out of his hand so that he could open the door. "They're getting through, Nick. We gotta hurry."

"I knew I should have left that duck urine on!" Mark snapped. "That'll teach me to bathe when I know better."

Nick could feel the putrid breath of the zombies on his neck when he finally slung open the door and fell into the store. Simi ran inside, Madaug started in, then cried out as one of the zombies grabbed him and yanked him back toward the street.

Caleb had to force himself not to expose his powers and use them as he fought the zombies off and let the other two into the store. He could feel the stank of dark magick. It permeated even the air he was breathing. Whoever controlled the zombies was a force to be reckoned with.

An ancient force.

Not as old as him by any means, but still someone comfortable with their powers who knew them intimately.

He'd fought it earlier. This time, the bokor had reinforced his or her strength. And because these zombies had no living force or will of their own, they were far more dangerous than the students had been.

Unlike the students, they had no attachment to life anymore. No lingering compassion or reason. They were evil souls summoned into the bodies of the dead.

This was the blackest of magick. The kind that not even he dealt with. Only a true dark spirit like the Malachai could summon an army this size and control it.

These were mindless killing machines.

Kind of like the Charonte, though Caleb had to give Simi credit. Unlike the others of her species he'd known in the past, she was holding her human guise and not breaking it to chow down on the zombies. Someone had trained her well.

Growling low in his throat, he hit the zombie holding Madaug. The zombie's skull broke, leaving its mandible to hang from a strip of tendon as some kind of cold green ew slimed his hand. It felt like two-day-old snot.

"Oh, gross!" Caleb wiped his hand against his shirt. "Zombie goo."

"Ooo," Simi breathed. "I wonder if it tastes like chicken? What do you think?"

Caleb scowled. "I think I'm never eating guacamole again as long as I live."

Ignoring them, Nick beat the other zombie back

until he was able, with Simi's help, to shove Madaug into the store.

"Hey!" Caleb snapped as he realized Nick was about to lock him on the outside with their attackers. He pushed the door open and glared at him. "No man left behind."

Nick scoffed. "This ain't the army, boy. It's every man for himself. Fall behind. Get eaten."

"I'll remember that the next time you're the one on the outside and I'm the one in the store."

Nick flashed an evil grin at him. "Yeah, but then the rules will change." He grabbed the door as another zombie tried to open it. "Ah no."

"What?" Caleb asked.

"You left the keys outside."

Caleb groaned at his stupidity, then helped Nick hold the door closed as more zombies swarmed. "What kind of idiot doesn't have one of those flipper lock things on their door?"

Nick gave him a duh stare. "Bubba. 'Cause all someone has to do is break the glass and then they can switch it open and be inside the store. You know

Bubba's Code: Always use keys." Which was why he had so many on his key ring.

Caleb felt his muscles bulge as he held the door tight while the zombies tried to pull it open. "I swear, Nick, I should throw you to them. After all, I don't have to outrun the zombies. I just have to outrun you."

"That's cold, dude."

Maybe, but if the zombies got in, he was going to sic Simi and her barbecue sauce on them, humans be damned.

"Stand back," Madaug said.

Nick looked over his shoulder to see Madaug with a rocket launcher. Oh, no way. Where on earth had he found *that*?

Was it loaded?

What a stupid question. It was in Bubba's store. Of course it was loaded and functional. And probably modified to take down half the city block whenever it was fired.

Nick widened his eyes. "That's not what I think it is, is it?"

Madaug shrugged. "I don't know, but I think you better duck."

They'd barely moved before Madaug fired at the zombies outside. The rocket exploded in the door, sending glass and zombie parts everywhere. Green and red ooze streaked through the night.

Simi actually licked her lips as if dying for a taste of it.

Nick gaped as more zombies headed for them. "Dude, for a genius that was really stupid. Now we have no door and, I could be wrong, but they look to be multiplying."

They heard the zombie converts they'd locked in the hidden room earlier—yelling for release—from the surveillance monitor Bubba had turned on earlier to make sure they were all right. Well, some were. Others were in the room crying for their mamas.

Meanwhile Bubba and Mark were outside whooping and hollering in all their glory as they fought off the undead. Nick ran to the back to get the ax.

I really need my arm functional again. Or better yet, a genetic implant that left him with one arm as a chainsaw like Ash in *Army of Darkness*. Now that he could definitely use right now.

Then again, he'd settle for both arms working.

A chill went through him as an image flashed in his mind of him being attacked by . . .

Not a raven, but the raven had been there, watching like a freaked-out guardian. And Nick's arm had been whole and working. . . . The images were in the back of his mind, but he couldn't focus on any one of them in particular. Just fleeting glimpses that were gone as fast as they'd appeared.

Had it been a dream?

But the memory felt real.

"Yee frickin' haw!" Bubba shouted.

Running back to Madaug and Caleb, Nick looked to see Bubba stunning the zombies with the cattle prod before he beat them with his bat. The man was having way too much fun while Nick was still worried about dying.

The zombies closed in.

Nick swallowed his fear and pulled Simi behind him to protect her. "Why hasn't one of the neighbors complained about this? Where are the cops when you need them?"

Caleb snorted. "Probably eating beignets. As the old saying goes, when seconds count, the police are just minutes away."

And it was looking like a killing field out there as panic took hold of Nick. Bubba and Mark were driving the zombies back like psycho ninjas, but even so the sheer number of the zombies was going to overwhelm them sooner or later.

Terrified, Nick watched as more came from the shadows. These seemed to be created and sent in. . . .

Not for kidnapping. These were here to murder.

Nick kept Simi from running around him to join the fray. She might be tall, but she'd be no match for the zombies, who continued coming while Madaug tried to reload the rocket launcher with another round.

He wasn't going to be satisfied until he blew all of them away.

Nick saw a flash of silver. Afraid it was more undead reinforcements, he kicked back a zombie, then froze as he recognized what was out there in the night.

Ash and Kyrian.

And as they joined the fight, he realized another thing. They were the ones who really fought like ninjas. Ash with a staff and Kyrian with a sword. It was incredible. While Bubba and Mark were fierce, Kyrian's moves were so graceful, they were like a violent ballet as he twirled, sliced one zombie, and then pivoted to catch another.

Nick kept waiting for Ash to use his powers, but for some reason he didn't. He merely used his staff to bash and deflect the zombies. Then he remembered what Ash had said. No doubt he was trying to remain incognito while there were witnesses around.

Though that didn't make sense if Ash could mind-wipe everyone. Could it be he simply enjoyed the fight like Bubba and Mark?

Between them and Bubba and Mark, the zombies didn't stand a chance. In only a few minutes, there were green bodies of ew littering the street.

Kyrian looked at Ash. "Too bad they don't disintegrate into dust, huh? I have to say I much prefer the monsters who clean up after themselves."

Ash laughed.

Bubba and Mark surveyed the damage. "I wonder why no one called the police about the rocket launcher? God knows my neighbors usually report it if I so much as fart in my backyard."

Ash planted the end of his staff into the ground. "Good question."

Kyrian pressed a button on his sword and compacted it down to the hilt. He slid it into his pocket. "I have a better one. How are we going to clean up this mess?"

Nick scoffed. "Nah, mine's even better. How do you hide a chainsaw in your locker at school?"

They all stared at him.

Nick gestured to the zombies that lay in pieces on the street. "I'm thinking they're not going to stop, and while the school has a strict no-weapons policy, I don't think the plastic sporks in the cafeteria are going to do much to combat them. I need protection, man. Serious protection." His gaze went to Madaug, who was still cradling the rocket launcher. "Okay, maybe not *that* serious. But still . . ."

Mark wiped the sweat off his brow. "It's like a friggin' zombie apocalypse. I always knew we'd have one in my lifetime. Everybody, but Bubba, told me I was crazy. Well look . . . who's crazy now?"

Nick had to bite his tongue to keep from saying it was still Mark who was crazy.

Caleb ignored Nick as he felt something peculiar in the air. . . . His gaze went to the two newcomers. He didn't know them, but he could feel their powers.

Like him and Simi, they weren't human either.

If he didn't know better, he'd swear the tallest one was a god, and as that being turned his head to Caleb, he was sure of it.

The other . . .

He was a powerful warrior—a servant of the goddess Artemis. One of a long line of ancient protectors who'd sold their souls to keep mankind safe from creatures like him.

Oh yeah, any other time and the two of them would be going at it like two women over the last gown left in their size at a bridal sale.

"Hey," Nick said, looking around. "Where's Simi? Anyone see where she went?"

Before anyone could answer, another wave of zombies appeared out of the darkness. These were even faster and uglier.

Ash looked at Bubba. "Get everyone out of here."

"And go where?"

"My house," Kyrian said. "It's on First Ave. Nick knows the way. I'll have someone there to let you in."

As they ran for the SUV, Nick saw Simi coming out of the store. She joined them and plopped down in the seat beside him.

"Where'd you go?"

"I'd tell you, but then I'd have to eat you and since the Simi likes Nick, she don't wanna hurt him." She grinned.

Okay . . .

Madaug dialed his phone as everyone belted themselves in. "I can't get Eric. You don't think anything's happened to him, do you?"

"He'll be all right," Bubba assured him. "Tabitha might be a little out there"—boy, wasn't that the kettle calling the pot black. *I guess everyone is someone else's weirdo.* "But she's good in a fight. They can take anything the zombie world throws at them. Vampires too."

"Oh, wait!" Nick panicked as he remembered his mom. "I'm supposed to be at my mom's club. She told me if I wasn't there by now, she'd come find me."

"And become a zombie hostage," Mark said. "I've seen it before. Countless times. The well-meaning hapless woman out to save her kid. Taken and eaten."

Bubba scoffed. "In the movies, Mark."

"Yeah, well, sometimes that happens in real life too, and this is definitely a time for it to happen 'cause that'd be just our luck. They take her and we all die trying to save her because she did something stupid."

Bubba turned his SUV around. "Let's go get her. 'Cause Mark's right."

Nick checked the time. "She still has four hours of work left."

Mark held up a gun. "It's all right. We'll get her one way or another."

Nick was horrified at the mere suggestion of pulling a gun on his mom. "You can't shoot my mom, Mark! Are you out of your mind?"

"I'm not going to shoot her. Calm down. I'm just going to tranq her a little."

Before Nick could protest, Bubba had the SUV parked. "Mark. You and the kids stay here."

Nick shook his head. "It's my mom, I'm coming."

Bubba started to protest, then must have thought better of it. "We don't have any time to waste. C'mon."

Nick led him to the back door of the club and knocked until John answered it.

The bouncer shook his head. "Boy, your mama is going to kill you."

"Where is she?"

"Green room."

Nick led Bubba down the narrow hallway until he reached the dressing room. He knocked on the door and waited.

His mom opened it. Her hair was teased out and her makeup thick while she was dressed in her bathrobe. The look on her face made his stomach head south.

"What have you got to say for yourself, Nick Gautier?"

"That I was attacked by zombies?"

She rolled her eyes. "Don't hand me that ridiculous story."

"No, Ma, I swear. Really!"

But she wasn't about to believe him. "Do you know what time it is?"

"Obviously time for me to get grounded again." He let out a deep sigh. Some days, it really didn't pay to be honest.

She narrowed her gaze at him. "That's right. I'm going to ground you until your grandchildren are old."

Bubba stepped forward, cutting her off. "Uh, ma'am? We do have a situation and we need for you to come with us."

She furrowed her brow as she looked at Bubba like he was crazy. "I can't leave. I have another set in a few minutes."

"With all due respect, ma'am, the zombies won't care and they won't wait."

"Oh good grief, Bubba. Would you stop filling my boy's head full of all that garbage? You've already got him fully convinced of everything but the tooth fairy and I'm waiting for him to come home with wings on, telling me that even it's real." She grabbed

Nick's good arm. "Get in here and sit in the corner until I decide how much restriction I'm giving
you."

"But Mom—"

"Don't you 'but Mom' me."

Nick looked at Bubba as a wave of helplessness
consumed him. Why would he have thought for one
minute his mother would listen? Not like she made a
habit of it.

Bubba shrugged and before Nick could stop him,
he shot her.

"Bubba!"

His mom let out a sharp cry before she staggered
back.

Bubba scooped her up in his arms as she swooned.
"Dang, Nick, your mom's a tiny little thing. Weird.
When she's awake, you forget she don't weigh noth-
ing at all."

"It's 'cause she's so fierce." He'd seen her stand toe
to toe with his father, who could dwarf a mountain,
and never blink or back down.

"She's going to kill us. You know that?"

Bubba ignored him as he carried her back toward the entrance.

John scowled at them as they walked past. "What's going on?"

"She fainted," he and Bubba said simultaneously.

"We're taking her to the doctor," Nick lied as he brushed past John. He hated that he had to say that, but John would never believe the truth and it'd probably get her fired.

"Boss ain't gonna like this. Not a bit."

Nick shrugged. "Can't help that she got sick. It happens." He ran ahead to get the car door for Bubba so that he could put his mom in as quickly as possible.

He fastened her seat belt before he took a seat next to her, while Bubba got back in the front.

Simi frowned. "She picked a fine time to take a nap. Was she really sleepy?"

Before Nick could answer, Bubba's phone started ringing.

Bubba pulled away from the curb before he answered it. "Ye-llo?" A dark cloud came over his features as if something bad had happened.

Nick's stomach tightened to the point that he half expected a diamond to form. What was going on now?

Gah, couldn't they catch a break tonight?

At least my mom's safe.

Bubba looked in the rearview mirror at Madaug, who visibly paled.

"What?" Madaug asked, his voice filled with the same dread Nick felt. "What's happened?"

"Yeah," Bubba continued, ignoring Madaug's question. "I'll tell him. Is there anything we can do?" He paused as he listened, and they all waited with bated breath. "I'll see you there." He hung up.

Nick leaned forward in his seat. "What happened?"

Bubba sighed before he answered. "We have another situation."

Great, just great. At this point, they really should be selling tickets for pay-per-view.

"That was Eric, Madaug," Bubba said.

Madaug swallowed as fear darkened his blue eyes. "They get attacked by the zombies?"

"Yeah, but they fought them off."

Madaug let out an audible sound of relief. "Then why you look so upset?"

"Eric went to your house and the front door was standing wide open."

Nick gasped in alarm.

Madaug's features turned to stone as his entire face blanched. "And?"

"He said it was a real bad scene."

Tears gathered in Madaug's eyes as he glanced around at all their faces. "My mom and Ian?"

"No sign of them. But Eric said he's calling the police right now to report it."

Nick's stomach tightened as he saw the raw agony in Madaug's eyes. "Dude, I'm so sorry."

Madaug didn't seem to hear him as he hung his head in his hands. "It's all my fault. All of this. Oh God . . . I just wanted them to stop picking on me. That's all I wanted. I didn't mean for anyone to get hurt. I didn't. Now my mom and brother are gone . . . probably eaten. What have I done? What have I done?"

Nick couldn't imagine how bad it must hurt to know he might have caused the death of someone he loved. Surely there was no worse pain in the world.

Madaug's agony tore through him and choked him up. He wished he knew what to say, but words wouldn't come.

Simi sat forward and patted Madaug on the back. "I'm sorry, little human. The Simi lost her mama too when she was little, but maybe your mama okay. She might be looking for you."

Madaug turned and hugged her.

Simi's eyes widened before she hugged him back. "It okay. You'll see. Just when you think nothing get better, it always does. Trust me. My akri says that tragedy and adversity are the stones we sharpen our swords against so that we can fight new battles. This just a minor skirmish and you'll be back in the fight. You'll see."

Madaug nodded, but as he pulled back, Nick saw the tears he was trying to hide. He lifted his glasses and swiped at his eyes. "I need to go to my house."

Bubba nodded as he headed that way.

They were all subdued the entire time it took them to reach Madaug's quiet upper-class neighborhood. On the outside, everything appeared calm and peaceful.

Just another night.

But there was nothing normal about any of this. Nick's gaze went to his mother's unconscious form. She was going to be so angry at him when she woke up. But better that than she be like Madaug's mom and be taken from him. He'd kill anyone who touched her, and that wasn't an idle threat. He knew he had it in him.

After all, he was his father's son.

As they approached Madaug's house, the police were everywhere. Lights flashed through the darkness as spotlights lit the entire street. Yellow tape cordoned off the yard, along with police barricades that had been set up to keep people back while they investigated the mess.

Caleb let out a low whistle as they left the SUV. "Anyone else getting tired of seeing the cops camped out?"

Nick didn't comment, but he couldn't agree more. "Simi? Would you mind staying in the car and keeping an eye on my mom?"

"Sure."

Tabitha came forward to meet them as they stayed back behind the police line. Her face grim, she pulled Madaug to her. "I'm so sorry, little guy."

"Where's Eric?" Madaug asked.

"He's inside with your dad."

Madaug left her to go to them.

Bubba looked at Tabitha. "What happened?"

She raked a hand through her hair as she glanced around the yard of police conducting interviews. "There was a really bad fight in the house. Madaug's room was ransacked and the kitchen's all bloody. The police think that someone broke in and killed their mom and Ian. They've called in cadaver dogs to start searching for them."

Nick winced at what she described as a wave of sympathetic pain flooded him. For a moment, he thought he might be sick.

"How's Eric doing?" Bubba asked.

Tabitha swallowed. "He's really messed up over it. He keeps saying that he should have been here to protect them." She sighed again. "What about Madaug?"

Mark shook his head. "He's been really quiet. Freaky, scary quiet. Like Eric, he's blaming himself. He keeps saying that if he hadn't created the game, none of this would have happened."

Nick met Caleb's gaze. "You feel as bad as I do for them?"

Caleb nodded. "I just can't figure this out. Where are all these living zombies coming from? If Madaug only had the one game . . . surely they're not all coming from that."

Nick scratched at the back of his neck. "Like Bubba said earlier, someone must have made a copy of it."

"Yeah, but doesn't it seem like it spread a little too fast?"

"What do you mean?"

Caleb narrowed his eyes on the cops. "I think there's something else at play here. Something just doesn't feel right about any of this."

Nick gave him a droll stare. "You mean other than

the dead zombies who tried to eat us a few minutes ago?"

"That's my point, Nick. This isn't just a game gone awry. I smell the hand of evil. Real evil."

Nick started to make a snarky comment at the hokiness of his tone and words, but thought better of it. While he still believed Caleb was a head case, in this he might, God forbid, be right.

There was something terribly wrong here. Even he could feel it.

Wishing he could help Madaug and Eric, he glanced over to the crowd of gawkers who'd come to see what was happening. A tall man in black who stood apart from them caught his eye.

He knew him in an instant and that recognition slammed into him like a fist in his gullet.

Ambrose.

Nick watched as the flashing light from the police car highlighted his sinister face. It cast shadows across the planes of his cheeks, making his eyes look inhuman. *And I thought my father looked evil. . . .*

Adarian had nothing on Ambrose.

With that thought came a bad feeling that Ambrose might be behind this. Wanting to get to the bottom of it, Nick started toward him.

Ambrose turned and his gaze locked with Nick's. In that single heartbeat, Nick swore the man's eyes turned a deep bloody red that glowed in the darkness. One second Ambrose was staring at him like he could kill him and in the next . . .

He was gone.

Nick came to a halt as he looked around the yard. No one seemed to have noticed the man who was now missing.

"What the heck?"

Caleb came up behind him. "What's wrong?"

"Did you see . . ." What was he supposed to say? Did you see my crazy uncle, Jason Voorhees? Do you think he could kill someone's mom and brother?

"Did I see what?"

Nick shook his head. "Never mind. It must have been a shadow."

Caleb scowled at him. "You all right? You look kind of pale."

Nick wasn't sure anymore. Suddenly, he felt dizzy and weird. For a second, he thought he might be sick until he felt a soft hand on his shoulder. Turning his head, he saw Nekoda behind him. Her pale face was gorgeous and she was the best thing he'd seen all day.

"What are you doing here, Nick?"

He'd never been happier to see anyone in his life. Before he could think better of it, he turned and hugged her close.

Nekoda froze at the unexpected contact. Never in her life had anyone held her like this. Never had they greeted her as if they were thrilled to see her. A wave of foreign emotion ripped through her entire body.

What was it?

And it wasn't just the emotion, it was the sensation of his arm around her. Of his breath falling against her cheek and the warm smell of his hair. It made her entire body hum and gave her an insane desire to bury her hand in his soft hair. Most of all, it sent a wave of chills over her. "Nick?"

Nick couldn't answer as he let the heat of her body

comfort his ragged emotions. How strange that in a night of chaos, she seemed to ground him.

"I'm sorry," he whispered, before he let go and stepped back. "I didn't mean to assault you. It's just been a really, really bad night and I'm glad to see a friendly face."

Nekoda trembled as he put his hand on her cheek. *He's my enemy.* A creature she was sworn to kill. But looking into those blue eyes, she didn't see a monster.

She saw . . .

Something that scared and shocked her to her core. *Don't let him charm you. It's not real. It's his powers. Nothing more.*

He is evil to the center of his soul.

But her compulsion toward him didn't feel like it was coming from him. It felt like it was coming from deep inside her. As if some part of her just wanted to be closer to him.

How utterly peculiar.

Unable to stand it, she pulled his hand away from her face and put enough distance between them that she could think straight. "You didn't answer my question."

He gestured over his shoulder, toward the house. "We brought Madaug home. What about you? What are you doing here?"

"I live nearby," she lied. She'd been summoned here by a violent wave of magick. It was like Nick's powers on steroids. If she didn't know better, she'd say it was him at his full strength, but he was still weak.

Still human.

And what she'd sensed had been mature and ready to take lives.

"I saw the police and came to investigate," she said.

"You shouldn't be out here. It's dangerous."

She frowned at him. "How do you mean?"

Nick glanced over his shoulder to where Caleb was staring at them with an odd look on his face. "There are things out here . . ." *Don't say zombie, moron. She'll think you're a loon.* "It's just a bad scene. Full moon and all. You should go home where it's safe."

"Are you . . ."—she narrowed her eyes as if searching for a word—"trying to protect me?"

Oh, he knew that tone. It was dangerous. "I'm not being a male chauvinist. I know a woman is just as capable of taking care of herself as a man, but there are things . . . I'm sure your parents are worried about you and—"

"You *are* trying to protect me." A broad smile curled her lips and did the strangest thing to his stomach. "That's so sweet."

Instead of slapping him, she actually kissed his cheek.

Nick's entire body erupted the moment her lips touched his flesh. Now he felt like the one in danger.

For the first time in his life, he didn't mind being called sweet. Not if it meant he got kissed with it. Of course, on the lips would have been infinitely better than the cheek, but so long as she wasn't slapping him and calling him an insult, he wasn't arguing with the location.

When she pulled back, her eyes sparkled in the low light. "Thank you for caring."

"My pleasure." *Idiot. What a stupid thing to say.*

But she didn't seem to notice. "All right. I better go. You watch yourself."

"You too."

He didn't move as she withdrew, and he took a

second to savor her scent that lingered around him. She smelled all womanly and good. And all he wanted to do was follow her home.

Caleb snapped his fingers in front of his nose. "Dude, she's not what you think."

He turned his head toward Caleb. "What are you talking about?"

"You need to stay away from her, Nick. Trust me. Girls ain't nothing but trouble."

Yeah, but it was the only kind of trouble he wanted to launch himself into headfirst and wallow there until he was pruny from it.

However, he wasn't about to admit any of that to Caleb, lest he revert to kindergarten and start telling her that Nick had a crush on her. Oh, the humiliation of *that*. "She's all right."

Caleb's eyes flashed with deep sincerity. "No, she's not. You need to listen to me, kid. That girl is your death."

Nick blew off Caleb's sinister Vincent Price tone. "You're an idiot." He headed back to the car where his mom was.

SHERRILYN KENYON

But as he reached it, an unbidden image went through his head. It was Nekoda . . .

Only she wasn't the girl he knew who made him laugh and who kissed him on his cheek. She was something else entirely. Dressed in armor, she looked like an ancient warrior, complete with a helmet and shield.

And a sword she was driving straight through his heart.

CHAPTER 15

Madaug was alone in his room, picking up some of the mess there and crying as he realized how badly he'd screwed up. It wasn't supposed to be like this. How could trying to protect himself have turned out so badly? How?

He'd accidentally ruined so many lives. . . .

I'm so worthless. Brian was going to prison . . . classmates had died, Scott's arm would be permanently disfigured, and now his mom and brother were probably dead too—eaten by the very things he'd created. *I should just throw myself under a bus. I'm not even worth the cost of a bullet.*

Suddenly, he heard whispering.

At first, he thought it might be the police outside the door with his dad again. But it wasn't.

It seemed to be in his ears—like it was coming from his own brain.

Lifting his head, he tried to locate the source, but he saw nothing except the police lights flashing from outside through the slats of his closed blinds.

Madaug . . . Filled with panic, his mother's voice was distinct. Undeniable.

"Mom?"

She didn't answer.

Great. I'm hallucinating. I've now lost even my sanity.

A light mist appeared outside his bedroom window. It dove and then formed a thin string that seeped up from his sill. In slow motion, it crawled along his desk like a creepy caterpillar until it gathered into a clump. Twirling and dancing, that clump solidified into an old, hideous, small woman who pointed an accusatory finger at him. "You are killing your mother and brother."

An image of them screaming appeared beside the miniature ghost.

Madaug put his hands over his ears. "Shut up! Don't hurt them!"

The old crone stepped closer to him as the image of his mother and brother faded. "Do you want to save them?"

What kind of stupid question was that? "Of course I do."

"Then you need to come to me."

He hesitated. "You're in my room. I'm already with you." Was she completely stupid?

"Not here, you imbecile. I need you with me."

What was he supposed to do? Guess randomly out of the millions of different locations in the greater New Orleans area? "Where are you?"

"The St. Louis Cemetery."

Oh yeah, right. He wasn't brain damaged enough to think it'd be that easy to get his mom back. If he showed up there, he'd have no leverage and the old ghost woman could do what she wanted to with both him and his mom.

Even Ian.

"You'll kill me if I do that."

The small woman laughed evilly. "I'll kill them if you don't."

Madaug wanted to slam his hand down on the table and squash her like a roach. But he knew it would only hurt him if he tried. She wasn't real. Just a ghost image with no real form or body. "Why are you doing this to me?"

"You're the one meddling with things you shouldn't have. Didn't you know that when you tamper with human will, dreadful things happen?"

"I wasn't trying to hurt anyone. That was never my intent. I just wanted them to leave me alone."

The woman shrugged. "Intentions don't matter. It's the end result we're all judged by. Evil in the name of good is still evil. And when you dance with the devil you seldom get to pick the tune."

"What's that supposed to mean?"

"It means the countdown on their lives is speeding up and the longer you delay, the more likely they are to die."

"Don't hurt them. I'm coming."

"You better be alone, *mon petit*, and bring your

Zombie Hunter game program or else. . . . You have thirty minutes to get here." She faded into nothing.

Madaug bit his lip as he cracked open the blinds to see his yard crawling with police. How could he get to the cemetery without being seen or followed?

There was no way he could walk there in that amount of time.

What was he going to do?

Starting to sweat, he went down the back stairs that led to the kitchen. He froze as he saw his brother and crew with Bubba, Mark, Nick, and Simi.

"I'll leave Mark here," Bubba said to Eric. "He can help out while I go drop Cherise and Nick at Kyrian's. Then I'll be back."

Eric nodded. "Just be careful."

"Will do."

Madaug slid out the back door while they were facing away from him and made his way through the shadows to the shed where his dad kept the lawn-mower. It was also where Eric's old Honda scooter was kept. He'd always called it the nerdmobile and now he was going to be forced to ride on it.

Gah, how awful.

But for his mom's life, he was willing to look like a total goober. He opened the door carefully so it wouldn't squeak and draw attention to him, then slipped inside the small wood shed.

As quietly as he could he made his way to the scooter and opened the gas cap. Just as he suspected, no gas.

Dang it. Eric? Couldn't you do anything right?

It's all right. You have a 160 IQ. You can think of something. He forced himself to calm down so that he could postulate options. As his gaze danced around the darkened room, an idea formed.

Grabbing the hedge clippers, he cut a piece of hose to make a siphon, then drained the riding mower and poured the gas into the scooter.

As soon as it was gassed up, he grabbed the keys off the wall hanger, the helmet that was covered in cobwebs, and pushed the scooter away from the house. His heart pounded with every step he made. Any minute he expected to be caught.

But luckily, no one saw him. The police were too

busy dusting for prints, talking to people, and standing around chatting to notice a kid rolling a bright red scooter across his backyard.

Actually, that was a scary thought. How oblivious could the trained experts be? If he didn't need them to be inattentive, it would horrify him. And later, when he looked back on this, he would be horrified. But right now, he kept his thoughts focused on his mom and brother.

With a relieved breath as soon as he was a block away, he got on the scooter and started it. It roared to life and shot down the street at a speed a rusted-out tanker would envy, but at least it was faster than walking.

And it would get him to the cemetery in time.

"I'm coming, Mom." He wasn't about to let anything happen to her, or even his brother. Ian might make him insane, but Madaug was the older brother and it was his job to protect Ian.

Even from brain-eating zombies.

* * *

Nick paused as a tingle went down his spine, making the hair on the back of his neck stand on end.

There was something . . .

He saw an image in his mind of Madaug, looking really goofy with a red Power Rangers helmet on his head while riding a red scooter, sneaking away from the house. He didn't know where it came from, but it was there as crystal clear as Bubba who was standing next to him.

"I think Madaug's doing something stupid."

Bubba scoffed. "And that would be different from normal, how?"

"Police! Stop!"

Nick looked over to where two officers had their guns drawn. His jaw went slack as he saw what they were focused on.

It wasn't Madaug.

It was more zombies.

Nick cursed.

The police didn't fire until the first zombie reached a cop and sank its rotted teeth into the officer's head.

Nick couldn't breathe as he saw more of them coming. "Oh my God . . ."

It was an army of the undead and they were moving straight at them like a pack of ugly hyenas. Why didn't they stumble like in a Romero flick?

No, they had to be attacked by super zombies. *Leave it to me.*

"There goes the neighborhood," Caleb said.

Nick shoved at him.

"Mark!" Bubba started for the house, but it was too late. More zombies were coming in from the back and they'd already gone inside where the others were. The house was now completely occupied by their enemies while civilians ran screaming only to get overtaken by the zombies.

Nick grabbed Bubba's arm to stop him from going in after Mark. "We have to go."

Bubba's features turned to stone. "Don't worry. I've seen that movie too. You go in to help your friend and they eat you instead. Mark's smart. He can escape. I believe that."

Simi got out of the SUV. "The Simi will go gets

him. You get to safety and I'll take care of them old nasty zombies." She pulled a bottle of barbecue sauce out of her coffin-shaped purse.

Nick wasn't sure about that either. "Simi—"

But she was already halfway across the yard, sauce in hand and whooping with eager delight.

Bubba shoved Nick into the car by his face.

"Arm! Watch the arm!" Nick shouted as Bubba's grip sent pain all the way through him.

Caleb climbed in beside him as Bubba got in, turned the truck on, and slung it sideways into the street. He didn't even slow down as he plowed through as many zombies as he could hit.

They growled and hissed as they tried to grab and hold on to the truck to get to them. But Bubba's swerving sent them flying.

Nick cringed as one took a header into a tree and splotted like a multicolored bug on a windshield. "I'm so glad my mom's not awake for this. She'd skin all of us."

"Dang," Caleb breathed as he crawled over the seat into the front. "How many zombies are there?"

Bubba swerved to hit another one—at least Nick hoped that one was a zombie and not some poor innocent pedestrian. "You gotta figure there's three hundred years of dead in New Orleans. While Mark and me have taken out a few dozen over the years . . . that makes for a lot of zombies."

Nick scowled. "But how could one bokor raise that many? Doesn't it suck juice out of them or something?"

Bubba shook his head. "Yes, and blood, unless they've made a pact with someone a lot more powerful."

"Someone like a god?" Caleb asked.

Bubba nodded at Caleb. "Yeah. Someone like a god."

Nick hissed as a pain shot through his skull. It was so intense it made his nose start to bleed.

Bubba snatched his head around. "You okay?"

Nick had no idea as he pinched his nose closed. "I feel sick. Real sick."

"You throw up in that backseat, boy, and I'll make you lick it up. I swear it. I'm still making payments on this thing and it's hard to get the smell of vomit out of the upholstery."

But it wasn't that kind of sick. Nick's head was spinning with images he couldn't understand. He saw fire and felt an unbelievable anger swelling.

It was his, yet not his.

Bubba looked over at Caleb. "He ain't turning into a zombie, is he?"

"No," Caleb said, scowling. "But he is turning kind of green. You got a bag or something in case he hurls?"

Nick ignored them. "We have to drop off my mom and find Madaug."

"What?" they asked simultaneously.

Nick caught Bubba's gaze in the rearview mirror as Bubba looked back at him. "Something bad's about to happen."

"Boy, in case it has slipped your oh so astute attention, something bad has been happening all day."

Caleb turned around in the seat. "Maybe we should go on then and find Madaug first."

"No." Nick looked at his mom, who was already going to be hotter than a nest of hornets flung against a house. "We take care of my mom first—she's my number one priority. I have to make sure she's safe."

"And then what?" Caleb asked.

"Then we break major zombie aaa . . . sss."

CHAPTER 16

Nick had his head against the glass, watching the road pass by as he struggled to keep from being ill. What was wrong with him?

"You're fighting me. Stop and you won't be sick."

He looked around the car to see if anyone else heard the voice in his head. His mom was still unconscious. Bubba was listening to the radio while Caleb sang along to Iron Man under his breath.

And as Nick looked at Caleb, he saw his friend's form change before his eyes. It was like he could see under Caleb's skin and that Caleb was no longer human. He was . . .

"A daeva. A midlevel class of demon. Not innately

evil. They were soldiers of an older time and place. Protectors or messengers for the ancient gods. In the case of Caleb, he was a feared general who is still capable of summoning and commanding legions of demons.

"FYI, Nick, not all demons are bad. Like people, they're complicated life forms with varying personalities and quirks. Filled with complex emotions, some are malevolent and some are good. In the case of Caleb, he's your protector. He would die to keep you safe.

"So before you judge him about being born a species he couldn't help any more than you could help yours, you should know that he's stayed in the background as a silent bodyguard who didn't step forward until he was needed to keep you safe.

"Really, do you think he's enjoyed being in high school with you and the others when he didn't have to be?"

Nick saw an image of Caleb with wings, his flaming orange hair long as he stood at the helm of a thousand demons, leading them to battle. His skin dark red, he had yellow eyes like a serpent's and he fought with the strength of a titan.

Nick shook his head. *I'm going crazy.*

"No, you're becoming aware of who and what you are. Of everything around you that has always remained hidden—just as I promised you you would."

Who are you? Nick asked silently.

"Ambrose . . . and I'm also here to protect you. Listen to me, Nick, and I'll teach you everything you need to fight the creatures who are going to come for you. The ones who'll ruin your life if you continue to live without the ability to see them and fight back."

Nick scowled. *I don't understand. Why did you run from me at Madaug's?*

"I wasn't running from you. I was trying to save your friend before the mortents hurt him. But like you, he didn't listen to me."

Yeah, right. Why don't I believe this?

"It's true, Nick. Remember the little girl in the alley? The one who attacked you?"

Duh. Not like I could forget that Wes Cravenesque encounter anytime soon.

Then again, they'd done something to him that he
had forgotten it. But now he remembered every single
detail.

WTH?

"I told you they were called mortents. They crawled
out of their hole, and this time, they claimed your
friend Madaug and his family. They want to use his
video game to control the living—because the living
still possess their souls and their free will, living zombies are immune to our silkspeech and powers of ma-
nipulation. We can't control them like we can the
dead. If the mortents can get the game from Madaug,
they can use it to control you in particular, and they
can build an army out of the living to attack the world."

*Why me? I don't understand why this is happening
and why they'd give two spits about controlling me. I
can't even walk across the floor without getting grounded.*

"Nick, you are key to some of the rawest, most potent powers ever created. The battles for your posses-
sion will scar you in ways you won't know until it's
too late. If you listen to me, I can save you."

I'm key? Dude, you seriously have me mistaken for someone else.

"No, I don't. I, better than anyone else, know exactly how powerful you are and what you can do. And deep inside, you feel those powers too. You've spent your whole life denying them. Saying it was Menyara or a sixth sense. It's not a buried sense. It's your birthright and you have got to embrace it or you will lose everything that matters to you."

And if I don't believe this crap?

Images of a dark, frightening hole flashed in his mind. He saw himself in the future looking a lot like Ambrose. Alone. Bereft.

Tortured.

Most of all, he was inhuman and cruel.

"If they can turn you evil, they will be rewarded and you will be ruined. And everyone you love will pay the price.

"Everyone."

Nick shook his head in an effort to dispel the horrific images. Terror choked him as he feared becoming the monster his father was. Of becoming the creature he'd just seen.

I don't want to be evil.

"You can't just say it and make it so. It's not that easy."

Of course it is. My mom tells me all the time that we decide between good and evil. What we are is completely *up to us.*

"And things drive us to make decisions that are beyond our control. Just like your mother. You know how much she hates dancing and yet there she is every night, right on time, often working double shifts to bring in more money. For you. And you haven't been betrayed yet, Nick. You don't know what that's like. What it does to you. The scars it leaves that never fade."

Not true. Alan, Mike, and Tyree had all betrayed me.

"And you want their blood for it."

I want to bathe in it.

"That's *exactly* what I'm talking about. That's the evil that's seducing you. The malevolent power that is crawling through your blood tempting you onto a treacherous path that will cost you everything you love and hold dear. You have to let that anger go before it's too late. Vengeance always turns inward and it will consume you until nothing's left but an empty hole that nothing can fill."

Nick bristled as he saw that night again—the glee in Alan's eyes as he pulled the trigger. *They shot me!*

"And they will pay, but not by your hand. Trust me. Karma has her own plans for them and what she has in store is more painful than you could ever dream."

I don't know about that. I have one great imagination. And letting it go is much easier said than done.

Ambrose laughed in his ear. "Believe me, I know."

All of a sudden, Nick saw Ambrose in the car beside him. Translucent, he manifested on the other side of his mother, leaning against the car door as if he really was another passenger.

His dark eyes filled with absolute misery, Ambrose reached out and touched Nick's mother's cheek. There was so much anguish on his face and tenderness in his touch that it made Nick's stomach clench. Ambrose touched her as if she were a ghost who'd haunted him for centuries.

Most of all, he touched her as if she were unspeakably precious. Someone Ambrose had never thought to see again. Even Ambrose's lip quivered while he brushed his hand through her hair.

You love her, Nick sent his thoughts to Ambrose.

Ambrose nodded, then met his gaze so that Nick could see the sincerity burning in his eyes. "I would do anything to keep her safe. Anything to keep you on the right path."

And it was then Nick knew he could trust him. There was no way to fake that depth of emotion. He meant every word he said. Even though it kind of grossed him out that his father's brother loved his mom he believed Ambrose was trying to help them.

The look on Ambrose's face seared him. "Will you trust me, little brother?"

I guess. But only as long as you don't betray me.

Ambrose gave a cocky grin. "I'm the last person who would ever do that, Nick. I would sell my soul and give my life to keep you from becoming what I am."

Nick nodded. *Then tell me what I need to know.*

"You're going to have to learn to take control of the zombies."

Nick laughed out loud, which caused Caleb to jump in startled alarm and glare at him. "Sorry," Nick said out loud. "I didn't mean to scare you."

Caleb snorted before he relaxed. "It takes more than *you* to scare *me*. Must be amusing in that head of yours, Gautier. But remember the rest of us aren't in there with you."

Yeah, only Ambrose seemed to have that power.

Nick returned his attention to Ambrose. Car lights shone through his body, making it shimmer in the darkness. *Can Caleb not sense you?*

"Only if I allow it."

And obviously, he wasn't allowing anyone but Nick to see and hear him right now.

What are you? he asked Ambrose.

"We"—he indicated the two of them—"are the last of a cursed race. Which isn't necessarily a bad thing as it's our prime nature to hurt others. When they're weak and hurting, we swoop in for the kill. But I'm hoping you have enough of your mother in you that you'll learn to curb those impulses and learn to let the things go that I never could."

Nick hoped so too. *I don't want to be anything like Adarian.*

That eerie red tint returned to Ambrose's eyes— not that Nick needed a reminder that the creature next to him wasn't human. "Neither did he and he's not quite the jerk you think he is. In time, you'll understand him better than you'll want to. And together, if we're lucky, we'll keep you from following in his footsteps. In the meantime, I have to teach you everything I know as quickly as I can."

What's the rush?

Orange flickered in his red eyes, like dancing flames. "My time's running out and soon I won't . . ." His voice trailed off.

You won't what?

"I won't care anymore. About anyone or anything . . . not even *you*." Ambrose took Nick's hand and manifested an ornate gold dagger in his palm. The pommel held an elaborate pattern that looked like a circle of ancient birds spiraling out. And on the cross hilt was a bloodred ruby that seemed to be radiating warmth.

Nick frowned at it. *What's this?*

"The seal of the Malachai. With that dagger, there's nothing you can't kill. Gods, demons, zombies . . . you name it or, more to the point, stab it and they'll all fall to you."

Why are you giving this to me?

"In part so that it won't tempt me, and so that you can cut through the zombies who'll come for you tonight." He took Nick's hand and laid his palm over the center of the dagger. "Close your eyes and imagine it the size of a pocket knife."

Do what?

"Trust me, Nick."

Nick did as he said and the moment he had the image in his mind, the dagger shrank. Gasping, he opened his eyes to see it no longer than his index finger.

Ambrose handed him the sheath for it, which was a matching size. "You can carry it with you anywhere you go. To make it bigger, just imagine the size you want it. It can be a sword, a dagger, or a knife."

Are you serious?

He nodded. "It'll even go through airport security. No creature or machine will ever detect it."

How is that possible?

That familiar sadness returned to Ambrose's face. "I'm going to show you things you never thought possible. Show you a world you never dreamed existed. And for that I'm sorry. But it has to be done and better I show it to you than you learn it the way I had to."

It was obvious from his words and demeanor that he was a summa cum laude graduate from the school of massive groin kicks. And as Nick watched him stare at his dozing mother, he couldn't help wondering one thing.

How old are you?

Ambrose sighed before he answered. "I've lived hundreds of years."

Nick gaped in awe. Ambrose didn't look a day over twenty-four. Was it really possible to live that long?

Then again, Ash had. And with that thought came another one that he was dying to know, even though in his gut he already had a good idea of what the answer was.

What about my dad? How old is he? 'Cause right now, Nick was going to bet he wasn't the midthirties he appeared to be, either.

Ambrose took his mother's hand into his and held it to his heart. "Much, much older than I am."

He'd suspected it, but the truth hit him like a cheap gut shot. He tried to imagine what it would be like to live through centuries. It had to be a lot of fun.

And extremely lonely.

Will I live that long?

"With luck, and I hope you live those years much happier than I have."

Meaning?

"Meaning, I need you to focus. If you want to save Madaug, you need to listen to me or the mortents will eat both of you Pop-Tarts for breakfast."

I'm listening.

Ambrose cursed as the car slowed down. "We're at Kyrian's house. This'll have to wait."

Nick started to ask what he meant, but the moment he looked out the window, he understood. There was a small crowd of people gathered in front of the house. Male and female, half of them carried baseball bats and staves. Interesting weapons that made him wonder what they carried that he couldn't see.

Nick looked at Caleb. "Uh, is it just me or is that half our class?"

"Yeah, I'm thinking it's a reunion or, since it is our classmates, a collection of idiots. Let's call it a meese. Like geese, only with morons."

Bubba pulled into the driveway, where Tad was issuing orders to the others.

Nick got out first while Ambrose materialized beside him.

Tad had his back to them while he spoke to a group that included Kyle and Alex Peltier, Stone, Casey, but oddly enough no Brynna. "Since there are only four Dark-Hunters in the city tonight, they're doing everything they can to combat the Daimons, who are taking advantage of the zombie situation to come out in force and feed and blame the deaths on them."

Nick frowned at Caleb while Bubba went to the back to get his mom.

"What's a Daimon?" Nick asked Ambrose.

"You really want to know?"

"Enlighten me."

A strange light flickered in Ambrose's eyes.

"Soulsucking vampires. While they drain humans of blood, they don't feed on that. They only drink the blood to kill you and then once you're dead and your soul leaves your body, they suck it into their bodies and live on its essence."

Nick took a step back in disbelief. "You're screwing with me."

Ambrose shook his head. "No I'm not, and you will one day be very intimate with several of them."

"I don't like your tone, Ambrose." Most of all, he didn't like what Ambrose was implying.

"You'll like it even less on the day you meet a Daimon named Stryker. But that's another story. . . ." Ambrose indicated Tad with a jerk of his chin. "He, on the other hand, is a good friend to have. Entertaining as all get out."

Nick scowled as he listened to Tad's speech while Bubba carried his mom into the house.

"Since the Dark-Hunters are busy, Eric needs us. For those who haven't heard, who are wondering why you were called, his mother and brothers are missing. Taken, we think, by the bokor. Eric doesn't know where they are." His gaze went to Stone and the Peltiers. "We need you guys to help us track them and find them."

Stone sneered at the Peltiers. "They can't track for crap."

Alex started for him, but Kyle caught him and held him back. "You don't want to kill the wolf, A. They taste like dry chicken."

Stone stiffened in outrage. "Who you calling a chicken?"

"Bock, bock," Alex said with a grin. "If the beak fits . . ."

This time several others came between them as Stone lunged for Alex.

Tad growled at them. "Were-Hunters down. This is not the time for y'all to be acting up. We need you."

Nick scowled. There was that word again. And in spite of what Tad had said, he was convinced it wasn't a gamer's term.

Russell turned around and saw him and Caleb. "How long have the mundanes been here?"

Caleb scoffed. "Not mundanes, dweeb. We have more right to be here than any of you."

Stone sneered at Caleb. "You're out of your element here, Malphas."

Caleb opened his hand. Just like Ambrose had done in the alley, he manifested a fireball. He threw it at Stone so that it landed at his feet and illuminated Stone's entire body. "Don't cross me, Scooby-Doo. I'm not an old man in a mask waiting to be thwarted by you meddling kids."

Tad nodded. "And Gautier is now working for Kyrian. It's not like he's not going to find out what we are sooner or later."

"And what are you?" Nick asked.

Carl Samuel, one of Tad's friends who had blond hair and blue eyes, stepped forward. "We're multigenerational Squires."

"Which means what?" Nick asked. "You prance around with tinfoil armor and plastic swords pretending to be knights?"

Carl laughed while Russ insulted both Nick's intelligence and parentage.

Tad ignored them as he answered the question. "We are humans in the service of the goddess Artemis who help her and her soldiers protect mankind from the evil that preys on us. St. Richard's is our New Orleans training ground for those of us who come from a long line of Squires."

"Yeah," Carl said. "It's why some of us haven't been real welcoming to you. We don't like being with mundanes who don't know about us. No offense."

No offense? Most of them had been royal jerks to him.

Carl indicated the Peltiers and Stone. "They're shapeshifters. Most of the football team is." His gaze went to Caleb. "We didn't know about you and your powers."

Caleb shrugged. "There was never any need for you to know about me, and none of you will know about me when you get up in the morning, either."

Stone snorted. "That don't work on us."

"Oh yeah, Scooby, it does. You and I have gone round many a day. I'm the reason you keep thinking you've had alien abductions."

Nick laughed. "I knew there was a reason I always liked you."

Caleb leaned forward, between Nick and Ambrose, then said in a low tone, "By the way, boss . . .
you're not as covert as you think, and I've heard everything you told the kid in the car." He looked straight
at Ambrose. "Nice coat, but I prefer the black suit you
had on the last time we met."

Ambrose made a Vader move that made it look
like something had grabbed Caleb in an invisible
choke hold. "Don't push your luck, Malphas."

Caleb relaxed as Ambrose moved away. "You
know, Nick, I like you so much better than that
prick."

For some reason, Nick wasn't sure that was a compliment.

"All right," Tad said, demanding everyone's attention again. "We need to break into four groups and
see what we can find."

Alex Peltier indicated Nick with his thumb. "I'll
head out with Bubba, Nick, and crew."

"All right. If anyone finds anything, remember to
call it in, and we move as a group. I don't want anyone
to be a hero. We don't need to die tonight."

Nick still wasn't sure what was happening as Alex came over to them. "Why did you pick us?"

"I like helping the newbs and most of the rest of them get on my nerves. If nothing else, Bubba and Mark are always good for a laugh."

Nick's stomach hit the ground. "Yeah, but I think the zombies ate Mark."

"What?" Alex looked shocked.

"Yeah," Caleb said sadly. "When we were at Madaug's house, the undead zombies attacked and we haven't seen or heard from him since. It's not looking good."

Alex appeared ill. "That's a shame. I really liked whenever Mark would drink too much and play cards with my uncles and Eros. It's highly entertaining."

Nick indicated the door with his thumb. "I'm going to check on my mom and Bubba. I'll be right back." He took a step, then paused and returned his attention to Alex. "Are you really a shapeshifter?"

Alex nodded. "You know the club Sanctuary on Ursulines?"

"Yeah."

"My family owns it and almost all of us are shape-shifters."

Nick shook his head. "Get out."

"Nah, for real."

Nick knew he wasn't kidding, but it was really too much to believe. "So what do you turn into?"

"A bear."

Nick laughed as he finally understood one of Sanctuary's long-standing traditions. "You the bear people wrestle for free drinks?"

"Nah. That's my uncle Quinn."

And on that note, Nick went inside to find his mom. Bubba was in the living room talking to Phil. He interrupted them only long enough to find out where Bubba had taken her, then he headed up to the guest room.

Entering the bedroom, Nick approached the huge bed that was decorated with maroon and gold, and looked down at his mom as she slept. She looked so frail against the dark gold sheets.

Protect your mama, boy. His father's voice rang in his ears, but he didn't need to hear his dad to know his obligations. He was the man of the house and it was his job to protect her.

Even when she didn't want it.

And right now, they had to go stop an apocalypse and hopefully save a friend. Not to mention the city that would be overrun by zombies soon if they didn't get to the mortents and drive them back to their hole.

Nick shook his head at the irony. Just yesterday his biggest concern was catching up in chem class after having been shot. Now it was saving the world.

I'm too young for this. . . .

"Unfortunately, you're not."

He turned at the sound of Ambrose's voice. "Where'd you go?"

"To get this." Ambrose handed him an old leather-bound book that was just a hair larger than a thin paperback novel.

Nick opened it, then frowned as he saw nothing but blank pages. "What is this? A journal?"

"Your grimoire. As you unlock your powers, incantations will appear that will allow you to further hone your skills. Pages will be added."

"Isn't that backwards? Shouldn't I have instructions first?"

Ambrose shook his head. "It doesn't work that way." He indicated Nick's pocket. "You still have the dagger I gave you?"

"Yeah."

"Pull it out and place it on the first page."

Nick set the book on the dresser since he only had the one arm. He pulled out the dagger and did what Ambrose said. The moment he did, a peculiar script wrote itself across the page in bloodred ink. He started to ask Ambrose what it said, but as he looked at it, he understood.

How could that be?

The veil is thin and so you see.
What lies beneath the surface tree.
In this regard they'll never fool.
But still be wary of becoming their tool.

Ambrose took the dagger from his hand and used it to prick his fingertip.

Nick cursed. "What are you doing?"

Ambrose didn't answer. Instead he let three drop of blood splash on the page. *"Dredanya eire coulet,"* he whispered as they fell. Then the blood droplets rushed in a circle before they exploded and added more words to the page.

Tonight the moon rises full.
And you will feel evil's pull.
Stand strong and fight them to the end.
Only by remaining faithful will you win.

Ambrose handed him the dagger back. "Any time you want advice or instruction, you can use that spell. In time, you'll be able to use it to find prophecy and foretell the future."

Nick gaped. "Really?"

Ambrose inclined his head. "And on that note, I have to go." He did look a bit pale, like something was draining his powers. "Good luck, Nick."

"Thanks."

Ambrose inclined his head before he faded out.

Nick took one last look at his mom, then the book, before he slid it into his back pocket. Steeled by determination, he left the room and went downstairs, where Phil and Bubba were still talking. He'd overheard Phil saying earlier that Kyrian had told him to come and look after him and his mom.

It didn't make sense to Nick that Phil would be at Kyrian's beck and call, but far be it from him to question it. If he knew anything it was that adults didn't like telling kids anything they didn't have to.

Phil smiled at him. "Don't worry, Nick. I'll protect her till you get back."

Bubba eyed Phil suspiciously. "I don't know if there's much you could do if someone broke in."

An insidious smile curved Phil's lips. "Don't let the suit fool you. I promise I'm a lot tougher than I look."

Nick frowned as he saw the strangest thing . . . it was a spiderweb tattoo on Phil's hand. Granted it was faint, but there was no missing it. It completely went against Phil's posh dress and upper-crust demeanor. "That's cool. You get it when you were young?"

Phil covered the tattoo with his other hand. "I did indeed."

"Nick?" Bubba said to get his attention. "We need to head out."

He thanked Phil for watching after his mom before he followed Caleb, Alex, and Bubba to the SUV. Nick sighed as he got in and took his seat. "Is it just me or has this been the longest night?"

Bubba snorted. "You do what I do, kid, and they get even longer."

Nick noticed there was a thick air of sadness around Bubba as he started the truck. "You're worried about Mark?"

Bubba bristled as if offended by the question, but Nick recognized that bluster. Bubba was definitely upset and concerned. "Why would I be worried about him? He's a tough little son of a biscuit eater. No zombie could get him. He's better than that."

But Nick could hear the truth in that gruff tone. Tough or not, it only took one hit to end a life, and that was what they were all keeping in mind as they headed out.

"So, Alex?" Bubba asked. "How you going to track?"

Alex held up a small handheld device. "GPS." He turned around in the seat to wink at Caleb and Nick.

Bubba wasn't so easily fooled. "How are you getting coordinates?"

"Madaug's cell phone."

"Ah, okay. Just tell me where to go."

Alex gave a sly grin as if he was holding back. After a second, he closed his eyes and Nick could tell he was using some kind of preternatural powers to seek out Madaug and his family.

While he did that, Bubba turned on the radio, which was playing an emergency broadcast signal that was followed by a newscaster telling them the mayor was issuing a citywide curfew due to a vicious outbreak of severe flu.

Caleb scoffed. "I told you they'd blame this on a disease."

Bubba turned left down Canal. "They don't want people to start panicking. For once I can't blame them. The more people on the street, the more vics in the morgue."

infinity

The newscaster continued. "The police are implementing a citywide curfew. All residents are urged to stay in while they secure the Quarter. Anyone found outside will be arrested."

"And all zombies will be shot," Nick added with a laugh.

"Should we head back?" Alex asked.

Bubba shrugged. "That's what common sense would say. What do you think?"

Nick leaned back in his seat. "Far be it from me to ever let my common sense get in the way of my stupidity. I say we press on. Caleb?"

He flashed a cheesy grin. "What's an arrest record anyway? Me, Alex, and Nick are minors."

"To infinity then."

Nick frowned at Bubba's words. "What's that mean?"

"It's something my dad used to say when I was a kid. To infinity, meaning you'd see something through to the end."

Nick didn't get it. "Infinity is never-ending."

"That's right, which means you keep going and

going no matter what happens or what obstacles you meet. Over, under, around, or through. There's always a way. And if you have to chase something to infinity, strap on your big-boy pants, hiking boots, and go."

Nick opened his mouth to speak, but before he could, something slammed into the SUV. One minute, they were fine.

The next, they were spinning out of control.

CHAPTER 17

Nick's head slammed into the glass so hard, he saw stars as the SUV rolled over and over, careening out of control. It felt like it was never going to stop, and it didn't until something catapulted them against the concrete wall of the I-10 overpass. They hit it so hard, he was amazed it didn't snap the truck in half.

Groaning, Nick saw Bubba lying unconscious, pinned between the steering wheel and seat. His brow was split and blood trickled down his face, dripping onto his shirt. Alex was breathing like a woman in labor as he tried to open his door. He was covered in blood with a split lip and swelling eye. But the most shocking was Caleb, who'd lost his human appearance entirely.

Whoa, not only was his skin red, but it glowed in the faint light. And those serpentine eyes with their diamond-shaped pupils were off the creepy weird chart.

Nick tried to move. But raw pain pounded through him, making it hard to breathe while Caleb tried to unbuckle his seat belt. One of his hands looked like it might be broken. Even so, Caleb didn't let it deter him at all.

"Alex?" Caleb said, his voice reverberating with a deep accent. "We're under attack. Can you get out?"

Alex made the sound of an angry grizzly. "Something has my powers locked. I can't do squat, not even undo my seat belt. Are your powers working?"

"No. I can't even hold my human form."

All of a sudden Nick smelled the pungent stench of sulphur and death.

Caleb cursed as he started kicking the side window. As soon as the glass was out, he grabbed Nick and shoved him through the opening he'd made. Nick hissed as agony erupted down his shoulder and arm from the manhandling.

Dang, it hurt.

Caleb climbed out and grabbed his good arm. Dragging him along behind him, Caleb was speaking in a language that Nick couldn't understand.

"Dude, I don't think we're supposed to be moving until the medics get here after a wreck like that. I think I broke something. We could sever our spines or something."

"You're about to break a lot more than your spine." Caleb turned and looked up over their heads. Cursing, he grabbed Nick and shoved him into a drainage pipe. "Don't move, and breathe only if you have to."

What kind of stupid comment was that?

Nick started to argue until he saw what had Caleb so worried. These were . . .

Flying monkeys?

You wish. 'Cause instead of being cute little blue things in weird suits and hats, the things after them were huge, ugly creatures that turned his stomach. With bald heads, talons, and Shar-Pei-like skin, they gave foul a whole new meaning. And they smelled like rotten eggs. No, they smelled like four-day-old powdered eggs that had been left to mold in the August sun.

Or Bubba's shoes . . .

Their stench was so pungent, it was all he could do not to heave.

Caleb turned to fight them. They swarmed over him like the birds in the old-timey Hitchcock film. Nick couldn't even see the outline of his body as they took him down.

Terrified, he fell back deeper into the drain, out of their sight. Pulling the sword out, he whispered a prayer for some serious divine intervention.

The sound of wings beat against the night like a thunderous heartbeat. Sweat beaded on his forehead as he considered his options. He couldn't see much of anything in the darkness. If he went out there to run, they'd see him and swarm him too.

Gah, what do I do?

"Nick?"

He froze as he heard his mother's voice and what

sounded like her sobbing. *It's a trick.* There was no way she could be here. None.

"They're hurting me, baby. Help me. Please!"

It's not her. It's not her.

But what if it was?

What if it's not?

He put his hand on the cell phone, tempted to call her and see. But if it was a trick, they'd hear him.

What do I do?

He tightened his grip on the sword as he heard something crawling along the ground outside. It sounded like it was coming closer. He looked down at the bright ruby in the hilt and hesitated. This was his only weapon. If he lost it, he'd be completely at their mercy.

No, wait . . .

He had something else that might help. At least he hoped it would. Pulling out the book, he crouched low with it and used his cell phone as a light so that he could see the blank pages. Repeating what Ambrose had shown him, he pricked his finger with the dagger and let his blood fall on the page.

"What are these things after me?" he breathed.

His blood drew a picture of them that was even uglier than what he'd glimpsed. Then words appeared underneath the image to explain what they were. *Ta-ahiki demons. Third subculture with limited powers. They are fetchers sent in to retrieve objects and creatures for their masters. In this case . . . you.*

"How did they immobilize Caleb and Alex?"

Beneath the picture, another image appeared. This one was a small medallion that was highly ornate. Once again, words appeared. *Star of Ishtaryn. Demon kryptonite. Will weaken and cage any demonkyn who comes into contact with it, which includes half-breeds such as you.*

And it's not good for werebeasts either.

The book had some serious attitude.

"So what do I do?" Nick asked it.

The blood crawled to the opposite page.

When all is said and all is done,
The best thing for you to do now is to run.

"Run" appeared as a giant, jagged word. Nick slammed the book shut, put it in his pocket, and did exactly what it said. He tore out of the pipe and hesitated as he saw the remnants of Bubba's SUV. *Please don't be dead.*

He barely had time to finish that thought before the demons saw him and reversed course. With a shriek, they turned like a flock of birds and came for him, wings flapping. He shrank the sword and put it in his pocket. With his head down low, he ran with everything he had.

For several minutes he seemed to be making ground.

Then, just as he was sure he'd escape, they dropped and shoved him hard. The motion propelled him forward, to the ground. Nick cried out as his shoulder and arm hit the street. The pain was so severe that for a moment, he thought he'd pass out from it.

Run! The word screamed through his mind. He pushed himself up, but the demons hit him again and again across his back. This time, they stabbed him with their talons repeatedly until the pain overwhelmed him.

Don't pass out. Don't you dare.

But it was too late. His sight was already dimming. The last thing he saw was Bubba's SUV bursting into flames and exploding.

Then everything went black.

Nick came awake to the worst pain imaginable pounding through his skull. He felt like someone was clawing out his right eye. How anything could hurt this bad and not kill him, he couldn't imagine.

Then he heard the faint sound of a little kid crying. Blinking open his eyes, he realized he was lying facedown on a cold earth floor in a tiny cell. The crying came from a boy around the age of ten who sat in a corner with his legs pulled tight to his chest. His brown eyes swam with tears as he sobbed against his knees.

"Shhh," Nick breathed. He didn't want the kid to be upset. But more than that, he didn't want the sound echoing through his head.

The boy looked up as he sniffed back his tears. "Are you going to hurt me?"

Nick started to tell him only if he kept crying, but luckily he caught himself before he traumatized the kid further. "No. Are you Madaug's brother?"

"You know Madaug?"

"Yeah."

"Is he okay?"

Nick grimaced as more pain laced through his skull. "I have no idea. Have you seen him?"

He nodded. "They brought him in here when they took my mama. Then they locked me in here and haven't been back. I'm so scared."

"It'll be all right." At least Nick hoped he wasn't lying to the kid.

"That's not what they told me. They told me they were going to eat my brains."

"Nah. Only older brothers do that."

The kid actually laughed. "My name's Ian. Who are you?"

"Nick."

"Can you get us out of here?"

Nick looked around. The room didn't appear to have a door or anything else, which meant no, he couldn't. But he didn't want to tell the kid that. "How did we get in here?"

Ian pointed to the wall to his left. "A door appears right there whenever they want in or out."

Nick got up and looked for a switch or trapdoor or something. But all he saw was the wall.

Figures.

He pulled out his cell phone and tried to call Kyrian. Big surprise, it didn't work. But at least he still had his book and the dagger. They weren't completely defenseless.

Yet he felt completely defeated as the magnitude of this situation hit him hard. How could he not? Everything had gone bad tonight. Bubba and Alex were dead. Tabitha, Eric, and Mark were probably dead too. And Simi and Caleb.

No one, including him, knew where he was.

What am I going to do?

He didn't see a way out of this.

"Ambrose?" he called, trying to summon his guardian to him.

There was no answer.

"Dude, c'mon," he called out to Ambrose. "You've popped in all night long. Can't you come the one time I actually want to see you?"

Of course Ambrose still didn't answer, 'cause, again, that would just be too easy.

Nick sighed in frustration. This was not how he'd imagined this day playing out. Yet here he was about to be eaten by demons or turned into a zombie.

Who'll take care of my mom now?

That wave of hopelessness washed through him only to be replaced by one of raw determination as he thought about his mom being left defenseless. He would not go down like this. Whining on the floor like the kid in front of him. He'd survived too much to just lie down and die like some cheap bimbo in a horror movie.

Oh no. He was Nick Gautier. A kid born standing up and talking back. No one ever got the better of him and he'd be damned if they were going to start now.

If what Ambrose had told him was true, he had powers inside him. Powers he should be able to use. All he had to do was figure out how to tap into them.

Pulling out the book, he used the blood incantation again. "How do I get out of here?"

Ian crept forward to see what he was doing, but he didn't say anything while he watched. The blood swirled around the page until it answered Nick's question.

Here you are and here you'll stay,
Until you learn a better way.

"Uh, hemoglobin, a little clarity would be nice. Could you be a little more specific for me?"

Born of time. Born of space.
First you must find your place.

"Can I get a yes or no from you? Are you going to tell me how to get out of here or not?"

Yes or no is not for me to speak.
Rather the answer is for you to seek.

Nick curled his lip in disgust at the cryptic answers. "Oh, you suck."

Suck and blow so you say.

But I'm not the one trapped with no getaway.

Anger ripped through him. "Leave it to me to find the only book known to sass its owner." Growling in aggravation, he slammed it shut and choked it.

Ian frowned at him. "What are you doing?"

"At the moment, wishing I could burn a book." It heated up in his hand to the point it was actually painful to hold. "Stop that!" he snapped at it.

It cooled down.

Nick raked his hand through his hair. How did he use those powers?

Closing his eyes, he concentrated like he did to make his dagger bigger and larger.

Nothing.

Except his headache got worse. A lot worse. *This is useless.*

"We're going to die, aren't we?" Ian asked.

Nick shook his head. "No, Ian, we're not. I'll keep you safe. I promise."

"What if you can't?"

"Dude, have a little faith. Okay?"

SHERRILYN KENYON

Sniffing back his tears, he nodded.

Nick had always wondered what it'd be like to have a brother or sister. He could see where they might get on his nerves, but the way Ian looked up at him like he was a hero . . .

A guy could get used to that. And it made him want to be worthy of that look.

The door in the side of the wall opened. Nick put himself between Ian and the tall, sinister figure who came through the newly created doorway.

It cocked its head as it stared at him and Ian. "Are you not pleased by your offering?"

Nick was perplexed by the question. "What?"

The black blob gestured to Ian. "Does he not meet with your satisfaction, my lord?"

"Satisfaction for what?"

Another figure stepped around him. This one was a small, tiny woman with dark tawny skin. She looked like a beautiful angel. "Your human sacrifice. We thought by now you'd have devoured him."

Ian's eyes widened as he stepped away from Nick. "I'm not going to hurt a kid."

They looked as baffled as he felt. Were they crazy?

An evil laugh rippled in the air around him. "Stand down, my children. He's not our Malachai yet. Our embryo is still thinking he's human. But he'll learn. Now bring him to me."

Ian started crying.

Nick refused to go without him. "I'm not leaving him alone. He's scared."

The female scowled. "What do you care?"

"I care a lot." Nick held his hand out for Ian, who took it and held it tight.

"Let him bring the small creature," the blob said. "There's no harm in it."

"Very well." The woman stepped back. "If you'll follow me."

Nick obeyed and the blob fell in behind them as the woman led the way down a dank hallway that reminded him of an old factory. "Where are we?"

"That's not important." She opened a door and stood back to let him and Ian enter first. Nick hesitated. Glancing around, he made sure there was no immediate threat before he moved forward.

Inside was a large room that definitely belonged to a warehouse. The rusted green walls had seen better years. There was dust, cobwebs, and broken glass every-where.

But that wasn't what was important.

It was Madaug, his mom, Eric, Tabitha, and Stone, who were all being held in a cage.

"Mama!" Ian ran to his mother to hug her through the bars.

Nick knew better than to be so relieved, as he saw the three demons who seemed to be in charge. He recognized the woman from the alley and the two men who had been with her. Now in human form, they were dressed all in leather. The men in black and the woman in bright bloodred.

Her blond hair was slicked back from her face as she approached him slowly like a predator. "You are ever a surprise."

He didn't know what that meant, but he was pretty sure it wasn't a good thing. "What's going on here?"

She gestured to the wall on his right, where a huge monitor was set up and a game was on pause. "Do you know the power of that game?"

"I know the power of all games. They're mesmerizing." His mom called them time-sucks because once you started playing, human concept of time slowed down. What seemed like five minutes of play equaled an hour in real time. Even Menyara had called them a tool of evil.

In this case, she might be right.

Nick saw the dazed look on Tabitha, Madaug, and Eric's faces. "What have you done to them?"

"They're the ones who played." She held a controller out for him. "Don't you want to join them in a match and beat their high score?"

The blob put his hand on Nick's shoulder and pushed him toward the woman. Suddenly, he felt trapped. Stifled.

It was a sensation he'd always hated. And one that ignited his temper.

She took the game off pause. "Look at it, Nicholas."

Nick tried to turn away, but the blob grabbed him and forced him to face it. He slammed his eyes shut. The blob grabbed him from behind and forced his lids open until he had no choice but to watch.

His breathing ragged, Nick struggled as hard as he could, but it was futile.

Before he even realized what he was doing, he was watching the central character—a blond man dressed in a long flowing coat—executing the army of zombies in an old cemetery as the game's mission scrolled across the screen. The impulse to play radiated through him until he had no choice except to obey.

In a world where ancient evil has been unleashed, there is only one hope for mankind.

You.

Your mission is to fight the zombies, humans who've been turned into mindless killers, through the cemetery to the ancient catacombs where an elixir was hidden long ago by a fair princess. Collect your items of protection and weapons along the way until you are virtually indestructible.

Your wits and your prowess are the only things that can't be taken away. But be warned. Even those closest to you can be turned and they will turn against you while you fight. The only way to power up is to eat the hearts of your enemies and to lay waste to as many as you can. Your experience points will dramatically increase the power of your blows.

Good luck, warrior.

May the ancient gods be with you.

The lights of the game flashed, entrancing him. Nick struggled to stay alert to everything around him, but he couldn't focus on anything except the main character. It was like the two of them were one. Like he was Necodemus the Necromancer fighting through the ever-growing army of zombies.

Every kill gave him a heart or weapon to collect. Every kill brought him closer to the catacomb. . . .

You are ours, a voice whispered in his ear.

Nick felt himself slipping into a fog. Completely unaware of everything around him, he played the game. It was like he stood on a precipice that allowed him to see straight into infinity. Time slowed and bent, the universe whispered secrets to him.

And with every kill he felt more powerful.

More invincible.

You are the Malachai. Those words whispered through his mind as images assaulted him. Images of him beating down his enemies. Of every bully, every Stone and Mr. Peters in his life getting exactly what they deserved. Not death—that would be too kind for their special breed of brutality—something worse. Much, much worse.

They became him. They were the ones who were mocked and belittled and laughed at, and made to feel like they were less than nothing.

Each and every one of them. Every insult. Every snide comment and look. It was all returned to them tenfold.

They begged for mercy while he gave to them the same amount they'd given him in his life.

None whatsoever.

Take that, you scum-sucking snipes. Eat your words and your cruelty. May you drown in it and die.

"He's ours now," the mortent leader announced. "Not made by evil, but birthed by human cruelty." She handed Nick a sword. "Now take your vengeance on the ones who've mocked you. Kill them and eat their brains."

Nick turned to Stone, whose eyes were large and filled with terror. Every nasty comment and insult he'd ever given Nick played through his head now. Right down to Stone getting him thrown off the team. To Stone trying to get him thrown out of school. . . .

Screaming in outrage, Nick ran at the pig so that he could gut him once and for all.

CHAPTER 18

Stone fell back in his cage, screaming like a four-year-old girl who'd lost her favorite toy as he held his arms up to protect himself and beg for his life.

Nick tasted vengeance and honestly . . .

It was sweet and satisfying.

But it wasn't filling, no matter how much he wanted it to be. In fact, it was hollow and cold. Even though he tried to tell himself Stone deserved nothing but the humiliation he'd heaped onto others' heads, that he deserved to die for what he'd done to other people, Nick couldn't buy it.

He finally understood what Ambrose had tried to tell him about Mike, Tyree, and Alan.

I don't want to be like Stone and the others.

To have no friends. No decency. To not be able to enjoy anything because he was too busy being jealous and petty over other people.

Stone was pathetic. He was weak.

Most of all, he wasn't worth Nick damning himself for. In the end, nothing could be crueler than leaving Stone to live his putrid life of false friends and petty jealousies. Friends who didn't really like him. Who only wanted to use him for what they could get.

Yeah, that was hell on earth and he wanted no part of it. While Nick could be happy wearing used clothes and living in squalor with his mother and Menyara, Stone couldn't be happy in a mansion with every overpriced toy and gadget his parents could give him.

How could Nick ever envy or want that?

He doesn't deserve to live. Think of all *the others he's tortured. The others he'll torture in the future if you let him go.*

Nick pressed the tip of his sword against Stone's throat as Stone wet his pants and wept. And still the voice in his head was unrelenting.

Spill the blood of your enemy and you will command armies. . . . You will be free.

No one will ever mock you again.

Ever.

He felt the cold hand of something evil on the nape of his neck, caressing him. "Do it," a soft, gentle voice urged. "Make yourself strong enough to command the respect of everyone you meet. Then no one will mock you ever again. You have to kill your enemies to have respect and be free of your past."

The mortent was right. The only way to be free was to kill his enemies and bury them deep.

But there was more than one way to slay them. Stone and his kind had already taken up too much of his past. Nick wasn't about to give them his future too.

All of a sudden, the dagger and book in his pocket heated up as something inside him was freed. Not by his hatred. Not by his need for revenge.

It was his sense of justice. A clarity of thought he'd never had before. He didn't want the respect of people who weren't worth wiping his nose on—people who weren't worth the spat-out gum attached to the bottom of his worn-out shoes.

The only respect he wanted was from himself and the people who really mattered in his life. The people who really loved and cared about him.

That definitely wasn't Stone or the mortents or any of the stuck-up snobs in his school or his principal.

It was from his mother and a bunch of Bourbon Street strippers who were raising him to be better. From people like Menyara, Liza, Bubba, and Kyrian.

Most of all, he wanted to be worth the respect and love of Nekoda.

"You got it." Nick stepped back and turned on the mortents. "My enemies aren't the bullies in my life." Honestly, people like Stone had made him strong and he was thankful for that. He'd found strength in his pain. Strength of character and dignity. The strength to hold his head high no matter what cruelty the world hurled at him. The very things Stone and his ilk lacked.

His enemies weren't the pathetic buttwipes who mocked and hated him for things he couldn't help.

His enemies were the ones who told him lies under the guise of being his friends. The ones who wanted him to be like them. To ruin his life and throw away everything he'd worked so hard to become.

He heard the book whispering to him. . . .

"*Arrasee-terra. Gitana mortelay dohn. Erra me tihani vassau. Pur mi.*" *Let me see truth. Never let flattery or hatred blind me. This is my life and I will live it wisely. For me.*

Not for them.

Nick threw his head back as an electric wave ripped through him. It was like a heated wire that connected every cell of his body. For one brief instant, he heard the breath of the cosmos.

"Kill him!" the mortent leader screamed.

Nick felt his arm heal instantly as he threw their sword at them. Pulling out his own, he made it bigger, then turned and broke the lock on the cage door.

Stone ran out, screaming, leaving the others behind.

"You flippin' coward." Nick kicked back the first demon to reach him as he kept them from Tabitha, Erik, Madaug, and his mother.

Ian was crying again as he tried to get his mom to wake up and see him.

Nick drove back the demons, but it didn't last long. Worse, they used Tabitha, Eric, and Madaug to attack him because they knew he wouldn't hurt them. Not while they were being used.

I need some way to shock them. . . .

"Where's a cattle prod when I need one?"

There wasn't even an outlet here. Was it too much to ask for a lightning strike? Yeah, okay, so the sky was clear, but still . . .

He cut across the blob demon and spun to fight the woman. All of a sudden, he felt his hand heat up as an image of Ambrose and Caleb conjuring fire went through his mind.

If they could conjure fire, could he conjure electricity?

What the heck? Might as well try. Worst thing that could happen is he'd fail and be killed by his friends.

Which was looking like the most favored outcome anyway.

Please let this work.

"Karatei!" He threw his hand out and what appeared to be a bolt of lightning shot from his fingertips to Madaug.

And it turned him into a goat.

Ah, crap.

Madaug ran at him and head-butted him backwards into a demon. Nick shoved the demon away and regained his balance. He glared at the goat as it eyed him. "Dude, I'm trying to help you."

But the goat didn't care; he ran at him again.

Trying to avoid a goat butt to his groin, Nick was completely surrounded while Ian kept crying for his mom to wake up. "I wish *I* could wake up from this nightmare."

Growling, he tried again to blast Madaug with his powers. The goat squealed and shook.

Oh, please don't die.

It'd kill Nick to know he'd done that to him.

The goat shuddered, then finally dissolved.

Nick's stomach hit the floor. Ah, crap. But no sooner had he stepped toward the goat's remains than it snapped up and Madaug returned to being a teenager.

Relief tore through him that he hadn't killed him. But it was short-lived as the zombies kept coming.

And Madaug was still one of them.

Worse, undead zombies were filling the room, while Tabitha and Eric tried to rip his arm off.

Nick twisted away from them. *I'm so dead. . . .*

He grabbed Ian's hand and pulled him behind his back before Ian's mom took a chunk out of the poor little guy. "Don't cry, kid. I'll protect you."

But who's going to protect me?

Now would be a good time for these supposed powers I have to kick in and help. Really . . . what were they waiting for?

He'd engrave an invitation, but by the time he finished it, he'd be zombie bits. His heart pounded as he realized how hopeless it was. They were growing in number and he was tiring at the same rate. Every time he swung with the sword, it took more out of him, and while they'd stumble back, he wasn't killing any of them. Honestly, he wasn't even slowing them down.

He was surrounded and they were hungry for what few brain cells he had left. But you know what? He wasn't about to give in or give up. If he was going to go out, it would be the way he'd come into this world.

Fighting for every single breath.

No one gets the better of me.

Ever.

Growling out loud, he fought the demons and zombies back with everything he had.

The walls around him shook and rumbled. Ian hid behind him, knotting his tiny hands in the tail end of Nick's shirt, as he tried to make it to a window or door so that at least the little guy would survive the night. But he was getting tired. His stamina was lagging.

A crash sounded to his right.

His stomach hit the ground as cold dread filled him. Expecting it to be more zombies, Nick backed away.

Out of nowhere, a huge gray extended-cab pickup

truck that had metal plates welded to it like a cattle scoop came through the wall, narrowly missing him and Ian. It careened through the zombies at a break-neck speed as if it was a lawnmower after crabgrass.

Nick froze as the driving style reminded him of his favorite redneck savant.

No, it couldn't be. . . .

They were dead. . . .

But even so a glimmer of hope ignited inside him.

A loud "Yee-haw" sounded as the truck doors were slung open and Bubba, Mark, Caleb, Nekoda, Simi, and Alex spilled out with weapons galore (well, not Simi; she came out bearing only a large bottle of bar-becue sauce while licking her chops, and interestingly enough, she wore a large white lobster bib). Mark was armed with a flamethrower as he ran for the first group of zombies.

Bubba stood in the door and propped his arms up on the top of the truck with a crossbow so that he could snipe at them. "Head down, Mark!" he shouted before he let fly an arrow that landed right between the eyes of the zombie in front of Mark.

Nekoda ran to Nick with a cattle prod. "Here, I'll trade you." She handed it to him, then took Ian from him and ran with the kid to the truck so that Bubba could keep him safe.

Nick used the cattle prod to zap Tabitha, Eric, Madaug, and his mom. They staggered back as their brains rebooted and they became human again.

Tabitha recovered the quickest. Snarling in anger, she grabbed the demon nearest her and snapped his neck. "Turn me into a zombie . . . you suck!" She jerked a set of sais out of her boots and went to town on their rotten hides.

How she remembered being a zombie, Nick had no idea, but he was too busy fighting off the others to worry about it right now. Eric pulled the metal belt off his waist, which turned out to be an iron whip, and took up a position at Tabitha's back so that he could guard her while Madaug took his mother to Bubba's truck to stay with Ian.

Simi was snapping off pieces of the zombies and laughing as she skipped around them, daring them to touch her. Meanwhile, Caleb, in human form, was fighting the three demons with moves Jet Li would envy.

Nekoda came out of the truck with a katana she brandished like a ninja queen. Nick froze as he watched her for a second. Dang, she was flexible and skilled.

He hissed as a zombie shoved him. Turning, he shocked it, then stabbed it with his sword.

And still they kept coming. Nothing they did seemed to matter. This new breed of zombie wouldn't be stopped. Not by hacking, burning, or stabbing. Dog, who trained them? The Terminator?

Nekoda screamed.

Nick turned to see two zombies on her like the last piece of steak in a dog kennel.

His heart sank. They were going to kill her.

Do something. Because if he didn't, they wouldn't survive this.

You will have the power to command the dead. . . .

Ambrose might have been on meth. Or he might have been telling the truth.

Hoping for the latter, Nick ran to help her. The first zombie he reached spun on him and bit him hard in the shoulder. "I'm really getting tired of this." Nick stabbed the zombie through the heart.

Still it kept fighting.

"Run, Kody!"

She refused. "Not without you." While he appreciated the thought, the girl was insane.

Nick put himself between her and them. "This isn't looking good for us. Is it too late to switch sides?"

Kody gave him a smile that made him weak in the knees and strong in resolve. "I have faith in you, Nick." And then she did the most unexpected thing of all.

She pressed her lips against his.

Nick was stunned as he tasted her. For an instant, time stood still as his breath mixed with hers and her tongue swept against his. This . . . this was better than anything he'd ever dreamed and it made his entire body heat up.

Great, I would get my first real kiss three seconds before the zombies kill me.

His luck never changed.

Kody cried out as a zombie ripped her from his

arms and slung her to the ground. A group of them descended on her.

Nick felt the book heating again in his pocket as it whispered to him.

To make the dead behave,
Total dominion you must crave.

Huh? What crack was the book on?

But no sooner had he thought that than he finally understood. It was something Brynna had done a report on in school last year. At the time he'd thought it stupid, but he finally got it.

Visualization. In order to make something happen, to become something else, you had to see it clearly in your mind. That was the first step of achieving success. Vague dreams never amounted to anything. Only those that were fully seen could manifest.

Just like with the dagger.

Thoughts had power. Negative and positive. They influenced everything. They could empower a person or rip them to shreds.

And hopefully, tonight, they'd save all their lives.

Closing his eyes, Nick saw himself like the character in the Zombie Hunter video game.

I will fear no evil for I am the baddest beast in the land. I am the power they can't tear down. And my will is law.

They will do as I say. The dead don't command me.

I command them.

Power, true power, comes from within. Not without.

Laughing as the He-Man chant went through his head, Nick opened his eyes.

And everything looked different. There was a haze around the people and a dull glow over the zombies.

More than that, he could actually hear the zombies in his head. No, not zombies. What he heard were the evil souls that the mortents had summoned to take over the dead bodies and reanimate them.

The body was only a vessel. And it was time to empty it and send them home. *All* of them.

To make the zombies fall and vanish.

A simple spell and touch you must brandish.

Nick shook his head to clear that gibberish. "Really, book, your rhymes seriously suck."

Fine then, Malachai, you try rhyming in a language not your own. You're lucky I'm even helping you. Not like I care whether or not you live or die. You know I can get a whole new master who'd be glad to have me . . . human. It spat that last word at him like it was the lowest insult imaginable.

Yeah, his book had some serious attitude problems. But at least it whispered the words he needed.

> *Ashes to ashes.*
> *Zombie head gashes.*
> *Dust to dust.*
> *Return to your graves you must.*

But the words sounded so much better in the book's native tongue, which were:

> *Tirre Tirre.*
> *Grauz sa ton.*
> *Dhani Dhani*
> *Madabauhn.*

Thank goodness he only had to say the latter to kill them. Along with one more bit.

He had to touch them too. Gross, but effective, and the moment he said the words and put a hand on them, they fell to the ground like a bunch of bad actors.

Bubba and the others stood back as Nick made his way through them until the only ones left were the three demons who hadn't been banished.

The mortents glared at him.

"This isn't over, Malachai," the woman spat at him, her eyes glowing deep in the dim light.

Nick scoffed. "Oh yes it is. I banish your smelly arses back to the holes they crawled out of. You do not command me and you never will."

Evil laughter rang in his ears. "You say that today, but come tomorrow . . . it's so much easier to go wrong than it ever is to go right. We will win this. You'll see. Before all is said and done, you will be on our side. This I promise you."

Nick didn't believe it for a second. "You should never underestimate the stubbornness of a Cajun guttersnipe. We wrote the book on cutting our noses off to spite our faces." Glaring at them, he used his new-found powers to banish them.

Tabitha wiped the blood off her sais onto her pant legs. "That's right. Get thee behind me, bitches. I don't got no time for you. Ha!"

Nick shook his head. "Good thing there's only one of you, right?"

Eric snorted. "You do know she has a twin sister?"

Nick didn't even want to contemplate that gene pool. Right now, he was merely glad to have the demons gone and his life not threatened.

At least hopefully not for the next hour or so.

Kody came running up to him. "Are you all right?"

Before he could stop himself, Nick pulled her into his arms and held her. He just needed to feel someone close to him who wasn't trying to eat his brains or kill him.

And God, she felt great.

"Yeah, I'm all right. How did you get here?"

She pulled back to gesture toward Mark. "I was

surrounded by zombies when he showed up with his monster truck and ran them down. He told me to get in and I didn't argue."

Nick laughed. "I think that's how I got sucked into all of this." But it didn't explain everything.

He went over to Bubba, who was packing up his crossbow and bolts into Mark's truck. It was so good to see him alive, even if he did have a gash and bruise on his forehead. Nick would have hugged him in relief too, but knowing Bubba he might shoot him for it. "I saw the truck blow up. I thought you were dead."

Bubba pointed to Alex. "I told you about those shapeshifters and their wicked powers."

Alex held his hands up. "You're lucky they worked. At my age, it's a rare thing that they do what I want them to, and they're what caused the truck to explode when I used them to get us out."

He turned to Caleb, who had his arms crossed over his chest as he cocked one arrogant brow. "Oh, they kicked my ass hard. I'll be limping for a few weeks, no doubt. But I'm a lot tougher than I look, and while they might have had me on the ground for a few, they weren't demon enough to keep me there."

Nick jumped as he heard something shattering behind him. Turning around, he saw Madaug at the gaming console, where he was smashing it with a pipe he must have found on the ground. He beat on it until both the machine and the disc were busted beyond repair.

Then he stomped both and ended up by jumping up and down on them.

Once he finished his tantrum, he went to his mom and hugged her close. "I'm so sorry for everything I did." He looked down at Ian and grabbed him too. "I'm so glad you're both all right. I don't know what I'd do if anything happened to you. I love you guys so much."

Ian grinned. "Does this mean I can come into your room whenever I want?"

Madaug shoved at him. "Don't push it, E. I'm not that grateful."

Eric and Tabitha joined them. "Thanks, Nick," Tabitha said. "We owe you."

Nick shook Eric's hand. "I would say any time, but really, next time zombies attack, call Bubba. He's the one ready to believe you. Remember the number: 1-888-Ca-Bubba. 'If he can't fix your problems one way, he'll fix them another.' There ain't no Nick in that slogan. After this, Nick's retiring to work for Kyrian as a go-fer. That's all I want to do. I don't want to know nothing about zombie slaying, duck urine, or anything else paranormal. Ever."

But Nick still had one person left to speak to.

Mark.

"How did you survive?" he asked as Mark left Simi, who was licking her fingers and joined them by the truck.

Mark flashed him a grin. "What? Did you forget the first rule I taught you, boy?"

Nick scowled as he tried to remember Mark's various rules for survival. "Duck urine chases away every living and unliving thing?"

"Nah, that's number six. Rule number one: I don't have to outrun the zombie. I just have to outrun you. How you think Eric and Tabitha got captured?"

Tabitha laughed. "Oh please. Inspector Gadget over there made a blowtorch out of Eric's art sealant and a lighter. I'm not sure the house is still standing, but he got us out of there and Simi covered the rest of our retreat. We'd have gotten away completely had Eric not tripped and I made the mistake of going back for him while Mark was hot-wiring a neighbor's car."

Nick laughed at more proof Mark wasn't completely insane. Never go back for the fallen unless you want to be captured or killed. Unless the fallen was Bubba, who usually had a larger calibre of weapons.

Mark sighed. "By the time I realized they weren't behind me, they were gone and I was sick over it. I really thought they'd gotten eaten. But luckily I saw your girlfriend under attack and, with Simi's help, was able to get her to safety."

Nick nodded as he ran all of that through his mind. He only had one question left. "So how'd they get Stone?"

"Stone was here?" Tabitha asked.

"Yeah, the coward ran out and left us the first chance he got."

Alex curled his lip. "You know, he's what gives werewolves a bad name."

Madaug's mom let out a deep sigh. "You know, guys, I've had enough excitement for one night. Bubba, can you take me home? Ian needs to be in bed. Madaug and Eric need to be grounded, and I just want to forget that I ever heard of anything preternatural. At least until I have to get up in the morning and deal with the Dark-Hunters."

"Sure."

Alex grinned at her. "So does this mean you're surrendering your Squire status, Mrs. S.?"

"Not on your life. It just means I need to rest." She lifted Ian up into the truck, then climbed in behind him. "Eric and Madaug . . . get your butts in here."

Eric gave Tabitha a quick kiss. "I'll call you later."

Bubba opened the door to climb in while Tabitha and Mark got in on the other side. "Let me run them home, then I'll be back to grab the rest of you."

Nick nodded as Nekoda took his hand into hers and held it tight.

He, Caleb, Simi, Alex, and Nekoda stayed behind.

Nick went over to the game and sighed. "You know, it was a fun game. But for the whole zombie conversion thing, he'd have made millions on it."

They all froze as they heard something rustling in the shadows. Nick pulled Nekoda behind him as Alex flashed himself from their group to the source of the sound.

A few seconds later, he threw Stone into the light.

Nick glared at him. "You loser dork."

"Ah, shut up, Gautier. You're nothing but trash anyway."

Nick grinned. "Yeah, but I'm trash with a seriously modified cattle prod." He stuck the tip of it against Stone's hip and sent him flying.

But it had an additional effect that Nick hadn't expected. Not only did it shock him, it turned him from human to wolf to human and back again.

"What the—?"

Alex backed up as Nick looked at him. "That's the bad thing about being a shapeshifter. You hit us with electricity and we lose control of our forms."

Gaping, he looked back at Stone, who would try to curse him during the few seconds he was a human as he flashed between forms. "How long's he going to do that?"

"You gave him a pretty good jolt. Probably an hour."

Nick laughed. "Bonus round."

Alex shook his head. "And on that note, I should get home too. I don't want to get grounded either. See you guys tomorrow at school." He disappeared into thin air.

Nick looked at Nekoda. "You're taking all of this weirdness in stride. Should I be afraid?"

"I almost got eaten by zombies tonight, Nick, and I rode in a truck with Bubba's driving. Some guy flashing out of the room and another one turning into a dog isn't exactly the scariest thing I've seen in the last few hours."

Simi came up to lean against Kody's shoulder. "Oh, the Simi thinks you've seen things much, much scarier than that."

Nekoda paled a bit, but didn't elaborate.

Nick pulled her away from the others so that he could speak to her with a little bit of privacy. Gah, this was awkward. There were so many things he wanted to say to her, but deep inside he was still afraid, even after everything they'd been through, that she'd shoot him down.

"Um, Kody ... I was wondering ..." He let his voice trail off as his fear mounted.

Just ask her out already.

Good grief, Nick, she kissed you.

Yeah, but she'd thought they were going to die. Now that they weren't dead she might be regretting that kiss. Wishing she'd saved it for someone who was better looking. Smarter.

Someone not dressed in a goober shirt.

"What?" she asked.

Man up, boy. You faced down demons tonight. How can you shirk now?

Then again, fighting demons was a lot easier than asking out a girl he really liked. They couldn't hurt his feelings.

With one word, she could crush him.

Just do it!

Taking a deep breath, he glanced away and spoke before he chickened out. "Would you like to go to the Café Du Monde with me tomorrow after school and grab some beignets? That is, if my mom doesn't ground me for life for letting Bubba tranq her?"

Time seemed to hang on forever before she spoke. "Sure. I'd like that a lot. But no more zombies, okay?"

In that instant, Nick felt like he could fly. "Yeah, all right. No zombies."

But in his head was the voice of Ambrose. *You only learned part of lesson one tonight, kid. You have nine more to go. Do you really think making time with a girl is the thing you should be focusing on?*

Honestly? Yeah. 'Cause when he looked into Kody's eyes, he could see into the future. There was something about her that warmed him, and after this night, he really needed that.

Especially given the challenges he would have to face in the future.

Lighten up, old man. This is my life, not yours, and I intend to make the most of it.

Ambrose flinched as he heard Nick's voice in his head with words that sent a cold chill down his spine. But he pulled back and left the kid alone to enjoy his victory.

"Unfortunately, Nick, you are living my life and God help us both, we're making all new mistakes."

He just hoped that this time they didn't kill everyone he loved.

As for Nekoda . . .

Ambrose had learned long ago to fear anyone he let near him whose past and future he couldn't see. Any time he'd made that particular mistake, the person had done their best to destroy him.

And in his gut, he knew Nekoda would be no exception.

A new face. A new chance.

But would it be enough . . . That remained to be seen.

EPILOGUE

✖

It was almost dawn before Bubba dropped Nick off at Kyrian's house. They'd had to run back to the store to let Brett and company out of the storeroom before Nick could face the dragon known as his mom.

Caleb stood beside him in the driveway while Nick looked up at Kyrian's mansion with holy terror gnawing on his gut.

"You ever had something you really dreaded doing?" Nick asked him.

"Yeah. It usually starts first thing in the morning when the alarm clock sounds and I know I have to go to school to learn stuff I already know."

Nick could definitely commiserate with that. "How do you stand it?"

Caleb shrugged. "You're my assignment, Nick. You do what you have to do or a bigger demon eats out your liver and uses your spine to pick its teeth."

The sad thing was, Nick wasn't sure he was joking about that. "Yeah, well, I just want to say thank you for everything you've done to keep me safe. I'm really sorry you got swarmed tonight and beat on so badly."

Caleb was completely stunned by the heartfelt words. Not once in all these centuries had anyone ever thanked him. Not even when he'd bled for them.

Nick held his hand out to him.

He started to mouth off, but changed his mind. He wasn't going to slap down someone who was being nice to him. It was too rare. "My pleasure, Nick." He shook his hand and inclined his head to Nick's newly healed arm. "By the way, you might want to keep that thing in the sling for a while yet. Your mom would freak out if you show up healed."

Nick tucked it back into the sling. "Good point."

He took a step toward the door, then stopped. "See you tomorrow?"

"Yes, you will. Evil always stalks you, kid." Caleb smiled before he turned into a raven and flew off.

Nick watched him vanish into the darkness.

What a screwed-up day this'd been. But at least he'd survived it, and he strangely felt better about himself and his future than he'd ever felt before.

I am so messed up.

Laughing, he went to the door and rang the bell. His fear returned a thousandfold while he waited for the inevitable.

A few seconds later, Kyrian opened the door.

He let out a relieved breath. "Thank the gods you're home. Your mother has made me insane since she woke up. Dang, she can nag with the best of them."

"No kidding, right? If it were an Olympic sport, she'd hold all the world records."

Kyrian let him in, then closed the door and locked it tight. He set the alarm.

His mom came running from the living room to grab Nick into a tight hug. "Oh my God, you're covered in blood! What happened to you? Where have you been? I swear I'm killing Bubba and Mark tomorrow. First thing. And you, Mr. Gautier, are grounded for eternity."

Nick started to ask if he could be exempted from restriction for his meeting with Kody, but decided to hold off until she calmed down. As mad as she was tonight, the answer would be no and then some.

"I'm sorry, Mom. It was just a crazy night and I didn't want you hurt."

"Hurt? Boy, if I'm not fired, it'll be a miracle."

Kyrian crossed his arms over his chest. "Well, if you're fired, Mrs. Gautier, I can get you another job."

She narrowed her eyes suspiciously at Kyrian. "Doing what?"

"Sanctuary is owned by friends of mine and I know they're looking for a cook and waitress. I could get you on there in a heartbeat."

That calmed her down. "Really? I've heard their waiters get the best tips of any place in New Orleans."

"Yes, ma'am."

She turned back to Nick and her anger snapped

right to where it'd been before her distraction. "But I better not be fired over your shenanigans or else. Now get upstairs to bed."

Nick was stunned by her order. "We're staying here?"

Kyrian nodded. "I've got to go to sleep and your mom can't drive a stick shift so I can't loan her a car. Rosa will be in in a few hours so if you need anything when you get up, just let her know."

"Come on, Nick." His mom headed for the stairs.

Nick followed after her.

Halfway up, he stopped and turned back to say thanks to Kyrian, who was in the middle of a yawn.

A yawn that showed him Kyrian had a set of long, sharp fangs.

Oh crap . . .

Here we go again.